"I'M TELLING YOU THAT T[...]
WANTS TO MARRY YOU, M[...]

Mr. Patterson said triumphantly. He [...] toward her, one of his hands grasping [...] knife and the other the large meat fork [...] ised to settle a vast amount of money on [...] return he will make you a duchess. [...] Sarah! Can you beat that?"

Sarah just stared at him out of appalled brown eyes. "You can't be serious, Grandpapa?" she said at last in a choked voice.

"Of course I'm serious! Do you think I would joke about a thing like this? I tell you, the Linfords came to me and asked me if I would be interested in such a match."

"But the Duke knew?" she demanded.

"Of course he knew. In fact, he told me not to tell you anything about the scheme, that he wanted to tell you himself." The merchant smiled complacently.

Sarah pushed back her chair and stood up. "I am sorry that you and the Linfords and the Duke have all wasted your time, Grandpapa, but I am not going to marry him."

Mr. Patterson looked stunned. "What?"

"I am not going to marry him," Sarah repeated. And then she ran out of the room.

ACCLAIM FOR JOAN WOLF'S *THE GAMBLE*

"*The Gamble* is a treasure of a book. Ms. Wolf's knowledge of the charming Regency era abounds. The plotting is exceptional—a totally different story line told with great warmth. The depth of her characterizations is, as always, right on the mark."　　　　—*Rendezvous*

"Ms. Wolf brings the reader another engrossing tale filled with engaging characters to hold your imagination captive. There is suspense, humor, poignancy, and a very clever plot to entice you, and only an author of Ms. Wolf's talents could combine all this and more to charm readers time and again."　　　　—*Romantic Times*

"Fast paced, highly readable . . . a bold, bright heroine. . . . The novel deftly depicts the flash and glitter of the season and will please Wolf's many fans."　　　　—*Library Journal*

"Two exquisitely drawn lead protagonists. . . . Just about everyone else in the subgenre is a pretender to Ms. Wolf's throne."　　　　—*Affaire de Coeur*

"Ms. Wolf is a dynamic author. Mystery and intrigue abound."　　　　—*Bell, Book and Candle*

"This is a nicely written story of love, acceptance, and self-worth. There's mystery and adventure here also. I think you'll enjoy this latest Regency."　　　　—*Old Book Barn Gazette*

"A top-notch read. . . . What fun you will have reading the incomparable Joan Wolf as she once again delivers the goods."　　　　—*Belles and Beaux of Romance*

Golden Girl

By Joan Wolf

The Deception
The Guardian
The Arrangement
The Gamble
The Pretenders

Published by Warner Books

Joan Wolf
Golden Girl

WARNER BOOKS

A Time Warner Company

WARNER BOOKS EDITION

Copyright © 1999 by Joan Wolf
All rights reserved.

Cover illustration by Stanislaw Fernandes
Hand lettering by David Gatti

Warner Books, Inc.
1271 Avenue of the Americas
New York, NY 10020

Visit our Web site at
www.warnerbooks.com

 A Time Warner Company

Printed in the United States of America

First Paperback Printing: October 1999

10 9 8 7 6 5 4 3 2

For all the wonderful people who have written to tell me how much they love my books. Your kind words are greatly appreciated.

PROLOGUE

September 1817

THE NEWS RAN LIKE WILDFIRE THROUGH THE exclusive men's clubs that lined fashionable St. James's Street, London.

"I say, Longworth," the Earl of West said to Viscount Longworth, as he came up to the latter in the dining room of Brooks's. "Have you heard? Cheviot went and put a bullet in his brain."

Viscount Longworth put down his glass of burgundy so abruptly that it spilled on the white damask tablecloth. "You don't mean it!"

West nodded his bald head solemnly. "I just heard the news from Lowry. He had it from his valet, who is a friend of Cheviot's valet."

The viscount scowled at the deep red stain his wine had made on the tablecloth. "Damme, but that's a shock."

He was referring to the suicide, not the stain.

The Earl of West carefully lowered his considerable bulk into the chair across from his friend.

"It is, of course," he said. "One suspected he was all to pieces, but I didn't know it was that bad."

"I heard he lost over a hundred thousand guineas at

Watier's the other night," the viscount said darkly, lifting his eyes from the tablecloth.

"Over a hundred thousand?"

For a man who was notoriously under the hatches, a hundred thousand was an enormous sum of money.

The viscount picked up his wineglass again and took a long swallow. "That's what finished him, I expect. He probably didn't have the ready to pay up."

The two men regarded each other somberly.

"So he put a bullet in his brain and left the mess for his son to sort out," West said.

"Looks that way, don't it?" the viscount returned.

The earl grunted.

The viscount looked more cheerful. "Well, what shall we have to eat, West?" he said, changing the subject. "They tell me the mutton is rather good today."

It was over a week before the news of the Duke of Cheviot's death reached his eldest son. Colonel Anthony Selbourne, Earl of Alnwick, was in Paris, where for several years he had been attached to the staff of the Duke of Wellington. He had just returned to his house after spending a few hours at the salon of one of Paris's leading hostesses when his butler met him with the news that his aunt and uncle, Lord and Lady Linford, had arrived from England and were presently ensconced in his drawing room.

For a brief moment, the earl's perfectly drawn brows drew together. Then his face regained its normally serene expression, and he said in his soft voice, "Thank you, Fanton."

The butler bowed, received the earl's hat and gloves, and then stood for a moment, watching as the slender young man crossed the hall to the drawing room. He opened the door, went inside, and closed the door behind him.

The butler signaled to a footman to relieve him of the earl's belongings, and then went about his business.

Inside the drawing room, sitting side by side on a pair of gilt Louis XV chairs, the earl found his Aunt Frances and her husband.

"My dear aunt," the earl said with his charming smile. "What a delightful surprise. I did not know you were in Paris."

He crossed the room to kiss her cheek.

He looked at Lord Linford in surprise as that gentleman rose to his feet and sketched a bow.

"Anthony," Lady Linford said, regarding her nephew with bright hazel eyes. "You never change—except perhaps to grow more beautiful."

"Sit down, my boy," her husband said, dismissing such feminine nonsense with a wave of his hand. "I am afraid we are here as the bearers of bad news."

In silence, the earl turned one of the Louis XV chairs to face his aunt and uncle, and sat down.

"Anthony," Lady Linford said, "your father is dead."

For a long moment, the earl maintained his silence. When finally he spoke it was in a voice tinged with irony. "Are you expecting an expression of grief from me?"

"No." Lady Linford sighed. "I can assure you that I have not come all this way merely to bring news that I know can only be welcome to you. It is much worse, Anthony. I'm afraid that your father killed himself."

The earl's light gray-green eyes widened with shock.

Lady Linford looked at her lap.

"What happened?" said the earl, who for a week now had actually been the duke.

Lady Linford looked up and hesitated.

Lord Linford said bluntly, "He went home one night and put a bullet in his brain, my boy. His valet found him in the morning."

Slowly and deliberately, Lord Linford extracted a paper from the inside pocket of his black mourning coat. He extended the envelope to the duke.

"He left this for you."

The duke took the envelope and stared at it for a long, silent moment. Then he ripped it open and took out the single piece of paper it contained.

The only sound in the room was the ticking of the great gold clock on the marble mantelpiece.

When finally the duke looked up, the slightly unfocused look in his eyes was the only sign he gave that what he had been reading was not just a courtesy note.

"What did he say, Anthony?" Lady Linford asked sharply.

Wordlessly, the duke handed her the note. Holding it so that her husband could see it as well, she read:

> My dear Anthony. Sorry to take the coward's way out, but I fear I just can't face the debacle I've made of my finances. I leave it to you to bail the family out. I have no doubt that you will.

It was signed merely, *Cheviot*.

"How bad is it?" the duke asked tensely.

"Only you will be able to discover the full extent of the damages, my boy," Lord Linford said. "What pushed Cheviot over the edge was losing over a hundred thousand guineas at Watier's. I gather he didn't have the money to pay the debt."

He handed the missive back to the duke, who took it

with fingers that were not completely steady. "A hundred thousand guineas!" he said.

"Most of it to Branford."

"Dear God," the duke said.

"Yes," returned his uncle.

The duke drew a long, deep breath. "What of my brothers?"

Lady Linford noted that he did not ask about his stepmother.

"They are in shock, of course," she replied. "I doubt if either Lawrence or Patrick knew the extent of your father's debts." She hesitated, then added, "The duchess is . . . very upset."

The duke's mouth curled with faint irony.

Lord Linford spoke next. "Your aunt and I thought you should hear this news from someone in the family, Anthony. Unfortunately, it will be common knowledge in Paris soon enough." The earl looked grim. "As far as I am concerned, it has already enlivened far too many conversations in London."

The duke briefly shut his eyes.

"I have thought about this very deeply, Anthony, and there is only one thing to be done," the countess said with convincing authority. "You must marry an heiress."

The duke looked at his aunt and his finely cut nostrils quivered. "Have you any candidates to offer me, Aunt?"

"Not yet, but I will have," she replied. Her strong face looked very determined. "Believe me, by the time you have wound up your affairs in Paris and are ready to come home, I will have found you a suitable wife."

"Dear God." The Linfords could see the pallor that lay beneath the duke's pale golden tan. He put a hand to his brow and shook his head as if to clear it.

"It is very bad, there can be no doubt about that," Lord

Linford said bracingly. "But there is one thing at least in which I agree with your father. If anyone can bail the family out of this dismal situation, Anthony, you are the man."

CHAPTER
One

April 1818

WILLIAM PATTERSON WAS AMAZED WHEN HE RE-
ceived a request from the Earl of Linford to call
at his house. Patterson knew that Lord Linford
headed the Treasury Board for the government, and all the
merchant could suppose was that the earl wanted his advice on some matter pertaining to government finance.

For William Patterson was enormously rich. He had
started life as the son of a poor cottager in Lancashire and
from those humble beginnings he had amassed a fortune in
the manufacture of cotton cloth. His humble origins would
always exclude him from a position in government, but he
was certainly one of the most formidable financial powers
in all of England.

He looked once more at the note that had been delivered
to his office in the city:

> I would very much appreciate your calling upon me
> at 17 Grosvenor Square tomorrow morning at eleven
> o'clock.
>
> Very truly yours,
> Linford.

*   *   *

Patterson leaned his broad shoulders back in his big desk chair and contemplated the note, a frown between his thick gray eyebrows. He was in his middle sixties, and his strong frame carried more fat than it had when he was younger, but he was still a powerfully built man.

An invitation to the Earl of Linford's house, he thought. *Well, well, well.*

In all the years that he had kept a home and an office in London, Patterson had never been to Grosvenor Square. That venue was restricted to the upper classes only; city merchants, however rich they might be, were not encouraged to taint its purity with the stink of commerce.

William Patterson was a hard and ruthless man. He'd had to be in order to achieve what he had achieved in his lifetime. But it never once occurred to him that he might refuse the Earl of Linford's invitation.

The following morning, at precisely eleven o'clock, a hackney cab dropped William Patterson in front of the home of the Earl of Linford. After instructing the cab to wait for him, Patterson approached the stairs that led to Number 17. Before he raised the knocker on the door, however, he paused to cast his eyes around the sacred environs of Grosvenor Square.

A pretty, formal garden lay in the center of the square, and around the garden's four sides were arranged a symmetrical panorama of elegant brown-brick houses with red dressings and stone cornices. The sun was shining and two children with hoops were playing in the garden under the watchful eyes of a nursemaid. A town chaise with an earl's coat of arms painted in gold upon its door drove past the waiting cab. Otherwise the square was empty.

Patterson lifted his hand to the polished brass knocker in front of him and rapped with authority on the heavy wood door.

It was opened almost immediately by a footman dressed in blue satin livery and a white wig.

"William Patterson," the merchant said gruffly. "I'm to see Lord Linford."

"Yes sir," the footman said. "His Lordship is expecting you. If you will come with me, I will take you to him."

Patterson followed the long, straight back of the footman across the marble-floored entrance hall. They proceeded down a wide passageway, past an elegantly carved staircase, then finally the footman stopped in front of a closed polished oak door.

He opened it and announced sonorously, "Mr. William Patterson, my lord."

"Send him in," came the earl's voice.

The footman held the door for Patterson and he entered the room slowly.

He saw immediately that he was in the earl's library, which surprised him. He had expected to be shown to an office.

He was even more surprised to find that a woman was in the room with the earl.

Linford stood up behind his desk and held out his hand. "Mr. Patterson," he said pleasantly. "I am grateful for your visit. Please allow me to introduce you to my wife, Lady Linford."

Patterson was too shrewd to allow any of the bewilderment he was feeling to show on his face. Instead he nodded gravely to the countess, who had remained seated, and murmured, "Pleased to meet you, my lady."

She inclined her head regally. "Mr. Patterson."

"Sit down, sit down," the earl said, gesturing to a chair that was drawn up to face the desk.

Patterson slowly lowered his big frame to a sitting position. He was dressed in the old-fashioned clothes he always wore: a full-skirted frock coat and buckled shoes. His still-thick gray hair was cut short, however, in the newest style.

"No doubt you are wondering why I wished to see you," Lord Linford said genially.

"That I am, my lord," Patterson replied.

He could not stop himself from casting a quick glance at the countess.

She gave him a gracious smile. She was a woman in her late forties and still quite good-looking. Patterson noted automatically that she had splendid breasts.

"I am not totally unacquainted with your family, Mr. Patterson," she said in a rich contralto voice. "Your granddaughter was at school in Bath with my own daughter for several years."

"Is that so, my lady?" Patterson replied.

"Yes. On one occasion Sarah even visited us at our country home in Kent."

"Did she, now?" Patterson said. "Fancy that."

In fact, he remembered perfectly the time Sarah had visited the Linfords. He had been hugely pleased to know that his granddaughter was hobnobbing with the aristocracy, and he had been acutely disappointed when she had not been invited again.

"She is a very pretty-behaved girl," Lady Linford said with gracious approval.

"She should be. She's had the best education that money could buy," Patterson said bluntly. "She's my only grandchild and I've had the raising of her since her parents died when she were but a little girl."

Lady Linford settled herself into her chair, much as her ancestors must have settled themselves upon their horses before advancing into battle.

"Mr. Patterson," she said, "it is about Sarah that we wished to speak to you today."

Patterson could not quite hide his amazement at this extraordinary statement. "Sarah?"

"Yes." Lady Linford made a motion with her hand that almost looked as if she were raising a sword. "My husband and I have a proposal to put before you, and we would greatly appreciate it if you would hear us out."

"Aye, my lady," said Patterson cautiously. He glanced at Lord Linford, but the earl was sitting quietly with his hands folded on the desk in front of him. Evidently this was Lady Linford's show.

"The proposal relates to my nephew, Anthony Selbourne, who is the Duke of Cheviot," the countess said.

Something flickered behind Patterson's blue eyes. Selbourne of Cheviot was one of the most famous names in all of Britain. Since the days of the early Middle Ages, it had figured in nearly every battle the country had fought, and in the lineup of numerous governments as well.

"Perhaps you are familiar with the Cheviot lineage," Lady Linford said.

"Aye, my lady," Patterson replied tersely.

What the bloody hell is this all about? he wondered.

"Then you know the position that my nephew occupies," Lady Linford went on. "I might add here that his mother was a French princess and through her he is related to half the royalty of Europe."

William Patterson had never been good at circumlocution. His was more the style of the juggernaut.

"My lady," he said with sharp impatience, "will you get to the point?"

The faintest look of annoyance crossed Lady Linford's face, and then it was smoothed away. She smiled. "Very well, Mr. Patterson. The truth is that my nephew has found himself in a very awkward situation. His father, the late duke, was not a good steward of his property. My own father, Anthony's grandfather, was also a profligate. Consequently, when Anthony assumed the title six months ago, he found himself in a position of near bankruptcy."

Light began to dawn in the merchant's brain.

"He needs money, eh?"

Lady Linford's face was grave. "He needs money badly, Mr. Patterson. I can assure you that Anthony is nothing like his father or his grandfather. He was bitterly opposed to my brother's reckless gambling. In fact, they had constant rows about it. After he finished school, Anthony left home and went out to the Peninsula. He fought in Spain for a number of years and then was part of our delegation to the Congress of Vienna. When Napoleon returned from Elba, he rejoined his regiment and fought bravely at the Battle of Waterloo."

Patterson was looking at her with shrewd blue eyes. "And what does this paragon of a duke have to do with my Sarah?" he asked.

For the first time, Lady Linford hesitated. She looked at her husband.

Lord Linford stepped in to answer the merchant's question. "Cheviot must marry a girl with money," he said. "Not to put too fine a point on it, Patterson, he must marry a girl with a great deal of money. His debts are enormous."

He paused to glance at his wife. When she said nothing, the earl continued, "We thought that your granddaughter might be suitable for our purposes."

Patterson shifted his bulk on his chair. "Let me get this straight, my lord," he said bluntly. "You are offering your nephew as a husband for my Sarah?"

The earl inclined his head. "That is what we are offering."

Patterson slowly ran his eyes around the comfortable book-lined room in which he sat. A portrait of one of Linford's ancestors wearing a white wig hung on the wall above the carved wood fireplace. A large globe was placed in one of the room's corners and the Persian rug under his feet was old but magnificent.

Patterson returned his gaze to the man sitting behind the large mahogany desk.

"Why pick a girl from the merchant class, my lord?" he asked with real curiosity. "Surely some blue-blooded heiresses must be available."

Lord Linford sighed. "Unfortunately, Patterson, most of the nobility have their money tied up in land. Cheviot has plenty of land—most of it heavily mortgaged, I'm afraid. What he needs at the moment is ready cash."

The merchant folded his arms across his massive chest and said bluntly, "So what you are saying is that the duke is for sale."

Lady Linford made a sound of indignation.

Lord Linford looked the merchant squarely in the eyes and replied with equal bluntness, "Yes."

Patterson's eyes narrowed. "How much?"

The earl looked a little pained. "That will be for the lawyers to arrange. But we are talking millions here, Patterson. Let me make that quite clear. The debts are crushing."

Patterson tipped his chair back a little and balanced it

on two legs. He knew he had the upper hand, and he was feeling considerably more comfortable.

"I already have plans for Sarah," he said. "She is to marry Neville Harvey."

"Neville Harvey?" Lord Linford drummed his fingers on the polished top of his desk. There was a frown on his aristocratic face. "Do you mean the owner of Harvey Mills?"

"The very man," Patterson said with satisfaction. "It has long been my dream to consolidate our two companies. The result will be a veritable cotton empire."

"I have not heard of any engagement between Sarah and Mr. Harvey," Lady Linford said sharply.

The merchant returned the two front legs of his chair to the ground. "Well, they ain't exactly engaged yet, my lady. Sarah only just came home from school."

The countess said firmly, "If nothing has been formally arranged between Mr. Harvey and Sarah, then I suggest that you consider our proposal, Mr. Patterson." A faint look of distaste crossed her face. "To speak in merchant's terms, we are offering you the best merchandise on the market."

Patterson was beginning to enjoy himself. "Well, I don't know . . . ," he began with feigned doubtfulness.

Lady Linford snapped, "We are offering you the Most Noble Anthony George Henry Edward Selbourne, Duke of Cheviot and Marquis of Newcastle, Earl of Alnwick, Baron Selbourne of Corbridge and Baron Selbourne of Bellingham. My nephew also holds the hereditary title of Warden of the Scottish Marches, a position held by the Dukes of Cheviot since the days of Edward III."

Lady Linford looked down her nose at the merchant. "*That* is what you are being offered, Mr. Patterson. *That* is the blood that will flow in the veins of your great-grandchildren. What can Mr. Harvey offer you that could possibly compare with that?"

She was right, and Patterson knew it. He was fiercely proud of being a self-made man, but he was English to the marrow of his bones. The superiority of the aristocracy was something that had been ingrained in him since early childhood.

To think of Sarah as the Duchess of Cheviot!

But Patterson was a shrewd merchant, and he knew enough not to give himself away. Let them sweat a little, he thought.

"You said his mother was a princess?"

"That is right," the countess replied grandly. "Through her, Sarah will be connected to the great families of France."

The merchant pretended to ponder this piece of information.

Then, "How old is this duke?" he demanded. "My Sarah is only eighteen."

"Cheviot is twenty-seven," the countess replied with admirable calm. "You need have no fear for your granddaughter if she should marry my nephew, Mr. Patterson. I can assure you that Cheviot will know how to make her happy."

The merchant snorted through his nose. "A ladies' man, eh?"

The earl answered that question. "Cheviot will know the respect that is due to his wife."

Patterson tried a different tack. "What makes you so sure my money won't go the way his father's money went?" he demanded of the earl.

"As I said earlier, Cheviot is not at all like his father," Linford replied calmly. "He is a very responsible young man. You will have nothing to fear for either your granddaughter or your money should she marry him, Mr. Patterson."

"Neville Harvey is a responsible young man, too," Patterson said triumphantly.

Lady Linford drew herself up in the manner of a knight getting ready for a joust. "Perhaps he is," she said icily. "But my nephew can make your granddaughter a duchess, Mr. Patterson. What can Mr. Harvey make her? The Queen of Cotton?"

The merchant narrowed his eyes as he acknowledged the accuracy of her thrust.

"You are an intelligent man, Mr. Patterson," the countess continued. "I do not think you will turn your back upon an opportunity to ally yourself with one of the greatest families in the country. Just think, someday your great-grandson might be a prime minister."

If he has my brains, he might very well, Patterson thought.

"You have a point, my lady," he said mildly. "I won't deny it."

The countess permitted herself a small smile. "Well then," she said, "I suggest that we bring the young people together."

The merchant looked at her speculatively. "And how do you propose we do that?"

Lady Linford's reply was prompt. "I will invite you and Sarah to visit us in Kent. My daughter Olivia, whom Sarah knows, will be there. And, of course, my nephew."

Patterson tried not to show his glee. He was to be a guest at the country home of the Earl of Linford!

"Very well, my lady," he agreed, his face carefully grave. "I won't object to the young people meeting. But if Sarah don't like this duke of yours, I ain't going to push her into marrying him."

Lady Linford smiled. "There is no question of that, Mr. Patterson. No woman in her right mind would not like my nephew."

The merchant snorted.

Lord Linford made a suggestion. "Perhaps it would be wise not to tell Sarah about this conversation, Mr. Patterson. It might cause her to feel constraint when she meets the duke. Let her meet him under seemingly ordinary circumstances. I think we can safely leave it up to Cheviot to do the rest."

The merchant grunted.

Lord Linford rose from his chair and held out his hand. Patterson heaved himself to his feet and took it.

"Shall we say that you will come to Hartford Court this Thursday?" the countess said pleasantly. She did not extend her hand. "There is no point in delaying this, is there?"

Not with all those creditors, Patterson thought cynically. *The sooner the duke gets his hands on Sarah's money, the better it will be for him.*

"Thursday it is," he said, and, turning, he stomped to the door and let himself out.

CHAPTER
Two

MAXWELL SCOTT CAME INTO THE LIBRARY OF THE Selbourne town house in Berkeley Square, and paused when he saw the duke sitting at the desk, his head lowered into his hands.

"Anthony?" he said with quick concern. "Are you all right?"

The duke looked up. "I'm fine," he assured his secretary. "I was just thinking."

Max scanned the familiar, beloved face of his employer. "You look tired," he said.

A small smile tugged at the corners of the duke's mouth. "I am tired," he admitted. "Tired of dealing with debts, debts, and more debts. It is a great pity that my father did not die ten years sooner. Perhaps then there might have been something left to salvage from his wreckage of the estate."

The secretary slowly crossed the room and came to a halt in front of the desk.

"Sit down, Max," the duke said wearily, and he gestured to a chair.

Maxwell Scott was not an ordinary private secretary. He had been a lieutenant in the duke's regiment on the

Peninsula, and when the inexperienced twenty-year-old Captain Lord Alnwick had been put in charge, the older, more experienced Max had kindly guided the young man through his initiation into the realities of war and leadership. In addition, Max had quite literally saved the duke's life at the Battle of Salamanca, hoisting the badly wounded young officer onto his own horse and leading him off the field to the dubious safety of the hospital tents.

When the duke had gone to Vienna for the peace conference, he had asked Max to accompany him as his secretary, and they had been together in that capacity ever since.

Max said, "It is a dismal situation, indeed." His face was filled with sympathy as he took the proffered seat.

"He even went through my stepmother's jointure," the duke said. He had taken his hands away from his face and they rested now quietly upon the desk in front of him.

Max's strongly marked brows flew upward. "How could he do that? I thought it was secured to her upon their marriage."

"It was, but somehow he managed to get hold of it," came the grim reply. "So now I have her to provide for, as well as my two half-brothers."

Max felt an impulse to reach out and put a reassuring hand over the duke's slender, perfectly kept fingers, but he refrained. He had learned long ago that his employer did not like to be touched.

He bit his lip and said regretfully, "I am afraid that I am the bearer of more bad news. I have just spent an hour with the president of your bank, and he feels that there is not enough security to justify the risk of a loan."

The duke looked bleak. "Unfortunately, he is right."

Max's heart ached to see that look. He searched his

brain to find some heartening words, but none came to mind. It truly was a dismal situation.

The duke sat back in his chair. "However, I believe my Aunt Linford may have come up with a solution."

"Lady Linford?"

"Yes. She has found me an heiress."

Max's widely set eyes flickered. "An heiress," he repeated slowly. It was the obvious answer to the duke's problems, of course, but . . .

"May I ask who?" he said.

The duke's expression was unreadable. "Her name is Sarah Patterson. She is the granddaughter of William Patterson, the cotton man."

Max was absolutely horrified. "A merchant's daughter?"

The duke steepled his fingers on the desk before him and regarded them thoughtfully. "The grandfather is enormously rich, and apparently he is willing to pay through the nose in order to see his granddaughter a duchess."

The horrified expression had not left Max's face.

The duke glanced at him. "It mightn't be so bad, Max." He sounded as if he were trying to convince himself. "According to my aunt, the girl was at school in Bath with my cousin Olivia. Lady Linford said she visited Hartford Court once and behaved quite like a lady."

"Are there no heiresses from the upper classes available?" Max asked.

"None with the amount of money that I need," the duke replied dryly.

Silence fell. The duke continued to look at his hands. His face looked perfectly serene, but Max, who knew him well, could see the tension he was trying to hide.

Finally, "I am sorry, Anthony," he said helplessly. "This must be most unpleasant for you."

"There is nothing else to be done," the duke said with weary resignation. "I simply must have money."

It never once occurred to either man that the lady in question might not be as amenable to such a glorious marriage as everyone expected her to be.

On the other side of town, the very same day as the duke's conversation with his secretary, Sarah Patterson returned home from a visit to the Royal Academy to learn that her grandfather wished to speak to her.

Sarah was surprised. It was not a time of day when William Patterson was usually to be found at home. She took off her hat and her pelisse and obediently went along to her grandfather's office.

She knocked on the door and when he called, "Come in," she peeked her head into the room and said, "You wished to see me, Grandpapa?"

"Yes. Come in, Sarah. I have some news for you that I think you will enjoy."

As Sarah crossed the floor, William Patterson regarded his granddaughter, regretting for perhaps the thousandth time that she was not a more imposing figure. Her long brown hair was smooth and straight and she wore it in an unfashionable chignon. Her eyes, unfortunately, were not blue like his, but brown like her Welsh mother's. Her features were delicate and unremarkable, her skin was not the creamy white of a proper Englishwoman's but had a tint of gold to it (another gift from her Welsh mother), and she was too small.

She sat in the chair next to his desk, folded her hands in her lap, and regarded him silently.

Sarah was too silent, he thought. She didn't have the

vivacity and sparkle one expected from a young girl. She was silent and solemn. No wonder she had not been invited back to Hartford Court.

"Where have you been?" he asked with forced geniality.

"To see the exhibition at the Royal Academy, Grandpapa."

He frowned in annoyance. "More painting?"

"I like painting, Grandpapa," came the quiet reply.

Mr. Patterson well knew that his granddaughter liked painting. As far as he was concerned, she spent far too much of her time indulging in that frivolous activity.

Painting! No one ever made any money by painting.

"You had something to tell me, Grandpapa?" she prompted.

"Aye." He recollected his good news and his frown lifted. "We have received an invitation from the Earl and Countess of Linford to visit their country home in Kent."

The words felt so good rolling off his tongue.

Sarah looked dumbfounded.

Should I tell her? William Patterson wondered. He scanned his granddaughter's puzzled face and decided that perhaps Lord Linford had been right. If Sarah knew about the Linfords' proposal, she would freeze right up when she met the duke.

Not that Patterson had any fear that Cheviot would reject his granddaughter. The man was clearly desperate for money. But pride made the merchant desire to see his granddaughter make a good impression.

"The Linfords have invited you and me on a visit?" Sarah asked cautiously.

"I done a favor for Lord Linford a while ago, and this is his way of thanking me, I suppose," he lied fluently. "We're to go this Thursday."

Sarah gave him a worried look. "I don't know if this is such a good idea, Grandpapa. I don't think we will quite . . . fit in . . . with the Linfords."

"Nonsense," he snapped loudly. His thick brows drew together. "You've been to visit there before. Linford even told me you were a very pretty-behaved girl."

"I visited Olivia," Sarah said. "And I was not comfortable at Hartford, Grandpapa. The Linfords are very different from us."

"They use a chamber pot same as we do," he replied crudely. "The only way they're different is that they have kept a record of their ancestors, while we have not."

A faint flush rose to Sarah's cheeks. She looked at her hands clasped in her lap and said nothing.

Patterson slammed his hand down upon his desk.

Sarah jumped.

"You have something a lot better than a list of ancestors, my girl," Patterson told her angrily. "You have money. You could buy and sell those fancy aristocrats with their lists of ancestors a dozen times over. Don't you ever forget that."

"Yes, Grandpapa."

"Look at me, Sarah!"

Her eyes jerked up to his face.

"We are going to visit Hartford," he said. "We will leave on Thursday."

Her flush had subsided, leaving her very pale. When Sarah was pale she looked washed out, Patterson thought with a scowl.

"Yes, Grandpapa," she said.

She never failed to irritate him. She was such a mouse; there was nothing at all of him in her.

"Go on, then," he said impatiently, waving her away. "I have work to do."

"Yes, Grandpapa," she said. She rose from her chair and walked gracefully to the door.

She was at least graceful; he'd give her that.

"And Sarah!" he called.

She turned.

"Be sure to take your best duds. I want to make a good impression on the Linfords."

"Yes, Grandpapa."

He scowled again as she shut the door behind her.

Sarah went up the stairs to her room, feeling as she always did after an interview with her grandfather, as if she had been battered by a hurricane.

She shouldn't feel that way, she knew. Her grandfather was not a violent man. But the sheer force of his ruthless personality never failed to overwhelm her.

Sarah slowly entered her bedroom. The chambermaid had tidied it and laid coal for a fire. She had also filled the vase on the window table with the fresh flowers that Sarah loved.

Sarah regarded the flowers absently, thought about her last visit to Hartford, and winced. Olivia had been fine. She liked Olivia. They had been friends at school and when Olivia had invited her to visit, Sarah had not thought twice about accepting.

But Olivia's mother . . .

From the moment Sarah alighted at the doorstep of Hartford Court, it had been clear to her that Lady Linford did not consider her to be a suitable friend for Olivia. The countess had never been impolite, but Sarah, who was acutely sensitive, had immediately divined that she was not welcome.

She had stuck out the visit and gone home with relief.

When Olivia invited her again, she had refused. The two girls had not seen each other since.

Now she was to go back. And with her grandfather!

Sarah sat on the edge of her bed and stared at the heavy flocked wallpaper which her grandfather had chosen and which she hated.

Whatever would the Countess of Linford make of her grandfather?

Suddenly Sarah grinned.

If I had to put my money on either of them, she thought with irresistible amusement, *I'd bet on Grandpapa.*

The grin faded.

If only she did not have to be there as a witness.

William Patterson was in high fettle for the entire three days before he and Sarah were due to leave for Kent. Sarah could not understand the reason for his extreme good spirits.

"Grandpapa is like a child waiting for his birthday," she said to Neville Harvey on Wednesday afternoon as they sat drinking tea in the red drawing room of the Pattersons' London house. "I had no idea that he was so impressed by the aristocracy."

"Well, you must admit that it is quite a coup for the son of a cottager to find himself invited to pay a visit to the home of an earl," Neville replied with a smile.

He was a nice-looking young man of twenty-nine, with a round face, dark blond hair, and blue eyes.

"I suppose so," she sighed.

"*You* don't seem overly impressed, Sarah," Neville remarked.

She picked up the Wedgwood teapot that was on the table in front of her and poured some tea into his empty cup.

"I've visited the Linfords before, Neville. It was not an experience I look forward to repeating."

He frowned. "Why?"

"Every time Lady Linford spoke to me she looked as if she were smelling something that had gone bad," Sarah said. She stirred some sugar into his tea. "It was quite clear to me that she did not think me a suitable friend for Olivia. Frankly, I couldn't wait to leave."

"If she felt that way, then she wouldn't be inviting you back," Neville pointed out reasonably.

He picked up his cup from the tea table and took a sip.

"It was the earl, not the countess, who was responsible for the invitation," Sarah informed him. "Apparently Grandpapa once did him a favor and this is his way of expressing his gratitude." She looked glum. "I only wish they had not included me."

"I'm sure you were reading something into Lady Linford's behavior that wasn't there at all," Neville said. "You're too sensitive, Sarah. There is absolutely no reason for Lady Linford to disapprove of you."

Sarah smiled at the young man who was sitting next to her on the sofa. "I am the daughter and the granddaughter of merchants, Neville. That would be more than enough to make Lady Linford disapprove of me."

Neville snorted. "You can buy and sell the Linfords a dozen times over," he said.

He took another drink of tea.

Sarah returned softly, "Not everyone puts as high a value on money as you and Grandpapa do."

She poured more tea into her own cup.

"That's not true," Neville replied with emphasis. He watched the graceful arch of her fragile wrist as she poured the tea. "Nothing in life is as important as money,

Sarah. Just you ask any poor soul who doesn't have any. He'll tell you."

Sarah squeezed a little lemon into her tea.

"I agree that one must have enough money to provide for the necessities of life," she agreed. "That is a different thing, however, from the accumulation of excessive amounts of money solely for the sake of having it."

"All right, then, go on and tell me what you think is more important than money," Neville demanded.

Sarah gazed into her teacup as if it might hold the answer to his question. "Well . . . I think painting is more important."

Neville gave her a look of mingled exasperation and affection. "Sarah, all of those great painters you so admire had to hang on the sleeves of rich men in order to be able to ply their trade."

A delicate pink color stained Sarah's cheeks. "A picture by someone like Mr. Turner is beyond price, Neville. The joy it can give one . . . the beauty . . . the way it can make you *see* . . ."

Her voice trailed off when she saw the amusement in his eyes.

"His pictures just look like blobs of color to me."

Sarah took a sip of her tea and didn't reply.

"It's that ladylike education you had," Neville said disapprovingly. "It's made you think that money is dirty somehow."

"I don't think that money is dirty," Sarah disagreed. "I realize that it is important. One has only to look at the poor wretches who live in London's slums to know that. It's just that sometimes it seems to me as if Grandpapa is so occupied with the making of money that he has never taken the time to reflect upon its uses."

Neville frowned. "Nonsense. Look at this house, Sarah.

Look at the horses and the carriage that take you wherever you want to go. Look at the meals that are set upon your table every night. Of course your grandfather understands the uses of money."

He sounded indignant, as if he felt her words were an indictment of himself as well as of William Patterson.

"I didn't mean to criticize," Sarah said softly. "I admire Grandpapa enormously."

"Well, you should." Neville's blue eyes were bright, his round cheeks very red. "Your grandfather understands the good things in life just as well as any earl."

Once more Sarah looked at her tea.

But he doesn't, she thought. *And neither do you, Neville. Neither of you understand anything about art or music or literature. All you understand is the making of money.*

Immediately she felt ashamed of herself for such a thought. Her grandfather's money had paid for the education that had enlightened Sarah about the finer things in life. She should not blame him for not having been given the same opportunity to learn that she had.

"I didn't mean to raise my voice to you, Sarah," Neville said stiffly. "I suppose I felt that you were criticizing me as well as your grandfather."

She lifted her head and made herself smile. "What an ungrateful wretch you must think me, Neville. I never meant to criticize you. You work very hard and you deserve to benefit from your talents and your labor."

He smiled back at her, placated. He put down his teacup, reached over, and removed the teacup from her hand. Then he lifted her hand to his lips.

Sarah's eyes flew to his in surprise. He thought that she looked like a startled deer.

"You're so sweet, Sarah," he said in a slightly husky

voice. He moved her hand away from his lips, but continued to hold it captive within his own. "We're a perfect match, you and I."

Sarah's hand went stiff with tension. "Because a marriage between us would consolidate Grandpapa's company with yours?"

He said reproachfully, "There's more to my feelings for you than that, Sarah. I want to take care of you."

"I'm neither a child nor an idiot, Neville," Sarah said irritably. She pulled her hand out of his. "I don't need a keeper."

"No, darling, what you need is a husband." He grinned at her. "And I'm the man for that, too."

CHAPTER
Three

SARAH SAT BESIDE HER GRANDFATHER IN THE PATTERson chaise, gazing out the window at the beauty of the Kent countryside. March had been warmer than usual and the grass was springtime green. A small stream ran alongside the road on Sarah's side of the carriage, and she looked with delight at its banks, so brilliantly colored with bluebells and violets.

Sarah loved the countryside. When she was a child, she had lived in the house in Lancashire that her father had bought for her mother, who was Welsh and hated cities. After her parents had died in a carriage accident, she had left the country and gone to live with her grandfather, first in his town house in Manchester, and then in London.

Mr. Patterson hated the country. He said it made him sneeze.

He was not sneezing at the moment, however. In fact, he was positively ebullient. Sarah had to hide her astonishment that something as simple as an invitation to visit the Earl of Linford could have provoked such euphoria in her hardheaded grandfather.

The carriage turned off the main road and began to

travel along a local lane. Three minutes later, it turned
again, this time into a wide curving gravel driveway that
was lined with rows of magnificent lime trees.

"Is this it?" Patterson demanded.

Sarah recognized the entrance to Hartford Court from
her previous visit. "Yes, Grandpapa. We're here."

Much as she was dreading this visit, she was very
happy to have arrived at their destination. She did not like
riding in closed carriages, and her grandfather wouldn't
allow her to open the window.

Patterson peered ahead. "I don't see the house."

"The drive is about a mile long, Grandpapa. We should
be coming upon it shortly."

"A mile-long drive, eh?" Patterson said admiringly.
"Linford owns a lot of property."

"It's a beautiful estate," Sarah said. "They have miles
of gardens, and a lake as well."

The carriage came around a curve and at last the house
was revealed to Patterson's eager eyes.

"Hmmm," he said through his nose as he took in the
large edifice that stood in the midst of a huge lawn that
was so well kept it looked like a carpet. Hartford Court
had been built during the time of William and Mary and
was a well-proportioned brick house with two symmetrical wings on either side of a central block.

"It's rather plain," Patterson said dubiously. His taste
ran more toward the rococo.

"It's quite elegant inside," Sarah assured him with a
smile. "And they have some lovely paintings."

Patterson shot her a dark look. "Hmmm," he said
again.

The carriage swept up to the front door of the building.
The door opened and a butler processed gravely along the

brick walkway to the drive. He was followed by two liveried footmen.

The butler opened the carriage door. "Welcome to Hartford Court, Miss Patterson," he intoned. "It is good to see you again."

"Thank you, Eliot," she returned quietly. "My grandfather, Mr. William Patterson, is with me today."

The butler peered beyond Sarah into the interior of the carriage. "Welcome to Hartford Court, sir," he said.

One of the footmen approached carrying a set of steps, and the butler assisted Sarah to alight from the chaise. She was followed by Mr. Patterson.

"The family is indoors," Eliot informed them.

He began to walk back toward the house, followed by Sarah and Patterson.

The front hall was tiled with black and white marble squares, rather like a chessboard. Waiting in the middle of the chessboard was a girl of about eighteen.

"Sarah!" she cried, and came running across the marble to envelope her much smaller friend in a hug.

"Olivia," Sarah said breathlessly. "How lovely to see you."

"I've been looking for you for the last three hours!"

Stepping back from Olivia's enthusiastic embrace, Sarah said, "You must let me make known to you my grandfather, Mr. William Patterson. Grandpapa, Lady Olivia Antsley."

Patterson bowed. "Pleased to meet you, Lady Olivia."

His shrewd eyes moved over the girl, taking in the golden blond hair, the bright blue eyes, the well-formed figure.

Damme, he thought. *She's going to make Sarah look even more like a mouse than usual.*

"How do you do, Mr. Patterson?" Olivia said. Her eyes

were shining with mischief. "My father asked me to take you to him as soon as you arrived. He is in the library."

"Thank you, Lady Olivia," Patterson said. "I am looking forward to meeting your father once more."

"If you will wait here for just one moment, Sarah, I will show your grandfather to the library, and then I will take you upstairs to your room," Olivia said.

"Certainly," Sarah replied. She was already gravitating toward a painting of a rural scene that hung on one of the walls.

"Come with me, Mr. Patterson," Olivia commanded, and she led the merchant across the marble-floored hall and down a wide passageway that led into the left wing of the house.

They stopped before a closed door. Olivia turned to the merchant, her eyes sparkling with mischief, and said in a half-whisper, "Does Sarah *know* why she has been invited to Hartford, Mr. Patterson?"

"Nay," the merchant replied. "I thought it best not to spring it on her too soon."

Olivia laughed. Her mirth was like the sound of bells ringing.

Patterson was not at all pleased that Linford's daughter had turned out to be such a beauty. However had she struck up a friendship with Sarah?

Olivia pushed open the door and said, "Papa, Mr. Patterson is here."

"Come in, Patterson, come in," the earl said genially.

And so, for the second time that week, Patterson walked into a library owned by the Earl of Linford. As had happened previously, he found Linford in the company of another person. This time the earl's companion was not Lady Linford, however, but a young man.

"I thought it would be a good idea for you and Cheviot

to meet," Lord Linford said genially. He turned to the slender figure who was standing by the window. "Anthony, may I present Mr. William Patterson to you."

A soft, clear voice replied, "How do you do, Mr. Patterson?" and the young man held out his hand.

It was done with perfect graciousness, and, rather to his surprise, the older man found himself crossing the room to the younger one.

"Pleased to meet you, Your Grace," Patterson said, taking the duke's slender hand into his own larger grip. For the first time he looked upon his granddaughter's proposed husband.

The sun shining through the large library window struck sparks of bronze from the duke's brown hair. His light eyes regarded the merchant steadily. His beautifully cut mouth was grave.

It was instantly clear to Patterson why Lady Linford had been so certain that her nephew would be able to charm Sarah.

"It was good of you to accept Lord Linford's invitation to visit Hartford," the duke said.

The merchant was annoyed to find himself acutely conscious of the difference between his own large, unfashionable person and the slender, elegant figure of the duke.

The young man was meeting his eyes with calm confidence.

He was not what Patterson had expected.

After the briefest of hesitations, the merchant decided he had better lay some cards on the table.

"I have told Sarah nothing about what Lord Linford and I discussed, Your Grace," he began. "She thinks she is here because Lord Linford invited me."

The duke nodded gravely.

From his place by the desk, Linford said, "Very wise. It will give Sarah a chance to become acquainted with Cheviot in a more natural and comfortable way."

"Hmmm," the merchant said. He continued to stare at the duke and his eyes narrowed.

"Do you have any questions that you would care to ask me, Mr. Patterson?" the duke said.

The merchant's eyes narrowed even further. He did in fact have a question, one that had been on his mind ever since he had first beheld the duke's face. William Patterson might think his granddaughter irritating, but he did not want to see her made unhappy. Or a laughingstock.

So he decided to speak bluntly: "I feel I must tell you that my granddaughter is not like the ladies of fashion you are probably familiar with, Your Grace. For one thing, she has been brought up to respect the marriage vow."

A flicker of some unidentifiable emotion showed for a moment in the duke's gray-green eyes. His voice was perfectly serene, however, when he replied, "I am glad to hear that, Mr. Patterson. I have a great respect for the marriage vow myself."

What kind of respect? the merchant wanted to ask, but for some reason he found himself hesitating. Incredibly, there was something about this impecunious young man that he, one of the richest men in England, found intimidating.

"Good. Then I think we understand each other, Your Grace," Patterson heard his voice say gruffly. He pulled himself together and held up an imperative hand, trying to establish the dominant position he felt he had lost. "But I have told Lord Linford that Sarah must agree to the match herself."

The duke responded with a faint smile. "Of course," he said softly. "Of course."

Lady Linford had very cleverly managed things so that the first time the duke met Sarah, they would be alone. She told Sarah that the company was to gather in the drawing room at six-thirty for dinner, when in fact the only other person who would arrive at six-thirty was the duke. Everyone else was to wait until seven.

It was with distinct reluctance that the duke betook himself downstairs at the appointed hour. He was dreading having to meet this girl. William Patterson had been appalling, and if his granddaughter was anything like him . . .

It doesn't matter, he told himself grimly as he approached the door to the downstairs drawing room. *This is not a matter in which I have any choice.*

The drawing room door was open and he stepped inside, looking to see if the girl had preceded him. A small figure in a simple white muslin evening dress was standing in front of Linford's Ruisdael landscape. The girl appeared to be utterly absorbed in the picture and did not turn around.

"I hope I am not disturbing you," the duke said.

She jumped a little, then spun to face him. "Of course not." Her voice was surprisingly husky. Her expression was that of a child who has been caught out in mischief. "I was just looking at this painting."

He crossed the drawing room's Persian carpet until he was standing beside her in front of the picture. "You must be Olivia's friend," he said.

She had a small, delicate face, which was almost engulfed by a pair of large brown eyes. Her skin was not the peaches and cream that was the standard of English beauty, but was instead a pale golden color. Her smooth brown hair was fastened at the back of her head in a simple chignon. She was neither plain nor pretty, he thought, but at least she looked like a lady.

She looked at him directly and her face registered none of the bedazzlement he was accustomed to seeing when people first beheld him.

His spirits began to lift. She did not seem to be at all like her grandfather.

"My name is Sarah Patterson," she said.

"How do you do, Miss Patterson," he returned. "I am Olivia's cousin. My name is Cheviot."

Her eyes widened as she recognized the name. "Cheviot? Not . . . not as in Duke of?"

"I am afraid so," he replied charmingly. He gave her one of his most engaging smiles. "But I assure you that I am fully as human as anyone else."

Her lips quirked in polite response to the smile, but her eyes remained grave.

"I see you were admiring this Ruisdael," he said, turning to look at the landscape himself. "Do you like Dutch painting?"

"Very much," Sarah said. She followed his lead and turned back to the picture.

It was an almost monochromatic painting of a river flowing serenely through a landscape of overhanging willow trees.

The duke said, "I have been to Holland and it always amazes me to see how the best Dutch painters manage to capture the quality of the light there."

Her voice woke to life. "But that is exactly it!" she replied. "It is the light that makes a picture like this so absolutely perfect."

He turned to her and found her smiling up at him, this

time with her eyes as well as her mouth. To his surprise, her small face had lit to beauty.

"Have you seen any of Mr. Turner's work, Your Grace?" she asked.

He shook his head regretfully. "I have not been in England for many years. I only returned home recently and I fear I have been too much preoccupied with business to have had much time for pleasure."

The enchanting smile died away from her face.

Clearly I had better familiarize myself with this Turner fellow, the duke told himself with faint amusement.

"Where were you residing when you were not in England, Your Grace?" she asked politely. "On the Continent?"

"In a manner of speaking," he returned. "Actually I was with Wellington on the Peninsula for several years. After that I was with the Army of Occupation in Paris."

She nodded and her small face grew solemn. "Do you know, sometimes I find it hard to believe that the war is really over? When I was growing up I used to think that it would last forever—or at least for a hundred years, like the war between France and England during the Middle Ages."

The duke, whose ancestors had fought at Crécy and Agincourt, was surprised and delighted that she knew about that long-ago conflict.

"If it had not been for Wellington, this war may well have gone on for a hundred years as well," he returned.

"It was terrible enough as it was." She sighed. "Two of the girls I was at school with had brothers killed in Spain, and another had a cousin fall at Waterloo."

Before he could reply, sudden color flushed into her cheeks. "I beg your pardon," she said. "I'm sure that you don't desire to discuss war casualties."

He smiled at her and said gently, "It is not a very cheerful topic for such a lovely evening."

He gestured to one of the eighteenth-century upholstered chairs that were scattered around the drawing room. "Won't you sit down, Miss Patterson? It appears that the rest of our party is late."

She moved gracefully toward the blue tapestry chair he had indicated, sat down, and looked at the clock on the green marble mantelpiece. "I was sure that Olivia said six-thirty," she said doubtfully.

"That is what she told me as well," the duke replied. He took the chair that was next to hers.

Sarah glanced toward the doorway and looked puzzled when she found it empty. The light from the chandelier shone on the top of her head, making her dark brown hair glow like polished mahogany. The duke looked at the long, delicate neck revealed by her drawn-back hair.

Lovely, he thought with pleasure.

"Is Mr. Turner a particular favorite of yours?" he asked.

She sat up straighter and moved her eyes from the door to his face. "Yes. The reason I mentioned him to you was that, like the Dutch painters, the use of light is a very important part of his painting. There is a luminosity about his work that I have seen in no other painter."

He raised an eyebrow.

"You are very knowledgeable, Miss Patterson," he said. "If you are ever in London you must pay a visit to Selbourne House and I will show you some of the pictures that are hanging there. There is a Canaletto painting of the Grand Canal in Venice that I think you will find particularly interesting."

Her lips parted and a dimple flickered in her cheek. "I

should love to see your collection of paintings, Your Grace," she said breathlessly.

He was astute enough to understand that she was not thrilled because she had been invited to visit the home of a duke; she was thrilled because he had offered her a chance to see some paintings.

He began to think that he could actually like this girl.

She folded her hands in the lap of her demure white muslin dress. He thought with relief that there was nothing about her clothes or her manners that gave away the fact that she was not a member of the upper class.

He could almost see her searching her mind for a new topic of conversation. He waited.

"Do you live in London, Your Grace?" she said at last.

"Not all the time," he replied. "My main residence is at Cheviot Castle in Northumberland."

She looked mischievous and the elusive dimple flickered again. "Actually, I knew that." Her voice altered slightly as she quoted from one of the most famous of old English ballads: " *'The stout Earl Selbourne, he doth lie/ In the castle of Cheviot.'* "

"I am humbled, Miss Patterson," he said with a laugh.

The look she gave him was charmingly skeptical.

To his own great surprise, he said, "Actually, I haven't seen Cheviot Castle for almost seven years—since before I left for the Peninsula, in fact."

She tilted her head and looked at him with sympathy. "Have you no family there?"

He replied a little ruefully, "I am not dragging my feet because I have no family there, Miss Patterson. I have been delaying because I am not overly anxious to see the family members who *are* in residence."

Her brown eyes were grave. "I see," she said.

Olivia's gay voice came floating from the doorway. "Have you two introduced yourselves?"

The duke glanced at the mantel and saw with surprise that it was seven o'clock. He turned to his cousin. "Yes, Olivia, Miss Patterson and I have introduced ourselves. It appears that someone told us the wrong time to come down to the drawing room."

Olivia gave him a radiant smile. "Darling Anthony, I'm so sorry."

"There is no need to apologize," he returned. "Miss Patterson and I have had a most entertaining conversation."

Olivia turned to her friend. "Is that true, Sarah?" she demanded. "Did he keep you entertained?"

Sarah's expression was reserved. "Yes," she said.

At this moment, William Patterson came into the drawing room. The duke looked at the bear of a man, dressed in an outrageous black frock coat and colored vest, who was lumbering across Lady Linford's exquisite carpet, and repressed a shudder.

"Well, well, well," Patterson said with rough geniality. "I see you are before me, Sarah."

Sarah stood up. "Yes, Grandpapa," she returned.

The duke also rose, watching as the merchant's blue eyes scanned his granddaughter's reserved face. He saw a look of impatience flash across the other man's heavy features.

"I am afraid that I am to blame for Sarah's being early, Mr. Patterson," Olivia said. "I thought Mother said we were to gather at six-thirty, and then when she changed it to seven, I forgot to tell Sarah." She gave the merchant a bright smile. "My cousin was early, however, so Sarah was not lonely."

"Good, good, good," Patterson said. He actually rubbed his hands.

The duke wondered if he always repeated himself three times.

They were spared further conversation by the arrival of Lord and Lady Linford. Lady Linford took one look at the gathering and said, "Shall we go in to dinner?"

They all gravitated in her direction.

"As we are almost a family party, there is no need to stand upon ceremony," Lady Linford said pleasantly. "Olivia, you will go in with your father, I will go with Mr. Patterson, and Anthony, you may escort Sarah."

Sarah looked amazed. As the lowest-ranking lady in the group, she should not be escorted by the highest-ranking gentleman.

The duke was annoyed. Between Patterson and Olivia and now his aunt, Sarah was sure to tumble to the scheme. None of them was being exactly subtle.

He moved to Sarah's side, took her hand, and placed it on her arm. "It will be my pleasure," he said, and began to walk her toward the door. The others fell in behind them, proceeding in the proper order of duke, earl, and commoner.

The duke looked down at the shining brown head of his dinner partner as they walked through the passage into the dining room and felt a rush of gratitude. It could have been a great deal worse.

CHAPTER
Four

SARAH TOOK A BITE OF HER DRESSED LAMB AND TRIED not to look as astonished as she felt.

Grandpapa must have done something very wonderful for Lord Linford, she thought, as she watched Lady Linford smile at something Mr. Patterson had said.

The contrast between the way she had been treated the last time she visited Hartford and the way she was being treated tonight was far too great for her not to notice it. On her previous sojourn, she had invariably been the last lady taken in to dinner. She had sat quietly, eaten little, and answered only when she was spoken to.

She had not been spoken to very often.

Tonight, however, she had been escorted to the table by a duke. She had been seated between the duke and her host, Lord Linford, both of whom were paying flattering attention to her. On the opposite side of the table, Lady Linford was being gracious to her grandfather.

It all seemed so unbelievable that Sarah wanted to pinch herself.

Lord Linford's attention was claimed for a moment by Olivia, and the duke, who was sitting on Sarah's other side, said in his soft voice, "Do you go often to the theater when you are in London, Miss Patterson?"

She turned toward him and, unbidden, a thought flashed across her mind: *Imagine what Michelangelo could have done with that face.*

Making an effort to keep her own face composed, she replied, "I very much enjoy the theater, Your Grace. I particularly like to watch Mr. Kean play Shakespeare."

Olivia joined the conversation from her place opposite Sarah. "Remember when we saw *The Merchant of Venice*, Sarah? I cried and cried for poor Shylock, but you didn't feel sorry for him at all. And you are the one who is usually so softhearted!"

"You were not the only one crying, if I remember correctly," Sarah returned with a smile. "Mr. Kean certainly played Shylock as if he were a great tragic hero."

"Then why didn't you feel sorry for him, Miss Patterson?" the duke asked curiously.

"I could not forget that pound of flesh," Sarah said. "He really was going to take it from poor Antonio, you know."

"So he was," said the duke.

Sarah frowned at her crystal wineglass. "If I were a Jew, I think it would upset me a great deal to see my race represented on the stage by such a vicious character."

The duke reached for his own glass of wine. He was on his third while Sarah had not yet drunk half of her first. "You must remember that Jews were not very popular during Shakespeare's time," he commented mildly.

From across the table, Mr. Patterson snorted. "They ain't too popular in our own time, either, Your Grace."

The duke's fingers loosely circled the fragile wineglass stem on the table. He had beautiful hands, Sarah noticed, finely articulated and immaculately kept. It was surprising that such an elegant appendage could also look so thoroughly masculine.

"Well, I, for one, certainly approve of them," the duke said pleasantly. "If it wasn't for the efforts of the Baron Rothschild, we would never have been able to finance the late war."

He was the most soft-spoken man that Sarah had ever met, yet his words carried a note of unmistakable authority. It was as if, now that he had spoken, the issue must be settled.

And it was all done with such invincible courtesy!

Sarah fully expected her grandfather to explode. To her stunned amazement, however, he did nothing of the sort. In fact, he said absolutely nothing. Instead he stared at the duke with what appeared to be an expression of approval in his hard blue eyes.

Lady Linford's voice broke the sudden silence. "Perhaps you did not know that my nephew fought in the war, Mr. Patterson." She signaled to the footmen that they could remove the dinner plates. "In fact, he was wounded twice—once at Salamanca and once at Waterloo."

Sarah glanced at the duke and found him regarding his aunt with unconcealed annoyance.

Olivia said with studied innocence, "Just how many horses *did* you have shot out from under you at Waterloo, Anthony? Was it three or four?"

His perfectly chiseled mouth tightened. "If you don't mind, this is a subject I would prefer not to discuss."

Lady Linford looked at Sarah, "Anthony is so modest. He won't ever tell you this, but he was decorated for bravery at Waterloo."

Sarah could see the tension in the duke's fingers as he gripped his wineglass.

Whatever is the matter with Lady Linford and Olivia?
she thought. *Can't they see that they are distressing him?*

She murmured some polite, inconsequential response
to the countess, then turned back to Cheviot and said,
"Have you ever seen any of Shakespeare's history plays
performed upon the stage, Your Grace? What do you
think of the battle scenes in them?"

Very slightly, his fingers relaxed. "The soldiers certainly manage to make a great number of speeches," he
said.

She laughed.

"Do you have a particular favorite among the history
plays, Miss Patterson?" he asked, smoothly following her
lead.

He lifted his glass and took a sip of the rich red burgundy.

"Henry V," she replied promptly.

"Ah." He held his wineglass in front of him and quoted
with a smile:

Once more unto the breach, dear friends, once more,
Or close the wall up with our English dead.

"That is certainly a thrilling passage," she agreed. "But
my favorite is the speech the King makes before Agincourt: 'We few, we happy few, we band of brothers.' "

His startling light eyes met hers and Sarah had the
strangest feeling that he had actually touched her.

After a moment he said, "That is my favorite as well."

As the footmen began to put the dessert plates upon the
table, Mr. Patterson announced loudly, "Sarah has had a
fine education, Your Grace. She's up to all the rig in
things like plays and operas and suchlike."

Sarah fastened her eyes on the crested plate that had

just been put in front of her. *Please, Grandpapa,* she thought imploringly. *Don't.*

"Well then, apparently she made better use of her time in school than Olivia," the duke returned. He looked across the table at his cousin. "What was it that you were telling me this morning on our ride? Something about Zanzibar being part of Asia?"

His voice was warmly teasing.

"Oh pooh, Anthony," Olivia returned. She tossed her blond curls. "Nobody cares where Zanzibar is."

"It is off of Africa, Lady Olivia," Patterson said complacently. "The east coast."

Sarah kept her eyes on her plate as Olivia made some reply to her grandfather. Then she heard a very soft voice say next to her ear, "Did you know that, Miss Patterson?"

She shot him a swift glance. His mouth was grave but his eyes were laughing.

Irresistibly, her own lips curled in response to that look. She said, "As a matter of fact, Your Grace, I did."

After dinner the ladies retired to the upstairs drawing room while the gentlemen remained behind in the dining room to drink their port.

The door had scarcely closed behind the women before Mr. Patterson fixed his gimlet gaze upon the duke and demanded, "Well, Your Grace, what do you think?"

There was a moment's pause. Then the duke said composedly, "I think your granddaughter is a very lovely young woman."

Relief surged through the merchant. Ever since he had met Cheviot in the library this afternoon, he had feared that the duke would humiliate him by rejecting Sarah. A man who looked like Cheviot would have little trouble finding himself an heiress who had more vivacity than Patterson's mousy little granddaughter.

The merchant's relief caused him to speak jovially. "I ain't never seen Sarah so animated as she was tonight. I think she likes you, Your Grace."

The expression on the duke's face was unreadable. "I hope she does," he replied. "I certainly like her."

Patterson beamed.

Lord Linford glanced at his nephew's face and said hastily, "I have always thought Miss Patterson to be a charming young woman. I know that my daughter is quite fond of her."

The merchant gave a triumphant grin. Neither of them could say enough good things about Sarah, he thought. The marriage was going to happen after all.

Money always wins in the end, Patterson thought complacently. *He's probably going to hold me up for a fortune, but it'll be worth it.*

For the shrewd merchant in Mr. Patterson had recognized as soon as he met the duke that if he bought this young man for Sarah, he would get value for his money. Cheviot was the real thing, Patterson thought, the genuine article. Instead of being outraged by the duke's unconscious air of command, as Sarah had expected, the merchant actually was reveling in it. He recognized it as a sign of his future son-in-law's elevated station in life.

I wonder if he'll wear his coronet when they get married, Patterson thought.

He leaned back in his chair and commented with confidence, "Sarah will make a grand duchess."

"I am sure she will," Lord Linford replied.

The duke said nothing.

Lord Linford splashed more port into his glass and drank it down as if he needed it.

"Well then," the earl said, as he returned his glass to the table. "When do you think we should broach the subject of this marriage to Sarah herself?"

"I'll tell her about it tonight," Patterson said. He was leaning back in his chair with his fingers steepled on his chest. He had taken only a single sip of the earl's excellent port.

"I do not think that is a good idea," the duke returned.

Over his tented fingers, the merchant stared at his future son-in-law in stunned amazement. It was one thing for the duke to make pronouncements as if they were an Act of Parliament; it was quite another thing for him to contradict William Patterson, the man who held the moneybags.

"Why not?" the merchant demanded with a scowl.

"Because I think it would be wiser to leave Sarah in ignorance for the rest of her visit. It will allow me the opportunity to make her comfortable with me," the duke explained. "Her nature appears to be reticent and I do not think that she will feel at all comfortable if she knows that I wish to marry her."

Reticent! Patterson thought derisively. *Well, he has taken Sarah's measure, that's for sure.*

He narrowed his eyes at the duke.

Cheviot was going serenely on, "Then, after we return to London, I will speak to Sarah myself."

His soft, gracious voice held all the calm confidence of a man who expects to have his way.

Patterson's scowl died away, but he maintained his narrow-eyed stare at the young man who was seated directly across the polished mahogany dining table from him.

Lord Linford was the one who shifted uncomfortably

as the oldest and the youngest man in the room stared each other down.

Finally Patterson said slowly, "All right, Your Grace. We'll do it your way."

Cheviot nodded and took a sip of his port.

Patterson continued to stare at the young man as he half-listened to what Lord Linford was saying.

Cheviot would be expensive, Patterson thought, but the more he saw of him, the more convinced he became that the duke was going to be worth it.

Olivia was playing the pianoforte when the gentlemen came into the downstairs drawing room to join the ladies. Sarah was seated to one side of the instrument on a white brocade Roman Empire–style sofa, and Lady Linford was seated in a gilt chair upholstered in flaming red satin.

The duke immediately went to stand beside Olivia at the pianoforte. From the look on his face, Sarah could see that he was utterly intent upon the music.

Olivia played brilliantly. Music, in fact, was the one thing in life about which Olivia was utterly serious. This dedication was the basis of her friendship with Sarah. The two girls had always understood each other's commitment to the particular art form that each loved.

When the last note of the sonata Olivia was playing had died away, she looked up at her cousin and lifted her perfectly arched eyebrows.

He smiled at her and said, "Play some Mozart, Olivia."

She nodded, and her fingers moved once more over the keyboard.

The duke moved to Sarah's sofa, sat beside her, and proceeded to listen to the music.

On the other side of the room, Mr. Patterson shifted his weight uncomfortably on the seat he had taken on a matching Roman Empire–style sofa. Sarah, who had learned years ago to be attuned to her grandfather's every passing mood, glanced at him nervously.

Much as Sarah loved to listen to Olivia play, she hoped her friend wouldn't go on for too long. Mr. Patterson did not have a great deal of patience with Mozart.

He did manage to contain himself until the piece Olivia was playing ended, however. Then Lady Linford surprised Sarah by saying, "Very nice, Olivia. And now let us ask Miss Patterson if she would mind entertaining us for a while."

Damn, Sarah thought daringly to herself. It was only in the privacy of her own mind that she allowed herself to say such a word.

"I'm afraid I don't play as well as Olivia," she said to Lady Linford.

"We perfectly understand that," the duke's quiet voice said from his place beside her. "There are very few people in England who play as well as Olivia."

Olivia, who had turned around on the piano seat, sent her cousin a radiant smile.

"Thank you, Anthony."

Lady Linford gestured her daughter away from the pianoforte. "Give Miss Patterson your seat, my dear."

Sarah rose to her feet with resignation, but before she crossed to the instrument, she glanced at the duke. "We had an ironclad rule at school that none of us was to be made to play after Olivia," she informed him. "She always had to go last."

He grinned.

Sarah crossed the drawing room floor and sat down at the vacant pianoforte. She knew she played well, but she had not been joking when she had told the duke about the girls at school insisting that Olivia must always go last.

The contrast between her friend's artistry and the playing of everyone else had been too depressingly obvious.

As she arranged her girlish white muslin skirts on the bench, it occurred to Sarah that during her last visit to Hartford, no one had evinced the slightest desire to hear her play the pianoforte.

She stretched her fingers, rested them on the keyboard, and began to play a section of a concerto by Haydn that she had always liked.

"Lovely, lovely," Mr. Patterson boomed as soon as he realized that she was done. "I'd say you were every bit as good as Lady Olivia, Sarah."

Sarah glanced at Olivia, who winked at her.

"Thank you, Grandpapa," Sarah said.

"You are very accomplished, Miss Patterson," Lady Linford said. The expression on her face was both pleased and relieved.

Sarah's brow puckered slightly. Suddenly she was overcome by the feeling that everyone else in the room knew something that she did not.

"What did you think, Your Grace?" Mr. Patterson demanded next. "Don't Sarah play well?"

Damn, Sarah thought with embarrassment. *What has got into Grandpapa tonight?*

"She plays very well indeed," the duke returned agreeably. "It must always be a pleasure to listen to someone who is as proficient on the pianoforte as Miss Patterson."

Her grandfather looked as if he had been expecting a greater compliment than that.

Sarah said firmly, "Thank you, Your Grace."

Then, instead of returning to her seat beside the duke, she went to sit next to her grandfather.

"Well, I thought you was every bit as good as Lady Olivia," he said, staring challengingly around the room.

She patted his hand. "Thank you, Grandpapa. I like to play the pianoforte, and I do it rather well. Olivia, however, is a musician."

Once again she looked at her friend.

Olivia's face had flushed with pleasure. "Thank you, Sarah," she said.

Sarah smiled at her.

Mindful of her duty as a hostess to entertain her guests, Lady Linford turned to Mr. Patterson and asked him if he would like to play a game of whist with her and Olivia and Lord Linford.

The merchant folded his arms across his brightly patterned vest. "I don't play cards, my lady," he announced. "Never had time to learn such foolishness."

Lady Linford looked stunned. Clearly she had thought cards would be the way to entertain Mr. Patterson.

"Sarah plays whist, Mama," Olivia said demurely. "Why don't you and Papa and Anthony and Sarah have a game, and while you play I will show Mr. Patterson the gardens?"

Sarah stared at her friend in amazement. What could Olivia be thinking of?

Olivia refused to meet her eyes, however. Instead she smiled gaily at Sarah's grandfather and said, "Our gardens are rather famous, Mr. Patterson."

Sarah's puzzled gaze went next to Lady Linford. She thought that there was little chance of that lady allowing her daughter to stroll about the gardens with the very vulgar Mr. Patterson.

"What a splendid idea, my love," Lady Linford said approvingly. She then made a motion toward the card table that was set in the corner of the drawing room, and said cheerfully, "Shall we, Miss Patterson?"

In a state of near shock, Sarah saw Olivia thread her

arm through Mr. Patterson's and lead him through the French doors that led outdoors into the garden.

She took her seat at the table and got another shock as she realized that her partner was not to be Lord Linford, but the duke.

She thought, as she picked up her cards and began to arrange them, *What on earth can Grandpapa have done for Lord Linford?*

CHAPTER
Five

WHEN FINALLY HE SOUGHT OUT HIS BED, THE DUKE was not in a good mood.

What a mull they are making of it, he thought in annoyance, as he closed the heavy bedroom door behind him.

His valet, who had been sitting on a stool awaiting him, leaped to his feet.

"Good evening, Clement," the duke said courteously. "Did they give you a good dinner?"

"Yes, thank you, Your Grace, they did," the man replied.

The duke stood quietly and let Clement slide his perfectly cut coat off of his shoulders and undo his perfectly arranged neckcloth.

During the course of the evening, the duke had seen how astonished and bewildered Sarah was by the very particular attention being paid to her by her host and hostess. The duke was well enough acquainted with his Aunt Frances to make a shrewd guess that Her Ladyship had not been nearly so attentive on Sarah's previous visit to Hartford.

He sat so that Clement could remove his evening shoes and stockings.

If his Aunt Frances didn't stop trying to throw him in the girl's face, she very soon would figure out what was going on. And this the duke did not want.

Sarah was intelligent; he knew that from the way she played whist. As his partner, she had consistently led into the strength of his hand, and she had confidently taken the winning trick of the set with the two of hearts, because she had been counting cards and knew very well that all the trump were out and that the two was the last heart left.

She was definitely intelligent.

The duke allowed his valet to help him into a black silk dressing gown, and then he dismissed the servant with a gentle good night. He did not get into bed right away, however. Instead he walked to the partially open window and stood there looking out into the darkness and inhaling the fresh scent of newly cut grass.

He was annoyed with his relatives, but otherwise his spirits were lighter than they had been in months. He stood in the darkened bedroom and breathed the sweet damp night air of Kent into his lungs, and for the first time he allowed himself to acknowledge how deeply he had dreaded meeting the Patterson girl.

He did not require that his wife be beautiful, but he could not have borne to live in intimacy with a woman who was loud and vulgar and crude.

He thought of Sarah's small, delicate face, of the elusive dimple in her cheek that came and went so intriguingly, and he let his breath out in a long sigh of heartfelt relief.

He thought he could live with Sarah.

He only wished that the others would stop pushing him

at her! He remembered how his Aunt Frances had informed Sarah that he had been decorated at Waterloo, and his mouth tightened with anger.

Aside from the fact that he did not like the idea of Lady Linford presenting him as if he were a particularly desirable piece of merchandise that Sarah should not let slip through her fingers, it always infuriated the duke whenever anyone tried to suggest that he was a war hero. As he well knew, the true war heroes were all dead. Thousands and thousands of them—all dead.

The duke always felt that he must not have done enough, simply because he had survived.

He pushed the drapes open so that the window was uncovered, and crossed the floor to the great carved fourposter where he was to sleep.

The house was silent.

He shrugged out of his dressing gown and climbed into bed in his drawers. It was how he had slept for all of those years in the hot climates of Spain and Portugal, and he had grown used to the freedom of near nakedness. The one time he had tried to put on a nightshirt, it had seemed excessively uncomfortable to him.

He turned down the lamp next to his bed, lay back against his pillows, stared upward into the dark, and reviewed his situation.

I have two more days here at Hartford to charm Sarah, he thought.

He had not a doubt in his mind that he could charm her. He had never yet failed to charm a woman when he exerted himself to do so.

Then, when we have returned to London, I will propose marriage.

Lord Linford had told his nephew that he had made it

very clear to Mr. Patterson that the marriage settlement was going to have to be enormous.

The duke thought of the scope of his debts and closed his eyes.

I am going to have to get her to agree to marry me quickly.

Unseen in the dark, his mouth took on a bitter line. Just once, when the news of his father's death had first been broken to him, it had crossed his mind that he did not need the title. He had enough money from his mother to allow him to live respectably. He could simply keep his commission in the army and continue to live the perfectly satisfying life he had been living for all of his adult life.

But centuries of responsibility had been bred into the duke, and he had scarcely hesitated before he had willingly accepted the burden his father had laid upon him.

At least he would see Cheviot again, he thought, as he stared upward into the darkness between his bed and its overhanging canopy. Unfortunately, the joy that thought brought him was tempered by the realization that his stepmother and two half-brothers would be at the castle as well.

As he had indicated to Sarah, it was not a meeting he was looking forward to. He disliked his father's second wife almost as much as she disliked him. As for his half-brothers . . . he had scarcely had enough contact with them to know how he felt about them.

Let me see, he thought. *Lawrence must be twenty-one and Patrick . . .* He did some figures in his head. *Patrick must be thirteen.*

Patrick had been little more than a baby when the duke had left for Spain, and Lawrence had been at school. Even before that, however, he had rarely seen either of them, as he himself had been at school during term, and he had always spent his holidays with friends.

In all the years of his growing up, he had done his best to avoid Cheviot Castle, which he loved with all his heart.

The first thing he must do however was make certain of this marriage, he thought, as he lay in the great four-poster of the state bedroom at Hartford Court. He couldn't do anything until he had money.

He shut his eyes and conjured up Sarah's face.

He thought that she, unlike her grandfather, had seemed remarkably unimpressed by his title.

I must make her fall in love with me, the duke thought. That would be the safest way all around.

His last thought before he fell asleep was, *She's really a lovely little thing when she smiles.*

Sarah arose before sunrise, dressed in old clothes, and quietly let herself out a side door of the house. She had with her a portable easel, an empty canvas, and her oil paints. She knew exactly where she was going: to the small knoll on the west side of the lake. It was a perfect position from which to observe the sun as it rose above the spring-green trees and still water of the lake below.

The first light was just beginning to touch the sky when Sarah arrived at her chosen spot. Her boots and the hems of her gown and cloak were soaked with dew, but she scarcely noticed. Efficiently, she set up her easel and paints, and as the first bursts of color lightened the sky, she went to work.

She was utterly intent upon her painting several hours later, when a horse and rider came cantering along the path that rimmed the far side of the lake. She paused for a moment to admire the beauty of the sight: the slim, elegant chestnut thoroughbred and the slim, elegant aristocrat on his back. In the early sunlight, the duke's uncovered hair shone with the same bright bronze as did the horse's coat.

The colors were in perfect contrast to the light in the sky, and Sarah wished she could stop them so that she could capture them in paint.

But the whole essence of man and horse was fluid motion. Useless to ask them to stop and pose; she would lose the beauty of the moment if she did that.

The chestnut and his rider disappeared into the trees and Sarah went back to her painting. Twenty minutes later, as she was working on the sky of her oil sketch, she heard the sound of a horse trotting up the path behind her.

She didn't turn her head. Perhaps he wouldn't notice her. Perhaps he wouldn't bother to stop. Perhaps he would just go away and leave her alone to paint.

She heard the sound of the horse's footfalls slow. Then a soft voice said, "Whoa, boy."

Damn, Sarah thought. She scowled at her picture. *He's going to bother me after all.*

The duke said, "Good morning, Miss Patterson."

Reluctantly, she turned her head. "Good morning, Your Grace."

"Please go on with your painting," he said. "I did not mean to disturb you."

Sarah needed no other encouragement. She wanted to finish this sketch before the light changed completely.

She nodded, picked up her brush, and went back to work.

Half an hour later, the full light of day was blazing in the sky and Sarah sighed, put down her paintbrush, and stretched her fingers and her back.

"I can see why you admire Ruisdael," the duke said in his quiet voice.

Sarah jumped. She had forgotten that he was still there.

She turned her head and found him standing several paces behind her, his horse's reins in his hand, his eyes fixed on her painting.

"Yes," she said. "The Dutch seventeenth-century landscape painters showed nature as it really is. I have always felt that our English landscape tradition is too . . . conventional to be real."

He nodded, his eyes still on her work. He said nothing else.

"It's just a sketch," Sarah heard herself saying. "I will do the real painting in my studio at home."

He nodded again. He was still looking at the painting.

"Do you admire landscape painting, Your Grace?" she said with an attempt at lightness. "It is not fashionable these days, I know."

"Where did you learn to paint like this?" he asked.

His voice was deadly serious.

"I had a wonderful teacher in Bath," Sarah replied. "John Blake. He studied for many years at the Royal Academy schools, so he was technically very accomplished. He taught me a great deal."

"A man like that was teaching at a girls' school?"

"He didn't teach at the school," Sarah said. "He had a studio in Bath and I took private lessons from him." She gave a little shrug. "I needed to know more than the school's art teacher could show me."

His eyes moved from the painting to her face and then back again to the painting. "How old are you, Miss Patterson?" he asked.

She was surprised by the question. "Eighteen," she replied, and looked at him in polite inquiry.

He smiled slightly. "You have quite a future before you, if you can paint like this at eighteen."

She flushed with surprise and delight. "Thank you.
That was a very nice thing to say." She hesitated, then
added, "My grandfather thinks I waste too much time . . .
'dabbling,' as he puts it."

"You are not a dabbler," the duke replied. His eyes
were once again on her canvas. "You are a painter. And a
painter should paint."

No one had ever talked to Sarah like this before except
John Blake.

"I own two paintings by Claude that I think you would
like very much," the duke said. He looked at her. "When
we return to London, you must come and see them."

"I should love to," Sarah said sincerely.

The chestnut thoroughbred, who had just about finished all the grass he could reach, tugged at the reins to
try to get the duke to move to a new spot.

"I had better get this fellow back to his stable," the
duke said. "He wants his breakfast."

Sarah smiled. "Perhaps I will see you back at the
house, Your Grace."

He put his foot in the stirrup and swung easily up into
the saddle. "I'm sure you will," he said, then turned the
horse and cantered off along the bridle path.

Sarah watched until he was out of sight, then she
turned to pack up her belongings. Her heart was full of ju-
bilation.

He said I was a painter!

It was like manna in the desert for her to have someone
take her work seriously. Her grandfather thought that
painting pictures was a waste of time.

"No one ever made any money out of paintings,
Sarah," he would say. And that, in Mr. Patterson's mind,
was that.

Even Neville Harvey, who had always been a good

friend to her, did not understand her passion for painting. He humored her, he told her that what she painted was "pretty," but she knew that he didn't begin to see the beauty that she was trying to paint.

Neville was like her grandfather. He didn't much like the countryside and was happiest when he was in the city. Commerce was what he understood. The changing light in the sky was a matter of supreme indifference to him.

She was very glad that she had come to Hartford and met the Duke of Cheviot. She hoped very much that he would remember his invitation to her to view his Claudes.

The duke had not been trying to flatter Sarah when he had called her a painter. In fact, he had been extremely surprised when he had seen the quality of her work.

It had given him a wholly new view of her. It had added to her substance.

He thought, *She is someone to be reckoned with, this girl.*

There was something in the canvas that she had done this morning that he had never before seen in another painting. It wasn't the technical accomplishment that had so startled him; rather, it was the quality of feeling the picture conveyed. There was an excited delight about the portrayal of different colors of light staining a sky with high clouds moving across its blue-gray expanse.

How on earth did a man like William Patterson come to have such a girl for a granddaughter? he wondered.

He remembered then that his aunt had said something about Sarah's mother being Welsh. Perhaps that would account for the difference, he thought. The Celts had always been sensitive to beauty.

He returned his horse to the stable and was beginning

to walk back to the house when it occurred to him that he had not seen any sign of a servant in the area where Sarah had been painting. She must have lugged easel, canvas, and paints out to the lake by herself.

He frowned. He had better go and help her carry them home.

It was a measure of his own gentlemanly instincts that he did not think of this as a means of currying favor with an heiress. He was truly appalled at the thought of a lady carrying such heavy items by herself.

He turned away from the house and began to walk in the opposite direction. At the end of the garden, he took the path that would lead him to the lake.

He had been walking five minutes through the woods when he met Sarah. She had taken the easel apart and it was hanging from her right shoulder by a strap; a canvas bag that must contain her paints hung off the other shoulder. In her hands she carried her wet canvas.

The duke strode forward. "You should not be carrying this heavy equipment by yourself, Miss Patterson," he said. "Why did you not ask a servant to carry it to the lake for you?"

"I did not feel that I could impose upon Lady Linford's servants," Sarah replied quietly. "And I assure you, Your Grace, that I am quite accustomed to carrying my own gear."

He stopped in front of her, blocking the path so that she had to stop as well. "Well, you shouldn't be. You will hurt your back by trying to bear this weight. Give the easel and the paints to me."

Steady brown eyes looked up at him. "I am stronger than I look, Your Grace. The weight is not hurting me."

He returned pleasantly, "Nevertheless, Miss Patterson, you will give the easel and the paints up to me."

She hesitated.

"It didn't occur to me until I had reached the stable that I hadn't seen a servant with you," he said. "Otherwise I should have assisted you sooner."

Sarah was beginning to grow annoyed. "I am not a child or a cripple, Your Grace. When Mr. Blake and I painted in the countryside around Bath, I always carried my own things."

"Yes, well, you are not with Mr. Blake now, Miss Patterson, you are with me. And I insist on taking that encumbrance from you."

"Oh, very well," Sarah snapped ungraciously. "If you want to play beast of burden, be my guest."

Carefully, she lowered her canvas to the path and propped it against her knees. Then she took the easel strap off one arm and handed it to the duke, who swung it over his own shoulder. Next she handed him the paints.

The easel was not light. The duke frowned and looked at Sarah's fragile neck. He imagined the groove that the strap must have cut into the delicate skin of her shoulder.

She leaned down and picked up her canvas.

"Ready?" she said to him.

His lips quirked. It was definitely a novelty having a lady annoyed at him for daring to help her.

"Ready," he said meekly.

She shot him a dark look and gestured him forward with her chin.

The duke, who was also much stronger than he looked, moved off easily.

They walked in silence until they had reached the formal gardens at the back of the house.

Then Sarah said contritely, "What a churl you must think me, Your Grace. I am sorry. Thank you for carrying my gear."

"You are very welcome," he returned.

A gardener who was out doing some early morning weeding paused in his work to bob his head and pull his forelock as they passed by.

The duke acknowledged him with a gracious nod.

Sarah stopped dead and demanded, "Is there something wrong with your eye?"

The gardener, who was an old man, replied in a reedy voice, "It be all right, miss."

"No, it isn't," Sarah replied. "It is all crusty. Have you seen a doctor?"

"N-no, miss," the gardener replied with wonder.

"You need some drops for it," Sarah said. "I will tell Her Ladyship that you must be sent to a doctor. What is your name?"

"Jenkins, miss."

Sarah smiled at him. A genuine smile that acknowledged him as a person. "The garden is beautiful, Jenkins," she said. "You do wonderful work."

The old man's face lit in response. "Thankee, miss. Thankee."

Sarah nodded and moved on.

The duke looked at her in wonder. He had not even noticed the old man's eye.

CHAPTER
Six

S ARAH DID NOT SEE LADY LINFORD UNTIL LATER THAT
morning, but as soon as Her Ladyship walked into
the very pretty morning room where Sarah was sitting with Olivia, Sarah told her about the gardener.

Lady Linford looked at her guest in astonishment.
"One of the gardeners has a crusty eye?" she repeated.

"Yes, my lady. It looks quite nasty. I'm surprised no
one has thought to send him to a doctor."

"Well," said Lady Linford. "I shall see that the matter
is attended to, Miss Patterson."

Sarah, who had no idea what a concession her hostess
had just made, replied, "Thank you, Lady Linford. His
name is Jenkins."

The countess hesitated, but it was perfectly clear that
Sarah expected her to do something immediately.

She rang the bell.

"Eliot," she said to the butler when he appeared in
front of her some thirty seconds later, "will you please
see to it that one of our gardeners, I believe his name is
Jenkins, is sent to the doctor? Apparently he has a crusty
eye."

Eliot was far too good a servant to allow his amazement to show on his face. "Very good, my lady," he said. "Will that be all?"

"Yes," said Lady Linford.

The butler left.

Olivia said, her voice bubbling with suppressed amusement, "I thought I would take Sarah to view the old Saxon church at Breedon this afternoon, Mama."

"That is a delightful plan," the countess replied. She arranged her mauve skirts gracefully upon the delicate pink silk sofa. "Will you invite Mr. Patterson to join you?"

Sarah said cautiously, "I rather suspect that Grandpapa will not be interested in an old Saxon church, Lady Linford."

"Very well," Lady Linford replied agreeably. "Do you think he would care to go out with a gun? Lord Linford would be happy to show him some sport, if that is what he would prefer."

The thought of her grandfather creeping through the woods with a gun almost made Sarah grin.

"I'm afraid Grandpapa does not shoot, either, Lady Linford," she said.

The countess did not look so agreeable as she had before. "Well then, what does he like to do? Is he a reader? Our library is extensive. I also have all the latest periodicals, if that is what he would enjoy."

Sarah shook her head regretfully, "I'm afraid not, Lady Linford."

By now the countess was frowning. "Perhaps he would like to spend the afternoon walking through the gardens."

"Flowers make him sneeze," Sarah said.

Lady Linford glared at her. "Really, Sarah! What am I to do with him, then?"

"He likes to eat," Sarah offered.

Lady Linford looked affronted. "I have, of course, planned an excellent dinner, but there are still many hours to fill before it is served."

Sarah sighed. "I'm sorry, Lady Linford, but all that interests Grandpapa is business. He doesn't do anything else."

If the countess had not been such a great lady, Sarah would have said that she looked flummoxed.

"We will take him with us to see the Saxon church, Mama," Olivia said firmly. "And Anthony can come, too."

Sarah had to suppress a smile at the expression of relief on Lady Linford's face.

"Thank you, Olivia," her mother said.

The thought of Mr. Patterson's likely comments when he viewed the Saxon church was enough to dampen Sarah's enthusiasm for the visit. There was nothing to be done, however. Sarah perfectly understood Lady Linford's frustration at trying to find something for her grandfather to do.

For the hundredth time she wondered what on earth had prompted the Linfords to issue such an extraordinary invitation.

The sightseers set off from Hartford in two carriages. Olivia and Mr. Patterson rode in the barouche, which was driven by one of the Linford grooms, and Sarah went with the duke in his phaeton, which he drove himself.

It was a lovely afternoon, sunny and warm enough for Sarah to be perfectly comfortable in a russet-colored bolero jacket worn over a plain tan carriage dress. She sat beside the duke in the high seat of the phaeton, her leather-gloved hands folded neatly in her lap, her small boots braced against the floor. On her head she wore a small russet velvet cap.

The duke's matched black horses were magnificent, and Sarah, who knew all about upper-class "bucks" and their reckless driving, was at first a little nervous. The duke proved to be an excellent driver, however. His horses went smoothly, steadily, and under perfect control. Sarah soon concluded she could rest easy that he was not going to overturn her in a ditch.

"I am surprised that you did not view the Saxon church on your last visit to Hartford," the duke commented as the phaeton rolled along under some large overhanging oaks, which were just starting to show green on their branches. "It is exactly the sort of place that would interest you." He turned his head and looked at her. "It would make a wonderful subject for a painting."

Sarah looked at her companion for the afternoon. He was wearing a black riding coat, tan trousers, and highly polished black Wellington boots. His neckcloth was intricately tied, although it was not overly high. In every way but one, he was a model of fashion.

He was not wearing a hat, and his hair, which was cut short, blew back from his face in the fresh spring breeze.

"Olivia was going to take me the last time I was here, but it rained, and then there was not time," Sarah explained.

He nodded and returned his eyes to the road.

Sarah glanced over her shoulder at the barouche that was following them, and said a little worriedly, "I wonder how Olivia is faring with Grandpapa."

She had been amazed by the carriage arrangements, having fully expected to be the one to companion her grandfather.

"She will do just fine," the duke replied serenely. "She

will ask him to talk about himself, and that will keep him occupied for the whole of the drive."

Sarah stared at him in wonderment. "That is true," she said. "How did you know that?"

He grinned, looking all of a sudden charmingly boyish. "All men like to talk about themselves, Miss Patterson. We are invincible egoists. Didn't you know that?"

Sarah kept looking at him. "I suppose I never thought about it."

"Well, you have been at a girls' school and you have no brothers," he said, excusing her. "But I assure you, Olivia will know just how to deal with your grandfather."

"Hmm," Sarah said thoughtfully. After a minute, she leaned back against her seat, unfolded and refolded her hands, and said, "So, Your Grace, would you like to tell me about yourself?"

He shot her a startled look. Then he laughed.

"You must be more subtle than that, Miss Patterson. You must ask me some leading questions."

On their left a pasture appeared, filled with ewes and lambs sleeping in the afternoon sun. The grass was very green and the hill behind the pasture was gold with new willow leaves.

Sarah furrowed her brow. "I'm afraid I'm not going to be very good at this," she murmured. "It just seems rude, somehow, to question a person about himself."

"You must do it tactfully," he said. He looked as if he were enjoying himself. "For example, you might ask me if I like horses."

Two of the lambs were curled up together, looking like two little balls of white fleece in the grass. Sarah smiled at the sight of them.

"Aren't those lambs adorable?" she said.

He glanced from the white bundles in the grass to her face, smiled, and said softly, "Yes. Adorable."

For some reason, Sarah felt warm color flush into her cheeks. She sat up straight on her seat and said primly, "Do you like horses, Your Grace?"

The remnants of his smile remained on his lips. Sarah found herself thinking that he had the most beautiful mouth she had ever seen.

"Yes, I do like horses," he replied. "Very much. I will not bore you with all the details, but I assure you that I am perfectly capable of talking for a half an hour straight about my horses."

"The drive to the Saxon church is half an hour," Sarah pointed out. "Go ahead and talk."

His amusement lingered.

"What do you want to know, Miss Patterson?"

She replied promptly, "What kinds of horses do you have? How many? What kinds of personalities do they have? Do you have a favorite one? How old were you when you first started to ride—"

"Stop!" The duke held up a hand. "It will take me a full hour to answer all those questions."

"Then we will have something to talk about on the way home as well," Sarah said.

A farmer's cart was coming along the road toward them, and when the driver saw the duke's phaeton, he pulled to the side and stopped to let them pass.

The duke nodded in acknowledgment.

Sarah said, "Good day. Thank you for letting us go by."

The farmer beamed back. "Good day to ye both."

There had been a child sitting next to the farmer on the front seat of the cart, and after they had gone by, Sarah said to the duke, "What a beautiful little boy."

The duke looked at her in puzzlement. "What little boy?"

"The little boy who was sitting next to the farmer. He had eyes as big as saucers."

A cloud of blackbirds rose from the wheat field on their left.

The duke said slowly, "You are very observant, Miss Patterson."

She looked surprised by his comment. Then she said in a tone of mock sternness, "No delays, Your Grace. You were going to tell me about your horses."

"Do you like horses yourself?" he countered. "Do you ride?"

She stared at him in exasperation. "I thought you were going to talk about *you*. Why is the conversation all of a sudden my responsibility?"

He laughed. "I don't want to bore you," he said. "If you don't like horses, we will find something else for me to discourse upon."

"I like all animals," Sarah said simply. "When I was a child I lived in the country and I had a pony and a dog and a duck, but when I went to live with Grandpapa I had to give them up. Animals make Grandpapa sneeze."

They were coming to a turn in the road and the duke slowed his team in case they met a carriage coming the other way. Sarah silently approved of his caution.

"What was your dog's name?" he asked.

"Bounce, because he jumped up and down all the time." She sighed. "I gave him to one of the village children. He was a friend of mine and Bounce knew him. Johnny promised me that he would take very good care of him, and I'm sure that he did."

"I have missed having a dog as well," he said. "I had two spaniels when I was a child, but then I went away to school and after that into the army. I've promised myself that as soon as I'm settled, I'm going to get a few dogs."

"That's nice," Sarah said wistfully.

"You know, I rather think we are starting to sound maudlin," he said.

She chuckled. "You're right. Cheer me up and tell me about your horses."

This time he obliged her. "Well, my favorite horse is a chestnut gelding named Sam."

"Sam?"

"Sam is a perfectly good name."

"Is he the horse you were riding this morning?"

"Yes."

"It's a crime to give a horse like that a name like *Sam*. He should be . . . Copper something or other."

He shook his head and his own hair gleamed copper in the sun.

"If you knew his personality, you would see that Sam suits him perfectly. He looks pretty fancy, I'll grant you that, but he is actually the most sensible animal in the world. I would trust him with my life. I *have* trusted him with my life. He's more intelligent and loyal than most of the people I know."

"That is quite an accolade," Sarah admitted. "Tell me more. What are some of the sensible things that he has done?"

The duke obliged with a story that made Sarah laugh. Then he told her another.

In an amazingly short period of time, she found that they had reached the Saxon church.

Sarah lay awake in bed that evening and relived in her mind the events of the afternoon. The Saxon church had been beautiful, with a central tower and one transept that actually dated from about the year 1000. The austere lines of the stone structure had been moving in their unaffected simplicity, and its setting, on higher ground some distance from the present village, was lovely.

Sarah curled up on her side in the warm, comfortable bed, and remembered how she and the duke had stood in the middle of the nave, with the sun coming in through the rounded windows. She remembered the words the duke had quoted in his soft voice: " 'The soul of man is like a sparrow, which on a dark and rainy night passes for a moment through the door of a king's hall. Entering, it is for a moment surrounded by light and warmth and is safe from the wintry storm; but after a short spell of brightness and quiet, it vanishes through another door into the dark storm from which it came. Likewise the life of man is for a moment visible; but what went before or is to come remains unknown.' "

"Yes," Sarah had breathed, looking around the beautifully preserved church.

Olivia's voice broke the stillness. "What is that saying from, Anthony?" She and Mr. Patterson had come up to them in time to hear the duke's words.

He turned to look at his cousin and replied, "It is from Bede's *Ecclesiastical History of the English Nation.*"

"Well, it must be a gloomy sort of book, if that is all he can say about a man's life," Mr. Patterson said, his voice sounding loud in the quiet of the little church.

"I wouldn't know if it was gloomy or not," Olivia said cheerfully. "I've never read it."

"Kind of small, this church, ain't it?" Mr. Patterson said next. "No nice colored glass or fancy carved screens."

"It is a Saxon church, Grandpapa," Sarah tried to explain. "They were very simple."

"Well, if you ask me, it sure ain't worth traveling miles to look at," Mr. Patterson pronounced. "It's kind of measly, as far as I'm concerned."

Sarah had seen the look Olivia exchanged with the duke, and she flushed with mortification.

"Perhaps your taste runs more toward the Gothic, Mr. Patterson," the duke had said with perfect courtesy.

"I like something bigger and fancier," the merchant replied. "If that's Gothic, then that's what I like. Not that I'm very big on churches," he added with a rough laugh. "I prefer banks any day."

"Banks are certainly important as well," the duke had replied suavely.

It's not Grandpapa's fault that he doesn't understand, Sarah told herself as she lay in the big bed in the middle of her lovely bedroom—a far larger and grander bedroom than the one she had been given on her last visit.

The duke was brought up surrounded by beautiful things. He went to school and read the Venerable Bede. Grandpapa did not have an opportunity to do any of that.

But the fact remained that Sarah was upset with her grandfather for his seemingly invincible cultural blindness.

It is one thing for him not to see the beauty of something himself, but he should not belittle other people for their appreciation.

As he belittled her, she thought. As he had always belittled her.

Miss Bates's School for Young Ladies had been Sarah's salvation from her grandfather. Mr. Patterson had sent her to this very fashionable school so that she would meet some members of the aristocracy and learn what he called fancy manners.

She had done both things, but in the process she had

also acquired an education. Sarah had been every teacher's favorite student, so eager had she been for knowledge.

It was at school that she had discovered art.

The only time Sarah had ever stood up to her grandfather was over her art lessons. Mr. Patterson had not wanted her to take instruction from John Blake. Sarah had insisted. She had had the school's art teacher write her grandfather a letter recommending the lessons. When that didn't work, she had asked Miss Bates herself to write a letter.

It was a measure of the headmistress's respect for Sarah's talent that she had done so.

Mr. Patterson had been furious. He felt as if he were being pushed, and no one pushed William Patterson.

He had gone to see Sarah in Bath and exploded.

To his great surprise, Sarah had not backed down. "I want to take these art lessons, Grandpapa. I will do everything else you ask of me, but I must take these lessons. I *will* take them, even if I have to pay for them myself."

"Pay with what, my girl?" he had asked scornfully. "The only money you have is what I give you."

"I'll find money somehow," Sarah had said. "I will take these lessons."

Eventually, Mr. Patterson had given in and paid for the lessons. He told her repeatedly that he was throwing his money away, but he paid.

Sarah had always tried very hard to feel grateful to her grandfather, but it was easier to think kindly of him while she was at school in Bath than it was living under the same roof with him.

Her alternatives to living with her grandfather were limited, however. She knew he wanted her to marry

Neville Harvey, but Neville Harvey was just a younger, more refined version of William Patterson.

Neville would never understand her passion to paint.

Sarah rolled over on her back and stared up at the rose-colored canopy that adorned her bed.

The duke understood, she thought.

Unbidden, his face materialized before her eyes.

You are a painter, Miss Patterson, and a painter should paint.

He might be a duke and look like a god, but he was also a nice man, she thought.

It's strange that I should feel more comfortable with him than I do with most of the people I have known all my life.

Suddenly Sarah realized the direction her thoughts were taking, and she scowled.

Don't be an idiot, Sarah, she scolded herself. *He is the Duke of Cheviot! He is only being polite to you, so don't let yourself think it's more than it really is.*

Still, she thought, it would be nice if he would invite her to view his Claudes.

CHAPTER
Seven

THE DUKE RETURNED TO LONDON IN A MUCH MORE
cheerful frame of mind than he had enjoyed when
he left.

"Miss Patterson is charming," he said to his secretary
the morning after his return, as they sat together in the library of Selbourne House going over the inevitable bills.

Max could not hide his surprise. "Charming?" he repeated. "Really, Anthony?"

"I found her so," the duke replied. He grinned boyishly. "I don't mind telling you, Max, I was scared to
death before I met her. Particularly after I had met the
grandfather! But she is a very well-mannered, ladylike
girl. It could have been much, much worse."

Max's dark eyes softened as he regarded his employer's relaxed face. He had not seen a smile like that
since they had returned to England.

"I'm glad, Anthony," he replied. "Such a girl must realize that this marriage will be an enormous honor for
her. Which is a very good thing, considering that the position she will be called upon to fill is one of the greatest in all of England."

The look the duke gave his secretary was distinctly

wry. "To be truthful, I'm not sure that she is at all interested in such a great honor, Max. She wants to be a painter, not a duchess."

"A painter!"

The duke nodded and the sun that was slanting in through the panes of the library window reflected off his hair.

He wears his own crown, Max thought a little painfully.

The duke said, "Actually, she is a very good painter. I saw a sketch she did while she was at Hartford, and it was quite astonishingly good."

"Good heavens," said Max.

The duke laughed. "Max, if old Patterson will settle four million pounds on me, she can paint everything and anything she desires. If I had my own choice, I would marry a girl from my own order, a girl who would understand the responsibilities of her position. But, as we both know, I don't have a choice. And this girl is intelligent. She can learn what she will need to know."

Max smiled and held out his hand. "I congratulate you, Anthony. It appears that your luck has finally reasserted itself."

The duke put his slim, strong fingers into Max's grip, and Max felt the familiar dizziness that Anthony's touch always managed to produce in him.

"I hope it has," the duke replied. He took his hand away and rested it on the arm of his chair. "There is one remaining fence that must be cleared, however."

Max cleared his throat. "What is that?"

The duke lifted his eyebrows. "Miss Patterson doesn't know about the proposed marriage. Patterson has said that he won't force her against her will, so in order to bring this off, I have to get her to agree to marry me."

Max looked at his employer's face.

"I don't think you will have any trouble getting her to agree to marry you, Anthony," he said.

"Well, I shall certainly do my damnedest," the duke replied fervently. "Then, perhaps, I can finally get rid of these!"

And he slammed his hand down upon the bills that were piled on the desk in front of him.

William Patterson actually dined with his granddaughter on the day of their return from Hartford Court.

"Well, I must say that the Linfords treated us well," he remarked between spoonfuls of oxtail soup.

He had been making this comment at ten-minute intervals ever since their carriage had driven away from Hartford Court that morning.

"Yes, they did," Sarah agreed, as she had been agreeing all day long. "The earl and countess were most attentive."

They were dining at five-thirty in the afternoon, much earlier than they had dined at Hartford, but Mr. Patterson did not like to be kept waiting for his food. Sarah, who was not very hungry, took a token sip of her soup.

Patterson said, "The duke certainly seemed to like you, Sarah."

"He was very nice," Sarah said.

Patterson gave her a piercing look over the soup spoon he was in the process of bringing to his mouth. "You liked him, then?"

Sarah wiped her lips with her napkin.

"Of course I liked him, Grandpapa. It would be impossible not to like such an agreeable man."

Mr. Patterson nodded with satisfaction. "Good, good, good," he said. "I liked him, too. He's a real duke,

Cheviot. I can always tell the genuine article, and he's it."

Sarah gave her grandfather an amused look. "Did you think perhaps he was an imposter?"

"Of course I didn't think he was an imposter," Patterson replied scornfully. "But there are dukes, and then there are dukes, if you know what I mean."

"I am afraid that I don't know what you mean," Sarah replied apologetically. "I didn't know that you were acquainted with any dukes, Grandpapa."

"Oh, I've met a duke or two in my time, my girl," William Patterson said. He had finished his soup and now he took a long swallow of claret, put down his glass, and said with distinct disapproval, "And I was a good bit surprised to find out that they can be just like anyone else."

Sarah could not contain a smile. "You don't think the Duke of Cheviot is like anyone else?"

Now that Mr. Patterson had finished his soup, the single footman who was serving them stepped forward to remove the dishes.

"No," Mr. Patterson answered his granddaughter. "It don't take even a minute before you know he's a duke. You'd know it even if no one told you who he was. Like I said, he's the genuine article."

Somewhat to her own surprise, Sarah found that she understood exactly what her grandfather meant.

"He liked you," Mr. Patterson said once again. "That was pretty clear, my girl."

A plate from Mr. Patterson's heavily gold-encrusted dinner service was laid in front of Sarah.

For the first time, she had an uneasy feeling that she saw where this conversation was heading.

She said carefully, "The duke was polite to me,

Grandpapa. He is the sort of man who would always be polite to a woman. Please do not refine too much upon any attention he might have paid to me. The Duke of Cheviot could never be interested in a girl like me."

The only word Sarah could think of to describe the expression on her grandfather's face was *smug*.

The back of Sarah's neck prickled.

"Is there something I should know about the Hartford visit that I don't know, Grandpapa?" she asked.

Mr. Patterson waited until the footman had finished putting the platters of food upon the table, and then he waved him out of the room.

Sarah sat with her empty plate in front of her and felt her heart begin to hammer in her chest.

Mr. Patterson picked up the carving knife and began to carve slices from the turkey that had been set in front of him.

"I don't know why you say that the duke wouldn't be interested in a girl like you," he said. The first slice of meat fell off the bird and he lifted it onto the platter that had been placed at his right hand.

"He would not be interested in me because he is a duke and I am a merchant's daughter," Sarah replied steadily. "I am not high-born enough for him to make me his wife, nor am I low-born enough for him to make me his mistress. He was merely being polite to a guest of his aunt, Grandpapa. That is all."

"So you think," Mr. Patterson said, the smug expression still on his face.

He slashed off a few more slices of turkey.

Sarah stared at the flashing knife and began to feel a faint sickness in the pit of her stomach.

Mr. Patterson went on, "You got one thing that the

duke ain't got, Sarah, and believe me, that cancels out all the difference between high and low birth."

The sick sensation in her stomach grew stronger.

"And what is that, Grandpapa?" she managed to say.

"Money, my girl. That's what you've got." Patterson pointed the carving knife at her chest. "And that's just what the duke ain't got. His father gambled away the entire family fortune. Cheviot may be a duke, my girl, but all he owns right now is debts."

Mr. Patterson gestured that Sarah should pass him her plate so he could serve her some turkey.

She didn't move. "What are you telling me, Grandpapa?"

"I'm telling you that the duke wants to marry you, my girl," Mr. Patterson said triumphantly. He leaned a little toward her, one of his hands grasping the carving knife and the other the large meat fork. "I've promised to settle a vast amount of money on him, and in return he will make you a duchess. A duchess, Sarah! And not just any duchess, but the Duchess of Cheviot! Can you beat that?"

Sarah just stared at him with appalled brown eyes.

"You can't be serious, Grandpapa?" she said at last in a choked voice.

"Of course I am serious! Do you think I would joke about a thing like this? I tell you, the Linfords came to me and asked me if I would be interested in such a match. At first I made 'em squirm, told him I planned for you to marry Neville Harvey. Then Lady Linford got on her high horse and informed me that all Neville could do was make you the Queen of Cotton, while her nephew could make you a duchess."

He chuckled and finally laid down his utensils.

"Damme, if she didn't have a point. I finally agreed and we made plans for you to meet the duke at Hartford."

"You told me nothing of this," Sarah said faintly.

Her grandfather gave her a shrewd look. "Lady Linford said I should keep it from you. She said you would feel skittish with the duke if you knew the real reason behind our visit."

The initial shock had begun to wear off and Sarah was starting to get angry. "But the duke knew?" she demanded.

"Of course he knew. In fact, he told me not to tell you anything about the scheme, that he wanted to tell you himself." The merchant smiled complacently. "But, as he'll soon discover, William Patterson ain't a man to be ordered about so easily, even by a duke."

Sarah pushed back her chair and stood up. "I am sorry that you and the Linfords and the duke have all wasted your time, Grandpapa, but I am not going to marry him."

Mr. Patterson looked stunned. "What?"

"I am not going to marry him," Sarah repeated. "I don't like to be deceived, and I most certainly would never marry a man who treated me the way Cheviot has!"

"He treated you like you was royalty!" Mr. Patterson roared. "Damme, what's the matter with you, girl?"

"I am not going to marry him," Sarah repeated. And then she ran out of the room.

Sarah locked herself into her bedroom and collapsed into the overstuffed chair that stood in front of the white wood fireplace. She was shaking all over.

I knew something was going on at Hartford, she thought furiously. *I could feel it.*

She thought of how she and the duke had just hap-

pened to meet in the drawing room the first night of her
visit.

It had all been arranged. Everything—the visit to the
Saxon church, the picnic the following day—all
arranged to give Cheviot a chance to charm her.

Sarah remembered the words he had spoken to her by
the lakeside. *You are a painter.*

She shut her eyes.

That hurt most of all. It hurt because she had believed
him. She had been so happy to have someone affirm her
talent, her vocation. She had hugged his words to her
heart as if they were a secret treasure. She had been so
happy.

He's despicable, she thought. *Utterly and completely
despicable. I wouldn't marry him if he were the last man
left on the face of the earth.*

She felt as if she had been betrayed. She had liked
him, and all the while he had been scheming against her.

He can go and find his money elsewhere, she thought
with furious contempt. *He's not going to get it from me.*

By the following afternoon, when Mr. Patterson still
had not been able to change Sarah's mind, he was forced
to write to tell the duke what had happened.

I ain't never seen Sarah so riled up, he wrote to his
granddaughter's prospective husband. *You'd best wait a
few days before you try to see her—give her a chance to
calm down. I'll talk some sense into her soon enough.*

"What is the matter, Anthony?" Max asked when he
saw the expression on his employer's face after he had
read Mr. Patterson's note.

The two men were standing in a small, elegant anteroom near the front door of Selbourne House. The duke

was dressed in a driving coat and had been on the point of going out when the note was delivered.

"I told him not to say anything," the duke said furiously. His eyes had turned more green than gray, something that they did when his emotions were aroused.

Max did not know what his employer was talking about, but the expression on the duke's face warned him it would be better not to ask again.

"*Christ!*" the duke said. He crumpled the note in his hand and threw it on the black and white marble floor. "He may have just ruined everything."

Max, who was standing in front of the black marble mantelpiece, ventured cautiously, "Who was the letter from, Anthony?"

The blazing green eyes swung around to Max's face. "It was from Patterson. Do you know what he has gone and done? He has told Sarah about the marriage scheme!"

Max did not quite understand why this should be making the duke so angry, but he was prudent enough not to say so.

The duke kicked the crumpled-up letter that was lying in front of his foot.

"That blundering fool may just have cost me four million pounds," he said bitterly.

Understanding dawned in Max's brain. "Miss Patterson does not like the idea?" he said.

"Of course she doesn't like the idea. No woman of any sensibility would—at least not the way Patterson must have put it to her. He probably presented it as a business deal!"

Max, who had been under the impression that it *was* a business deal, said nothing.

The duke ran his fingers through his hair, a sign that

he was very agitated indeed. Then he cursed, long and fluently, in Spanish.

At last he said, "Left to myself, I think I had a good chance of pulling it off. But now . . . !"

He was literally vibrating with fury. Max, who had been at the duke's side for most of his adult life, had never seen him this angry.

Max said quietly, "You may pull it off yet. You must go to see Miss Patterson, Anthony. You know women. You will know what to say to her, how to charm her."

The duke shook his head. He regarded his secretary out of eyes that had suddenly grown very bleak, and said, "You don't understand, Max. Sarah Patterson is different from most girls of her age. She is . . ." He frowned, searching for the words he wanted. "She is a *person*."

A warning sounded in Max's brain.

But the sight of the duke's distress wrung his heart.

He is so perfect, Max thought. *It is outrageous that he should be beset by all these petty concerns.*

Once he has the money he needs, he will be happy again.

"It is imperative that you go to see her, Anthony," he said firmly. "Do not delay. The longer she is left to the persuasions of her grandfather, the worse it will be for you."

The duke sighed. "You're right, Max." He picked up his hat from the small table where he had laid it down when he had taken Mr. Patterson's note. He smiled at his secretary. "You always give me good advice, my friend."

That smile had its usual devastating effect on Max. His voice softened as he replied, "She won't be able to resist you, Anthony. No one could."

The duke set the high-crowned hat upon his shining

locks. "I hope you are right, but I wouldn't bet the castle on it."

Max went to the window and watched as the duke swung up into the high seat of his phaeton and moved his blacks off down the street.

CHAPTER
Eight

W HEN ONE OF THE FOOTMEN INFORMED SARAH that the Duke of Cheviot had called and wished to see her, her first impulse was to refuse.

She put down the pen with which she had been writing a letter at the sofa table in the upstairs drawing room, and drew breath to tell Robert to inform the duke that she was not at home. Before she could speak, however, the young footman said with almost comical reverence, "I have put him in the front drawing room, Miss Patterson."

It was then that Sarah realized the bedazzled Robert had already let Cheviot know she was in the house.

Damn, Sarah thought. She reflected a moment, then decided that she was going to have to see him sometime—her grandfather would insist upon that—and perhaps it would be better to get it over with right away.

"Very well, Robert," she said a little grimly. "I will come."

She glanced down at the simple sprig muslin dress she was wearing and resisted the temptation to smooth her hair, which was simply tied back with a pink ribbon, like a young girl's. Instead she arose, walked calmly out into the passage, and went down the staircase to the most formal of the three drawing rooms that graced Mr. Patterson's London house.

The butler was standing at the bottom of the stairs, awaiting her. "The Duke of Cheviot is here, Miss Patterson," he said, with even more reverence in his voice than Robert's had held.

"Thank you, Crashaw," Sarah said.

"Shall I bring some refreshment to the drawing room, miss? Tea, perhaps?"

"No thank you," Sarah said to the elderly man whom she had known since her childhood. "I will send for you if I need you."

She had no intention of offering any hospitality to the perfidious duke.

Sarah opened the drawing room door, stepped into the room, and closed the door behind her. She could feel the anger seething inside her, and she struggled to push it down.

She did not want to give him the satisfaction of knowing that he had disturbed her in any way.

He was standing next to the purple and gold velvet sofa that lay at right angles to the graceful alabaster fireplace. Sarah noticed that her servants had already taken his hat and driving coat and gloves.

Well, he would be getting them back soon enough.

"Your Grace," she said, and stared at him with undisguised hostility.

Somber, gray-green eyes looked back.

One forgot, she found herself thinking, that he really looked like this.

"Damn," the duke said. "It's even worse than I feared it would be."

His words surprised her, but she knew exactly what he meant. "Yes," she said, and hostility was in her voice as well. "It is."

He gestured with one slender, ringless hand. "It really isn't quite as ugly as it appears to be, Sarah. I'd like you to know that."

"I don't want to know anything," Sarah said. "I just want you to go away."

She had only moved a few steps into the room.

He did not try to approach her. "I don't blame you," he answered from his station by Mr. Patterson's ugly sofa. "I deceived you, and you are angry. You have every right to be angry, but I ask you to allow me just ten minutes of your time, so that I may tell you how all this came about."

"I know how it came about," Sarah said. "You need money."

A look of ineffable weariness came across his face. "I need a huge amount of money," he agreed in that soft, deceptively gentle voice of his. "My patrimony from my father was a pile of debt that amounts to over two million pounds."

Sarah could feel her eyes widen with shock at the figure he named. "Two million pounds!"

"That is what I said." He gestured toward the sofa and the chairs that faced it. "Might we sit down? Please? I will not keep you long, I promise."

Much to her surprise, Sarah found herself walking slowly into the room. The duke moved to stand in front of one of the large wing chairs that were placed opposite the purple and gold sofa, and, after a moment's hesitation, Sarah seated herself on the sofa.

He sat down in the chair. His face looked tense but his voice maintained its usual easy register as he said, "You see, after my father's suicide, I . . ."

A muffled sound from Sarah caused the duke to pause. He looked at her expression and then he shrugged wearily. "He couldn't face the disaster he had made of his life, and so he bowed out."

"Leaving the disaster to you," Sarah said.

His smile was wry. "I must confess that I had a brief impulse to bow out as well. I had made a perfectly satisfactory life for myself in the army and I had no great desire to leave it." The smile faded. "However, the reality is that I am now the head of the family and I cannot turn my back upon that responsibility. I have two half-brothers whose lives must not be destroyed by my father's profligacy—not to mention my stepmother, who has been left virtually penniless."

She had no intention of offering any hospitality to the perfidious duke.

Sarah felt a treacherous feeling of sympathy creep into her heart.

Do not dare to feel sorry for him, she commanded herself.

She said in a hard voice, "So you decided that the only way to remedy your financial situation was to marry a girl who had money."

"Yes," he said. "But I must stress to you, Miss Patterson, that I regarded such a marriage as one that would confer benefits upon both parties. I would receive the money I so badly needed, yes; but my wife would receive one of the highest titles in all the country. It is worth something, you know, to be the Duchess of Cheviot."

"I'm sure it is—for some girls," Sarah said, making it very clear by her tone of voice that she was not one of those deluded creatures.

He nodded slowly. "I saw almost immediately that such an honor meant little or nothing to you. It meant a great deal to your grandfather, and I'm afraid I just assumed that you would feel the same way. But . . . it was obvious to me that you didn't."

Some of the anger Sarah had been trying to contain broke through her outward composure.

"Why wasn't I told?" she demanded. "Why was I forced to go through that pitiful charade at Hartford, when everyone else knew what was going on except me?"

He regarded her, and the beautiful line of his mouth was grave.

"My aunt decided that you would feel uncomfortable if you knew the circumstances behind the visit. She wanted to give you an opportunity to meet me without any accompanying baggage to get in the way."

"She wanted to give you a chance to charm me, you mean," Sarah accused him.

A faint smile tugged at the corners of that grave mouth. "Well . . . yes."

Sarah moved her gaze from his mouth to his eyes. "I liked you," she said. "I thought you were a nice man. And all the time you were lying to me."

"I never lied to you," he said. He was returning her look steadily. "I didn't tell you everything, that's true, but I never lied to you."

Sarah's look of scorn was her reply.

He leaned slightly forward in his chair. "Sarah, I want you to listen to me carefully. I think you should marry me and I want to tell you why."

Sarah's expression changed from scorn to incredulity.

"Just listen to me," he said. "I beg you."

His soft voice did not change, but Sarah sensed the desperation that lay beneath those quiet words.

She set her mouth.

A full thirty seconds ticked off the clock.

Then, "All right," she said. "I'll listen, but that is all."

"Thank you."

She thought all of a sudden that he looked much more tired than he had appeared at Hartford. For the first time since she had learned the truth, it occurred to her that he was trapped in a situation that was not of his making.

She supposed she should not blame him for trying to get out of it in the only way that was open to him.

Only she was not going to be the means that he used.

He said, "I went to Hartford Court to meet you with the expectation that you would be eager to become the Duchess of Cheviot." His smile was endearingly crooked. "Not because of my great charm, but because nearly every woman I know would like to hold such an exalted position.

"Then I met you and I saw that you were different. Being a duchess wasn't important to you; what was important to you was painting."

Sarah could feel her face hardening. This was his worst sin as far as she was concerned, his false compliments about her painting.

He saw what she was thinking. "When I saw you with your easel by the lake that day, I admit that I didn't take you very seriously. I asked to see your work, thinking that I would praise it and tell you how pretty it was."

His eyes held hers captive, refusing to release them.

"And then I saw what you were doing."

Sarah's hands had closed into fists in her lap. She glared at him, daring him to try to fool her again.

"At first I was shocked," he said. "Then I was enormously relieved."

Sarah frowned in confusion. "Relieved?" she repeated. "Why should you be relieved?"

"You see, I knew that I had found the one thing that I could offer you that might make you agree to marry me."

Sarah stared at him, bewilderment written all over her face. "I don't understand you."

"You are a good painter, Sarah, but in order for you to become a great painter you need to expand your sensibility by furthering your education. You need to look at many paintings by artists who have the same interest as you in the creation of light and atmosphere. You need to go to Amsterdam, to Paris, to Italy—the places where those pictures are to be found."

He leaned a little more forward in his chair, as if he were reaching out to her.

"If you marry me, I will take you to those places, Sarah," he said.

Sarah's fists were closed so tightly that her nails were biting into her palms. She couldn't say a word. She just looked at him.

"Who else do you know who will do that for you?"

His voice seemed to be coming from very far away.

"Your grandfather?" the voice went on. "This Harvey fellow whom you thought to marry? I'll wager that neither of them have any notion of the quality of your work. They probably think your painting is about as serious as I had thought it—before I actually saw what you could do."

"They don't even think it is that serious," Sarah said in a thin, strained voice. "They think it's a waste of time."

He didn't look surprised by this revelation.

"You have the potential to be a very fine artist—if your talent is allowed to grow and to mature. If you marry me, I will promise to give you every opportunity for that to happen. I have the entrée into homes whose owners have paintings you need to see."

Sarah could feel the sudden, hot color flood into the pallor of her face. She put trembling hands up to her mouth and stared at him over them.

Paris, she thought. *Rome . . . Amsterdam . . . perhaps even Venice!*

"You are diabolical," she whispered.

He shook his head. "I am offering you a partnership," he said. "As my wife, you can go where you wish to go and do what you wish to do. No one will question the Duchess of Cheviot if she should choose to exhibit her paintings at the Royal Academy. What do you think the Academy would say to Miss Sarah Patterson if she submitted a picture to the selection panel?"

"The Royal Academy would never take anything from me," Sarah said in the same whispery voice as before.

"If it was good enough, they would take something from the Duchess of Cheviot."

Sarah drew a long, uneven breath.

He was right.

But . . . marriage?

She faltered, "Perhaps . . . if I had more time to get to know you . . ."

The look on his face was indescribably bleak. "I don't have time, Sarah. I am going to lose most of my property if I don't pay off the mortgages immediately."

She bit her lip.

"Sarah." He got up from his chair and came around to sit beside her on the sofa. He reached out and took one of her small, trembling hands into his.

"You said before that you liked me. Well, I like you. That is not such a bad basis for a marriage. And I honestly believe that you will be happier with me than you would be with someone who thought that your painting was a 'waste of time.' "

He had enormous sexual magnetism, and if he had chosen to exert it at that moment, he would have lost her. What he did instead was hold her hand and look gravely into her eyes.

"I think I probably would be, too," Sarah said shakily.

He started to smile.

"Does that mean you'll do it?"

Sarah's eyes glittered with sudden defiance. "Yes. I will."

As he drove his phaeton away from William Patterson's house, the duke felt almost weak from the intensity of his relief.

Thank You, God, he thought fervently as he skillfully inserted his team into the flow of traffic heading toward Piccadilly.

Then, with even greater fervor, *Thank you, Sarah. You won't regret this, I promise you.*

For the duke had every intention of honoring the promises he had just made. He would take Sarah all over Europe and show her every single painting that she wanted to see. If she desired further instruction, he would see to it that she got it.

The duke had been brought up in houses that were filled with great art, and he did not take Sarah's talent lightly. He had never expected to find himself married to a woman whose chief priority did not lie in simply being his wife, but, *So be it,* he thought. He would never complain. After all, he would have her money.

Instead of going to his club as he had planned, he drove back to Berkeley Square. He would get a note off to Patterson in the city to tell him that Sarah had come around.

They were going to have to negotiate the marriage settlements.

The duke was under no illusion that such a negotiation was going to be either easy or pleasant. Patterson struck him as the type of man who would try to bargain over every penny.

He would leave the initial discussions up to his lawyers, but he knew that he was going to have to intervene if he was to get the amount of money that he needed.

It was not an attractive thought.

The duke was still thinking about the settlement process when he walked into the library of his town house.

His secretary was in the process of removing a folder from the blotter on the top of his desk.

"Anthony!" Max said. "I was going to go over these charges from Tattersalls again." He looked closely at the duke's preoccupied face and said in dismay, "You were not successful?"

The duke's preoccupied expression was instantly replaced by a look of radiance. "I was successful indeed, Max. She has agreed to marry me."

The secretary looked at the duke's lucent face and a flash of memory brought back to him the occasion when the two of them had first met.

Max had been a lieutenant of Dragoons Guards, in the regiment that the duke had been assigned to when he had first come out to the Peninsula as Captain Lord Alnwick.

Max clearly recalled the antagonism with which the men of his unit had greeted the news that they were to be commanded by a twenty-one-year-old earl who had only just left Oxford. But the means of advancement in Wellington's army was purchase price, and the son of a duke had the means to catapult himself over the heads of far more experienced men.

Max had gone to his new commander's tent, expecting to find a cocky, abrasive, army-mad youngster who thought he knew everything there was to know about leadership and war.

Instead, he had been welcomed by a soft and gracious voice saying, "Come in, Lieutenant Scott. I am very glad to meet you."

Then the new captain had stepped forward into the light.

At twenty-one, Anthony's beauty had been so blindingly pure that it had struck Max like a blow to the heart. He had taken the hand the young captain had held out and barely managed to utter a coherent answer.

By the time Max had left his new commander's tent some twenty minutes later, he had been Anthony's slave. Max had determined then and there that no other new officer in the history of the army would be able to boast of having a mentor as thorough and as dedicated as Max would be to young Lord Alnwick.

Then the flash of memory faded, and Max was no longer in a tent in Portugal but in the library of Selbourne House, and Anthony was looking at him a little questioningly.

At twenty-seven, the duke had lost that morning-of-the-world look that had so stunned Max at their first meeting. But in other ways he was even more beautiful. Just seeing him, just hearing his voice, could cause Max to grow dizzy with happiness. He felt now Anthony's profound relief, and he rejoiced for him.

"I knew you could do it," he said.

It was impossible for anyone to resist Anthony.

"I wasn't sure if I could," the duke replied. He laughed

shakily. "She will make an unusual duchess, to say the least, but I am very, very grateful to her."

"Nonsense," Max said gruffly. "There is no need for you to be grateful, Anthony. You are offering her a prize that is fully as valuable as any she may confer upon you."

"I've told you, Max," the duke said. His light eyes were very bright. "She doesn't care about being a duchess."

"I wasn't talking about the title," Max said. "I was talking about you."

CHAPTER
Nine

SARAH HAD THOUGHT THAT THE WORST PART OF HER decision to marry the duke would be having to endure her grandfather's gloating. Rather to her surprise, she had been more upset by the unexpected reaction of Neville Harvey.

He had burst in upon her the morning of the day after her interview with the duke. It had been raining earlier, and Sarah was working in the room she had set up as a studio, when Crashaw entered to inform her that Mr. Harvey had called and insisted upon seeing her.

Sarah frowned with annoyance. She was standing in front of her easel, putting the finishing touches upon a watercolor she had done of Green Park, and she did not relish being interrupted.

Under the circumstances, however, she supposed she could hardly refuse to see Neville.

"All right," she told Crashaw reluctantly. "Tell him I will be with him in a few minutes."

"Yes, Miss Patterson," the butler said, addressing her with solemn reverence. He bowed as he left the room.

Crashaw had taken to treating her like royalty ever

since he had learned that she was to marry the Duke of Cheviot. Sarah found it very irritating.

She cleaned her brushes first, then went upstairs to her bedroom to wash her hands and wipe a smudge of paint from her cheek. She was wearing an old paint-stained dress, but it never occurred to her to bother to change. Neville was used to seeing her in such garb.

When she had finished tidying up, Sarah went out into the passage, which contained two exceedingly mannered and boring landscapes, and down the stairs. Once on the first floor, she turned in the direction of the front hall.

She stood for a moment in front of the drawing room door, bracing herself to meet disapproval.

Neville had a right to be distressed, she told herself. After all, he had expected to marry her himself. He would be deeply upset at the loss of the long-anticipated merger between his company and Patterson Cotton.

She took a deep breath and walked into the room, prepared to be met by disapproval and disappointment. She was not prepared to be met by fury.

His words ripped across the room. *"How could you do this to me, Sarah?"*

She blinked and stared at him in surprise. He was standing in the exact same place the duke had stood the day before, and his face was white with anger.

"W-what do you mean?" she said stupidly.

"You know very well what I mean!" He took a few steps forward so that he was standing next to the wing chair the duke had sat in. "Your grandfather has just told me that you are going to marry the Duke of Cheviot!"

Sarah sternly quelled her impulse to run out of the room.

"Yes," she replied in a deliberately quiet voice. "I am."

"Well, you can't." Neville's round, pleasant-looking

face was flushed now instead of being pale. "You have promised to marry me."

Sarah made herself come a little farther into the room. She said as reasonably as she could, "I never promised to marry you, Neville. It was your father's idea and Grandpapa's to unite the two businesses by our marriage. I don't recall that I was ever consulted on the matter."

"You never objected," he cried. "You knew what was planned for us, and never once did you tell me that you didn't want to marry me."

Sarah had to admit that this was true. In fact, she had always vaguely assumed that one day she would marry Neville. It was something that her grandfather had talked about for so long that it had almost seemed as if it were a fact of life to her. But marriage had always been a long way in the future, and she hadn't thought about it often.

"Sit down, Neville," she said, "and let us discuss this in a reasonable manner."

He flung himself into the duke's chair, and Sarah crossed the room to sit upon the sofa. The formerly affianced couple regarded each other over the sofa table.

Sarah folded her hands in the lap of her paint-stained dress and said quietly, "You see, Neville, Grandpapa has changed his mind. Now he wants me to marry the duke."

Neville's blue eyes blazed. "I know that very well, Sarah. I couldn't believe it was William Patterson I was listening to this morning! He is all puffed up with the importance of your being the Duchess of Cheviot. He even asked me if I knew that one of the duke's ancestors was in a play by Shakespeare!"

With a flash of amusement, which she quickly suppressed, Sarah recalled mentioning to her grandfather the fact that the Earl of Cheviot was a character in one of Shakespeare's history plays.

Neville's voice took on a note of distinct bitterness. "What I can't for the life of me understand is how *you* have let yourself be talked into this match. Are you as bedazzled by a title as your grandfather is?"

"Of course I'm not, Neville," Sarah replied. "You know me better than that."

"I thought I did, but the Sarah I know wouldn't care about being a duchess."

"I don't care about being a duchess," Sarah repeated.

"Then, for God's sake, why have you agreed to marry him?"

For a fleeting moment, Sarah thought she might try to explain her motives to Neville, but the truculent look in his blue eyes made her change her mind.

He would never understand.

She said instead, "I am going to marry him because Grandpapa wishes it. I owe a great deal to Grandpapa, Neville. He has raised me since I was five years old. If I can make him happy by this marriage, then I am bound to do so."

"Sarah." A desperate note had entered Neville's voice. He leaned toward her. "Think about what you are doing. In marrying Cheviot you will be marrying into a way of life that is completely foreign to you. You won't be happy in such a position. You will be completely out of your depth. Marry me, and you will be able to live in the world you are accustomed to, the world you were bred for. And I will make you happy. I swear it."

Sarah looked at the boyishly round face, blue eyes, and dark blond hair of her oldest friend. Neville had been a part of her life ever since she had come to live with her grandfather. He had been fifteen years of age at the time, and astonishingly kind and patient with the unhappy, withdrawn little granddaughter of his father's friend.

She liked him very much.

But he didn't understand the need that drove her. And the duke did.

"I went to school with girls from the aristocracy," she said. "That way of life is not as foreign to me as you may think."

Neville pounded his fist on his thigh. "Don't you understand? He doesn't care about you, Sarah. *He's marrying you for your money!*"

Sarah was starting to get angry. "Well, Neville, you were going to marry me for Grandpapa's company," she retorted. "I don't see that there's very much difference between the two of you."

"I don't give a damn about Patterson's company!" he almost shouted. "I want to marry you because I love you!"

The breath whooshed out of Sarah's lungs.

In vibrating silence, they stared at each other across the sofa table.

Finally, in a more moderated tone, Neville said, "I've loved you for years. Didn't you know that?"

Still wordless, she shook her head.

"Well, I have. I never said anything because I was waiting for you to grow up."

Sarah ran her tongue around suddenly dry lips. She had to say something, but she didn't know what.

"Neville," she tried, and her voice came out like a croak.

At that, he moved, swiftly crossing the space between them and sitting beside her on the sofa. He took her hand into his.

The whole scene was so like the one she had played with the duke the day before that it was uncanny.

He said, "I was waiting for the right time to tell you . . . and then, to be hit with this!"

She stared into blue eyes that held an expression she had never seen in them before.

"Sarah," he groaned. "Oh God, Sarah . . ." He was still holding her hand, and now he pulled her toward him roughly, bent his head, and kissed her.

Sarah's whole body went rigid within his embrace. His mouth was pressing hard against hers, mashing her lips against her teeth. She felt as if she couldn't breathe. His hands on her shoulders hurt, they were gripping her so hard.

She tried to push him away, but her struggle only seemed to make him more determined.

"Sarah," he muttered again, and the pressure of his mouth on hers increased.

She tried to pull her head back and away from him, but he followed her.

She pounded on his shoulders with her fists. Against his mouth, she was making noises of protest.

It finally dawned on Neville that she was not a willing participant in this love scene, and he straightened up and let her go.

Sarah shot to the far side of the sofa and regarded him out of dark and frightened eyes.

"I'm sorry," he said in a voice that was much huskier than his usual tone. "I didn't mean to frighten you."

Sarah said shakily, "I think you should go now, Neville."

His mouth twisted. Then, slowly, he got to his feet. For a moment he stood there, looking down at her.

"Think about this, love," he said. "If you were frightened by the kisses of a man whom you have known for almost all your life, how will you feel getting into bed with a man you don't know at all?"

Sarah didn't answer, just continued to stare at him out of wide, fearful eyes.

"The duke will want more than kisses from you, Sarah. He will want an heir. Think about that and decide if you still want to marry him. Will you do that for me?"

"I . . . yes," Sarah said.

He smiled, and for the first time that morning looked like the even-tempered, pleasant man that she knew.

"Good girl. Don't let your grandfather bully you, Sarah. You do what is best for you."

She nodded two times.

"I will see myself out," he said.

She nodded once.

"I love you," he said. "Remember that."

She wet her sore lips. "Yes, Neville. I will."

With palpable reluctance, he walked to the door. He turned once, as if he would say something more, then shrugged, pushed it open, and walked out of the room.

Sarah huddled in the corner of the sofa.

The Duke will want more than kisses from you, Sarah. He will want an heir.

Neville was right, she thought. Of course the duke would want an heir. In his mind, that was probably the chief function of a wife: to produce future heirs for the dukedom.

Dear God, Sarah thought in despair. *What have I done?*

Sarah was so upset that she couldn't go back to her painting. She longed to get out of the house and just walk and walk and walk, but she was in London, not in the country, and one had to be careful where one walked in London.

To add to her troubles, the duke was coming at five o'clock to take her driving in the park. The formal announcement of their pending marriage would be in the *Post* tomorrow, but Sarah knew that her appearance beside the duke this afternoon would serve to alert the world to what was coming.

The duke had chosen the time of five o'clock for a purpose. At five in the afternoon, Hyde Park belonged to England's upper class. Its bridle paths were filled with dashing carriages drawn by beautiful horses, and with elegantly dressed riders perched atop equally beautiful hacks. It was the time of day when the *ton* went forth, to see and to be seen.

Her appearance beside the duke this afternoon would be as good as a marriage announcement.

Why did I have to be born a girl? Sarah asked herself despairingly, as she paced around her bedroom. *If I were a boy, I could apply to the schools of the Royal Academy. I could do what I want to do—which is be a painter and not have to marry anyone!*

All too soon the clock on her mantelpiece read four o'clock, and the housemaid who helped Sarah with her buttons and her hair was knocking on her door. It was time to get dressed to go driving in the park.

Sarah put on an unadorned rose-colored afternoon dress with a matching bolero jacket. She regarded herself critically in the pier glass and saw a small, brown-haired, extremely ordinary-looking girl.

She did not look at all like a duchess. If she married the duke, she thought, she supposed she would have to get a grander wardrobe.

If she married the duke . . .

She remembered how Neville's mouth had crushed hers that morning, and she shuddered.

All too soon, the housemaid was reminding her that it was time to go downstairs to the front drawing room to await the duke's arrival.

Crashaw announced him promptly at five, with such a flourish that Sarah almost smiled.

Her fiancé entered the room with his usual quiet air of regal distinction. Sarah said, "You have impressed Crashaw no end, Your Grace. He is now treating me as if I were a royal princess and not the tiresome little girl he used to scold when she dripped paint on the floor."

He crossed the room to stand beside her in front of the mantelpiece. All of his movements looked light, balanced, and athletic. He said, with a trace of amusement, "Don't you think it is time for you to stop calling me 'Your Grace'?"

Sarah, who couldn't imagine calling him anything else, looked uncertain.

His amusement increased. "My name is Anthony."

Sarah was steadfastly regarding the floor in front of the fireplace hearth. "Yes, I know."

"I would very much like to hear you say it."

She felt as if a hard knot were growing in the pit of her stomach.

How can I possibly marry this man when I can't even bring myself to say his name? she thought wildly.

"What is wrong, Sarah?" he asked quietly.

She continued to stare at the floor.

He waited for her to reply.

At last she said, her voice sounding very small and breathless, "I am afraid."

After a time, when he still did not speak, she dared to

glance up. Their eyes met and held, and there was no amusement in his light gray-green gaze.

"I see," he said gravely. He reached out and took her unresisting hand into his. He brought it to his lips, pressed a kiss into her palm, and said very softly, "You have nothing to fear from me, little Sarah. I promise you that. Everything will be all right." He folded her fingers over his kiss. "Trust me."

The hard knot in her stomach had been replaced by an unfamiliar, fluttery sort of feeling.

She gazed up at him, her lips slightly parted.

He released her hand. "It will be all right," he repeated, and smiled at her.

For some reason, Sarah's heart had started to pound.

He said softly, "My phaeton is at the front door. Are you ready? I don't like to keep my horses standing."

Sarah made an heroic effort to pull herself together. "I'm ready," she announced. And with steady steps she accompanied him out to the curb and allowed him to hand her up into the carriage.

The drive through the park went much as Sarah had imagined it would.

"Perhaps we should just have made a sign for the back of the carriage: 'Her Grandfather Is William Patterson, the Cotton Man,' " she said a little tartly, as they parted company with the eighth carriage that had stopped them.

He looked suddenly bleak. "Is this so unpleasant for you? Would you like me to take you home?"

She wished she had held her tongue. "Of course not. I'm sorry, Your . . ." She paused. "I'm sorry—*Anthony.* That was a very rude thing for me to say."

He shook his head. "You were simply stating the obvious. Of course all the *ton* knows the state of my affairs.

The near bankruptcy of the Selbourne family has been a favorite subject for gossip ever since my father died."

His voice was calm, but Sarah could sense the bitterness he was hiding under the quiet words.

"Tell me about the rest of your family," she said, thinking it would be a good idea to change the subject. "You said you have two half-brothers and a stepmother?"

"Yes." He was looking straight ahead, between the ears of his horse. "They live at Cheviot Castle in Northumberland."

"How old are your brothers?" she said encouragingly.

"Lawrence is twenty-one and Patrick is thirteen."

He didn't say anything more.

"Is that all you have to say about them?" she demanded.

He sighed. "I am sorry, Sarah, but I scarcely know my brothers. I was six when Lawrence was born, and when I was eight I went away to school. After school I went into the army. I probably haven't seen my brothers in eight years."

Sarah was horrified. "But didn't you have leave from the army? Didn't you get a chance to come home?"

"I had leave," he said, "but I didn't come home."

Sarah's painter's eye saw the tension that underlay the perfectly tranquil facade of his face.

"Was it your father or your stepmother you were avoiding?" she asked.

He shot her a look. "You are very perceptive."

She lifted her eyebrows. "It doesn't take a genius to see that there has to be a reason for you to have stayed away so determinedly."

The corner of his mouth quirked. "It was the both of them, if you must know. I couldn't bear to see what my father was doing to the estate. All we did was quarrel, so it was best for me not to go home at all."

"And your stepmother?"

He shrugged. "She has always resented my existence. If my father had not already had a son before he married her, then Lawrence would have been the next duke."

Sarah thought to herself that his home life sounded pretty dismal.

He said briskly, "Now that we are on the subject of my family, I suppose I should tell you the bad news. We are going to have to go directly to Cheviot after we are married. It is imperative that I assess the situation there and see that certain repairs are undertaken. According to my steward, my father has done nothing for the tenants or the land in over twenty years."

"Good God," Sarah said.

"Good God, indeed," he agreed rather grimly.

"It doesn't sound as if you have very many happy memories of your childhood home," Sarah said.

"I was only four when my mother died and one's memories of that age are dim," he agreed.

After a moment's silence, she said, "I was five when my parents were killed."

He turned his head to look at her. "How did they die?"

"In a carriage accident. Some drunken young lordling had taken the reins of the mail from the regular coachman, and he ran it right into the open carriage in which my mother and father were driving."

He was silent.

"I do have some happy memories of them, though," Sarah said.

"I suppose I would have a few myself, if I tried to remember."

"Duke!" They were being hailed gaily by a young

woman sitting next to an elegantly dressed gentleman in a phaeton whose seat was even higher than Cheviot's.

The duke courteously stopped his horses.

"Such a lovely day for a drive in the park," the young woman said. She was wearing a stylish blue carriage dress and a dashing bonnet that only partially covered her golden curls.

"Yes it is," the duke agreed. "Lady Maria, may I present my companion, Miss Sarah Patterson. Miss Patterson, this is Lady Maria Sloane, and her brother, Lord Henry Sloane."

Sarah produced her politest smile. "How do you do, Lady Maria, Lord Henry."

Two pairs of eyes raked her from head to toe.

Sarah couldn't resist glancing at the duke. He was looking amused.

"We are all looking forward to the time when your mourning period is over and you can join formal society again, Duke," Lady Maria said.

"Thank you," Anthony replied.

"Are you enjoying your drive, Miss Patterson?" Lord Henry asked.

"Very much," Sarah replied. "It is a lovely afternoon."

Out of the corner of her eye, she saw the duke's little finger twitch his left rein. His off-side horse threw up his head.

"Better not keep the horses standing any longer," Anthony said blandly. "Good day, Lady Maria, Lord Henry."

"Good day," Sarah echoed pleasantly.

They drove off.

"I saw you twitch that rein," Sarah said.

He laughed.

"For how long do you think we will need to stay at Cheviot?"

"A few months, at least." He turned to look at her. "And then I will take you to Paris."

Sarah's face lit to beauty.

Perhaps I made the right choice after all, she thought, as the duke drove his horses along the lake at a spanking trot. The fresh spring air smelled lovely after the morning's rain, and it was wonderful to be outdoors.

"I can probably find some good things to paint in Northumberland," Sarah said.

"There is the castle itself," he said. "And the sea, and the Roman Wall, and the pastures will be filled with wildflowers in May."

"How lovely," Sarah said with satisfaction.

"Duke!" a feminine voice cried.

As Anthony slowed his horses, he grinned at her.

Unaccountably, Sarah felt happy.

CHAPTER
Ten

LADY LINFORD WAS THE ONE WHO INFORMED SARAH'S grandfather that, as the duke was still technically in mourning for his father, his wedding was going to have to be a quiet one.

This news came as a heavy blow to Mr. Patterson, who had pictured a grand marriage ceremony, with the duke wearing his robes and coronet, and all of the nobility of England in attendance.

What a splash that would have made in the city!

It was not to be, however. Lady Linford explained to him, in her most forceful manner, that official mourning was not a social rule that could be violated with impunity.

"A large wedding would put dear Sarah in a very bad light, Mr. Patterson," the duke's aunt said. "And we do not want to do anything that might jeopardize her acceptance by the *ton*."

Once Mr. Patterson had reluctantly been brought to understand this fact of upper-class life, he suggested putting the wedding off until the duke's mourning period was over.

It was the duke himself who made it clear that he could not wait that long.

Then Sarah said emphatically that she did not want a large wedding under any circumstances, and Mr. Patterson found himself blocked on all sides.

Like a frustrated bull, he was forced to channel his thwarted energy into something else—in this case, the negotiation of the marriage settlement.

He demanded to see a list of all the duke's debts.

He demanded to see a list of all the duke's assets.

He demanded to see copies of all the mortgages.

He demanded that the duke submit to him a financial plan showing the projected solvency of the Selbourne family for the next twenty years.

All of the early negotiations on the duke's behalf were done by Maxwell Scott and the duke's lawyers, but in the end, as he had suspected would happen, the duke was forced to sit in himself.

It infuriated Max to have to watch Anthony being so invincibly patient and courteous as he answered the barrage of encroaching questions put to him by the vulgar cotton merchant and his equally vulgar man of business.

They are like flies buzzing around a purebred stallion, Max thought angrily, as he watched the duke's profile silhouetted against the light from the library window behind him.

Why does he endure them? Why does he not just swish his tail and flick them away?

But Max knew the answer to those questions. The duke had no choice but to be polite to the hucksters from the city. He needed their money.

In the end, however, it was the duke who prevailed. This outcome did not surprise Max, who knew that behind Anthony's soft, gracious manner lay a will of iron. Even the ruthless, bull-like dynamism of Mr. Patterson eventually gave way before the Duke's always-courteous insistence that he must have four million pounds or the deal would have to be called off.

Then, once the merchant had given in and agreed to the amount, the duke stunned Max by arranging to tie up a quarter of a million of those precious pounds in a trust fund for Sarah.

"I thought you needed every penny of that four million to pay off your mortgages and to repair the neglect of your farms," Mr. Patterson said with heavy sarcasm, after the duke had stated his desire for the trust fund.

"I do need it, but it is necessary for Sarah to have money of her own," the duke replied with perfect serenity. "I will make do with the three and three-quarter million that is left."

"Make do!" the merchant boomed. "Let me tell you, Your Grace, that there ain't no other man but me, in all these British Isles, who could afford to part with that much money as a marriage settlement!"

"You are probably right," the duke agreed with a charming smile. "You have been very generous, Mr. Patterson. That is why I did not ask you for the quarter million pounds for Sarah, but am taking it from my own funds instead."

To Max's astonishment, Mr. Patterson threw back his head and roared with laughter. "Damme, Your Grace, but you're a lad after my own heart. *Your own funds!*" He took off the spectacles he wore to look at figures and wiped tears of merriment from his eyes. "I'll tell you what. Join me in Patterson Cotton and we'll both make such a fortune that *your own* four million pounds will look paltry in comparison."

Max shuddered at the very thought.

Anthony laughed. "That is a very generous offer, Mr.

Patterson, but I do not think that I will have the time to devote to such a demanding enterprise."

Patterson replaced his spectacles. "True, true. And dukes don't set up with cotton merchants. I know that." He peered at his future grandson-in-law over the spectacles he had just donned. "But you'd make a damn good merchant, Your Grace. A damn good one."

"Thank you, sir," the duke said, and actually managed to look as if he appreciated the compliment.

Sarah, of course, was aware that negotiations over the settlement were going on, but she did not ask either her grandfather or her fiancé anything about them. It was not a subject upon which she cared to dwell. She knew very well that Anthony was marrying her for her grandfather's money; she just did not think that it was necessary to keep reminding herself of that fact.

Lady Linford had taken charge of shopping for the future duchess's bride clothes, and she dragged Sarah, with Olivia present to lend moral support, into literally every shop on Bond Street that sold female clothing.

They bought morning dresses, afternoon dresses, carriage dresses, evening dresses, pelisses, jackets, hats, gloves, muffs, stockings, reticules, and hair ornaments. Sarah suspected that, since her grandfather would be paying for her bride clothes, Lady Linford wanted to make certain that she had enough to wear for the next few years.

In some ways, Sarah found the Countess of Linford to be very like her grandfather. Lady Linford was an aristocrat, of course, but the ruthless force of her personality battered on Sarah's spirit in the same way her grandfather's did. It was easier to give in than to argue—especially since Sarah did not really care about the clothes that were of such all-consuming interest to the countess.

The one shopping expedition that Sarah did care about was the visit she paid to the shop where she bought her painting supplies. She wanted to arrange to have a complete shipment of everything she would need sent to Cheviot Castle in Northumberland, and she got the duke to accompany her on this particular errand. He was, she thought, the one person who was capable of understanding that this matter was of urgent importance to her. She could not paint if she did not have her supplies.

They arrived at their destination in Knightsbridge in the early afternoon, and the duke left his groom to hold his horses while he accompanied Sarah into the painting supplies shop and small gallery she had been patronizing for five years.

"I may be a while, Anthony," Sarah warned her escort.

"Don't worry about me," he replied peacefully. "I shall amuse myself by looking around."

True to his word, he moved off to look at the frames and paintings that the proprietor had hung in hopes of making a sale. Halfway through her order, Sarah glanced around to check on him and was grateful to see that he appeared to be browsing with perfect contentment.

Her grandfather or Lady Linford would have been impatiently demanding that she hurry up, she thought. She had been wise to ask Anthony to bring her.

When she had finished placing her order, she took the list of items from the merchant and went over it carefully to make certain she had not forgot anything.

"I'll have these things to you by tomorrow morning, Miss Patterson," the merchant said.

Sarah looked up at him in surprise. Then she laughed. "I don't think it will be quite that easy, Mr. Shields. They are not going to my grandfather's house this time. I am going to be married, you see, and I want them to be sent to my new home."

The small, gray-haired shop owner looked delighted. "Married? Well now, Miss Patterson, and who is the lucky man?"

"I am," came the duke's soft voice from somewhere just behind Sarah. Then he was standing at her side. Mr. Shields looked at Sarah's future husband, and his eyes widened.

"Allow me to present Mr. Shields to you, Anthony," Sarah said. "He is the proprietor of this lovely shop." She looked back to the merchant. "Mr. Shields, His Grace the Duke of Cheviot."

Mr. Shields's already-widened eyes nearly popped out of his head. "Good heavens," he said.

The duke maintained his invincibly courteous expression, but Sarah could see amusement pull at the corners of his mouth. "How do you do, Mr. Shields," he said.

The merchant bowed and said breathlessly, "How do you do, my lord."

The duke did not correct his erroneous term of address. He said instead, "This package of supplies should be sent to the Duchess of Cheviot at Cheviot Castle, Northumberland."

"Aye, my lord. I shall be certain to do that." Slowly, the merchant's wide-eyed look transferred itself from the duke to Sarah.

She gave him a warm smile. "If I have forgot anything, I will write to you and perhaps you will send it to me? I have the highest regard for the quality of your goods, Mr. Shields."

"Of course I will, Miss Patterson!" the merchant replied fervently.

"Then, if you have finished your purchases, Sarah, perhaps we might go," the duke said.

As they walked toward the front door, Sarah said, "You have been very patient with me. Not once did you complain about being forced to keep your horses standing."

"That is because I told Holmes to drive them around while you shopped," he replied with imperturbable serenity. "He should have them back by now, however."

In fact, the duke's phaeton and gleaming black horses were just pulling up to the front of the shop when Sarah and Anthony arrived on the sidewalk. The duke's groom, a middle-aged man who had a distinctly army look about him, grinned at the duke and said, "They're a right handful this morning, Your Grace."

The duke assisted Sarah to the front seat of the phaeton, then went around and got in on the driver's side. Holmes handed him the reins and shifted to the groom's seat behind them.

"What do you say to a little drive through the park?" the duke proposed to his fiancée. "Holmes is right. These horses need some exercise."

Sarah, who had long ago stopped being nervous when she drove with Anthony, gave him a sunny smile.

"I'd like that," she said.

He smiled back, and turned his team in the direction of Hyde Park.

The wedding of the Duke of Cheviot and Miss Sarah Patterson took place on the third of May at the Grosvenor Square home of the Earl and Countess of Linford. Those present included Lady Olivia Antsley, who was bridesmaid to Miss Patterson; the Earl and Countess of Linford; the bride's grandfather, Mr. William Patterson; and the groomsman, Colonel Colin Melville, a friend of the duke's who had come all the way from Paris in order to stand up with him.

Mr. Patterson was bitterly disappointed with the meager ceremony. The duke didn't even wear his coronet, let alone his robes of state. Instead, he stood before the Reverend Mr. Allensby dressed in a plain black evening coat and snowy white shirt and neckcloth. It was true that the coat fit him very nice, Mr. Patterson thought gloomily, but no amount of simple elegance could console the merchant for the absence of the coronet.

The bride wore an evening dress of the palest pink gauze over an underdress of white satin. Her hair was drawn smoothly back off her face and a wreath of pink roses circled the shining chignon at the nape of her neck.

Considering its outrageous cost, Mr. Patterson thought that Sarah's dress was far too plain. She had told him that she was too small to carry off a lot of ornamentation, but he didn't agree. He had also hoped that Sarah would wear the Cheviot diamond tiara that the duke had said would be hers, but she had not done that, either.

All in all, they looked just like anybody else, Mr. Patterson thought grumpily as he listened to the exchange of wedding vows. It was a bitter disappointment.

Still, Sarah was now a duchess. There wasn't another man in the city who could claim to have a granddaughter in such an elevated position.

This thought cheered him up and he even drank the champagne toast to the newly married couple.

The wedding breakfast might have been attended by a small number of people, but the food provided by Lady Linford was lavish. Mr. Patterson watched Sarah as she deftly managed her plate and at the same time responded easily to the remarks of Lord Linford, and he thought that her education, which had cost him so much, had been worth it after all.

Damme, if the girl didn't know how to behave just like a duchess!

The food was delicious, and Mr. Patterson even unbent so far as to take a second glass of champagne.

An hour later, while he was talking magnanimously to Lord Linford about some stocks he thought the earl should buy, Mr. Patterson happened to glance around and notice that his granddaughter was no longer in the room.

"Where's Sarah?" he demanded of the earl.

"Changing her clothes, I expect," Lord Linford replied. "You know that the young couple are to spend the weekend at a small estate owned by one of Cheviot's friends in Sussex. If they wish to arrive there in time for dinner, they must leave shortly."

"I suppose that's so," the merchant agreed gruffly. He looked around the room again and saw that the duke had disappeared also.

"Ain't they going to say goodbye?"

"I'm sure they will, Mr. Patterson," the earl replied reassuringly.

Ten minutes later, the duke reappeared, dressed in a riding coat and highly polished Wellington boots. He stopped by the punch bowl to talk to Olivia.

Five minutes after her new husband had arrived, Sarah herself came into the drawing room.

For her going-away outfit she wore an elegant frock of almond-green cambric muslin, with a matching bonnet and a pair of outrageously expensive French kid gloves.

Mr. Patterson had nearly exploded when he saw the bill for those gloves, but Lady Linford had told him that French kid was essential for a woman in Sarah's position.

He had paid the huge bills for his granddaughter's

bride clothes, and thought with satisfaction that from now on, the cost of Sarah's position would have to be borne by her husband.

Sarah had joined the duke and Olivia, and Olivia was hugging her and laughing. Mr. Patterson made his way across the room toward his granddaughter and her husband.

"Well, well, well," he said genially, as he reached the small party that was gathered near the punch bowl. "Getting ready to leave, then, eh?"

"Yes, Grandpapa," Sarah said in a low voice.

Mr. Patterson looked at her critically. She was too pale, he thought. When Sarah had color in her face, her skin looked pretty, but when she was pale, she looked sallow.

Mr. Patterson stared with annoyance at his granddaughter's pallor. Virgin fears, probably, he thought cynically. Patterson's eyes flicked to the duke. Cheviot would know how to take care of that.

"Since we will be riding in an open carriage, I would like to reach Hamilton Hall before it begins to grow chilly, Sarah," the Duke said tranquilly. "I think it will be best if we leave immediately."

"Why're you driving in an open carriage?" Mr. Patterson growled. "Don't seem healthy to me."

"I get sick sometimes when I am cooped up inside a carriage, Grandpapa," Sarah said. "It is better for me to be out in the air."

Mr. Patterson recalled several occasions from Sarah's childhood when she had given evidence of such a failing.

"What! Do you still heave up your guts when you travel?" he asked incredulously. "I thought you would have grown out of that."

Sarah flushed, and he thought she looked much prettier.

"Well, I haven't, Grandpapa," she said.

"You didn't get sick when we rode in my carriage to Hartford Court."

"It was a short ride," she replied.

"There is no need to worry about Sarah, Mr. Patterson. I will take very good care of her," the duke said.

Sarah's grandfather winked at her new husband. "I'm sure you will, Your Grace," he said.

The duke's eyes flickered, but his facial expression did not change.

"Are you ready, my dear?" he asked Sarah gently.

"Yes." Her voice sounded almost comically resolute. "Yes, I am."

He put his hand on her elbow. "Then let us go."

"Goodbye, Grandpapa," Sarah said, and leaned forward to kiss him on his cheek.

"Goodbye, Duchess," Mr. Patterson replied gleefully.

Then the duke was steering his new wife toward the door. In a moment they had passed out into the hall and out of the sight of those left behind in the Linford drawing room.

It was done, Mr. Patterson thought with satisfaction. His great-grandson would be the Duke of Cheviot.

CHAPTER
Eleven

SARAH SAT BESIDE HER HUSBAND IN THE FRONT SEAT OF the phaeton, and felt as if the ring on her finger was burning into her flesh. The gold circle was hidden by her tan kid glove, but she knew it was there. To her quivering nerve endings it felt hot as a horseshoe that has just come off the blacksmith's forge.

Out of the side of her eyes, she sneaked a look at the duke's profile. He was concentrating on the road ahead, which was filled with afternoon commercial traffic.

The solemn words of the promise she had made only a few hours before resounded in Sarah's mind:

I, Sarah Elizabeth, take thee, Anthony George Henry Edward, to be my wedded husband, to have and to hold from this day forward, for better or for worse, for richer or for poorer, in sickness and in health, to love, cherish, and to obey, till death do us part.

She had promised to love, cherish, and obey a man who was as different from her as the night was different from the day. With a sinking feeling in the pit of her stomach, she thought that in accepting Anthony George Henry Edward Selbourne, she had also accepted a way of life whose complexities and distinctions were as foreign to her as would be the protocol at the court of Süleyman the Magnificent.

It doesn't matter, she told herself resolutely, as she stared straight ahead at the busy London street. *All that matters is that he has promised to help me to paint.*

She clasped her hands tensely in her lap as the duke expertly maneuvered his horses around a broken-down vegetable cart.

I can survive anything as long as I can paint.

It never once occurred to her that she might not be able to trust him to honor his promise.

They stopped once on the road at a famous coaching inn to give the horses a rest and a drink. The duke took Sarah into a private parlor and procured some lemonade for her and a beer for himself. Then they were back in the phaeton again.

It was five o'clock in the afternoon by the time they reached the duke's friend's estate, and Sarah was feeling extremely weary. She had not slept well the night before, and between the wedding and the journey into Sussex, it seemed to her jangled nerves as if the day had been going on forever.

And the worst part was yet to come.

"How charming," the duke murmured as he drove the phaeton up the driveway of the small estate of Hamilton Hall. Dutifully, Sarah looked at the place where she was to spend her wedding night.

Hamilton Hall was a pretty gabled manor house set in a lovely surrounding of meadows and woods. The walls of the house were of rich gray-yellow stone, and the tall chimney stacks were of mellowed brick. It was not a large property, the duke had told her, which was why he had chosen it for their brief wedding trip.

"A small house will be more cozy," was his explanation. He had not seen Hamilton Hall himself, but had assured her his secretary had gone down to Sussex to take a look at it and had pronounced it acceptable.

As she looked at the pleasing picture in front of her, Sarah understood that her husband had not wanted to overwhelm her with the undoubted grandeur of his own estates, and she felt a flash of gratitude for his consideration.

She knew she was not yet ready to cope with palatial ducal splendor. First she had to cope with being married.

The duke drew rein before the front door, said, "Stand," in a firm no-nonsense voice to his horses, and went around to Sarah's side of the phaeton. Without asking her leave, he reached up, put his two hands around her waist, and lifted her down.

Sarah felt the color flush into her cheeks. He had never done that before.

As her feet touched the ground, the front door opened and two servants advanced quickly down the front steps.

"Welcome to Hamilton Hall, Your Grace," the two cried in unison as they came to a halt in front of Sarah and the duke.

The housekeeper—for she could be nothing else—was a plump, gray-haired, comfortable-looking woman who was beaming all over her round rosy face as she dropped into a deep curtsey. The man bowing beside her was thin as a rail and bald as a billiard ball.

Sarah, who still could feel the touch of the Duke's hands on her waist, struggled to regain her composure.

"How do you do," the duke said with his charming smile. "You must be Mr. and Mrs. Watson. Mr. Lawton told me that I could rely upon you to look after my wife and me these next few days."

"That you can, Your Grace," Mrs. Watson assured him. Her face was luminous with pleasure.

Sarah managed to say, "What a lovely house, Mrs. Watson. It must be very old."

"It were built in 1634, Your Grace," the housekeeper announced proudly.

The duke was looking around. "I thought my groom had come down before me, but I don't see—"

"Here I am, Your Grace," someone called, and Sarah turned to see a man running toward them from the far side of the house. As he got closer she recognized the military-looking groom who had taken charge of the duke's horses the day they had gone to the paint shop.

"Ah, Holmes. I was afraid you had got lost," the duke said.

His voice was perfectly pleasant, but the groom looked anxious. "I was inside the stable and didn't see you drive in, Your Grace."

The duke nodded. "Well, you can take these horses 'round to the stable. They've had a long afternoon and they're tired."

"That I will, Your Grace. Right away." Holmes climbed agilely up to the phaeton seat, picked up the reins that the duke had wrapped, clucked to the horses, and began to drive them toward the back of the house.

Mrs. Watson gave Sarah a sweet smile. "You must be tired as well, Your Grace. Your maid is here and has unpacked all your clothes. You must let me take you and His Grace up to your rooms. I'm sure you will want to wash and change after such a long journey."

"Thank you, Mrs. Watson," Sarah said gratefully. She followed the housekeeper into a front hall that had beams in the roof and dark paneling on the walls. Sarah thought that it had probably looked much the same two hundred years before.

She noted automatically that there was a clock, a mirror, and a piece of tapestry hanging on the walls, but no paintings.

The housekeeper led them through the hall and up a lovely carved oak staircase to the second floor, where she turned left and pushed open a door.

She turned to them and said, "Here is the main bedroom, which Mr. Lawton said you was to have."

Sarah slowly walked into the room which she was to share with her husband. This room was also paneled, but it was much brighter than the downstairs had been, as the paneling was painted a pretty pale green color. The wide-planked oak floor was partially covered by an attractive rug, and there was a charming window seat built into the alcove formed by four tall windows. A chaise longue stood in front of the fire, which had been lit.

"There is only the one bedroom?" asked the duke.

"Aye, but there be two dressing rooms, one for the master and one for the mistress, Your Grace," the housekeeper explained anxiously, and she pointed to the oak doors set into opposite walls of the bedroom.

"I see. It is all very nice, Mrs. Watson," said the duke.

She smiled, reassured, and turned to Sarah. "I will have hot water sent right up, Your Grace."

Sarah managed to nod.

"We should like dinner to be served at seven, if that wouldn't be too much trouble," the duke said.

"Not at all, Your Grace! Not at all!"

With another beaming smile, the housekeeper hurried out of the room, leaving the newlyweds alone.

Sarah had not looked at her husband since they had come into the house. Now she heard him say, in a sympathetic voice in which she was sure she could detect the faintest trace of amusement, "My dear, I told you not to worry. Everything is going to be all right."

Sarah squared her shoulders, turned to look at him, and announced firmly, "I am not worried."

There was definitely a gleam of amusement in those gray-green eyes of his. "I am very glad to hear that, because there is no reason to be."

Maybe not for you, Sarah thought tartly. The amusement irked her.

Out loud she said with dignity, "I am rather travel-stained and weary, Anthony. I believe I shall retire to my dressing room and rest before dinner."

His voice when he replied was perfectly grave. Too grave, she thought in annoyance. "A very good idea. I believe I shall do the same."

"Well then," Sarah lifted her chin. "I shall see you later."

He nodded. "At dinner."

She marched determinedly to the door in the left wall and jerked it open.

Inside was a man.

Instinctively, Sarah jumped backward.

"Is that you, Currier?" the duke's soft voice inquired from behind her back.

"Yes, Your Grace," the valet said.

"You must have opened the door to my dressing room, my dear," the duke said blandly. "Yours is over there."

Sarah did not even glance at him as she recrossed the room to the opposite door. She opened it and inside was the maid Lady Linford had hired for her.

Without another word, Sarah stepped into her sanctuary and, with extreme firmness, closed the door between her and her husband.

* * *

The duke did not rest in his dressing room but instead took a walk down to the stables to see how his horses were to be housed. Holmes was briskly currying one of the splendid black geldings in his stall, and he and the duke had a comfortable chat about the facilities, which were small but perfectly adequate. Then the duke took a walk around the property, which included an old walled garden and a very pretty pond. By the time he returned to the house, it was time to get dressed for dinner.

Once he was attired in the proper evening garb of black coat and formal knee breeches, he thought about going along to Sarah's dressing room to see if she was ready. Then he decided that his appearance would only alarm her and instead he went downstairs to wait for her in the paneled drawing room, which was furnished with large pieces of oak furniture that probably dated from the reign of James I.

The duke was not really looking forward to his wedding night. He was a man of extensive sexual experience, but all of his partners had been women who were already well versed in the joys of the flesh. He had never before had to deal with a virgin.

It was a nuisance, the duke thought. He was going to have to be very careful. He did not want to hurt or frighten her. If he did that, the consequences for their future relationship would be very ill indeed.

He wondered if she even knew what was going to happen between them once they were in bed together. She had no mother. Indeed, she seemed to have no female relative who might have advised her about her marriage duties. It was one of the things that marked her as a girl of the merchant classes. A girl of his own class would never have been so solitary.

He heard the rustle of a skirt and turned to see his wife coming in the doorway. She wore a cream-colored evening dress, which was cut lower than anything he had ever seen her wear before. He noted with interest that her breasts were not as small as he had thought, and that her skin glowed like pale gold against the creamy silk.

"Did you manage to rest for a while?" he asked courteously as she walked slowly into the room.

"Yes," Sarah said. "Thank you."

"I decided that I would rather stretch my legs, so I took a walk about the property. It is very pretty. Tomorrow we will explore it together."

"That would be nice," Sarah said.

The duke, who had dealt with frightened recruits for years in the Peninsula, decided that the best way for him to handle this situation was to distract her attention from what she was afraid of and focus it on something else. Consequently, he began to tell her about one of his cousins, the Prince of Margaux, who had a splendid collection of paintings at his chateau that he would arrange for Sarah to view.

His ploy was successful and carried them all the way through dinner. He told her how the prince's father had sent his paintings to England before the revolution, thus saving them from destruction by the republican mobs, and how they had been restored to the chateau after Napoleon had abdicated the first time.

Sarah listened intently, asked intelligent questions, and even ate some of her Pheasant à la Braise.

When dessert was served, however, all of the animation left her face and she stopped meeting his eyes.

The duke sighed. *Might as well get the deed over with,* he thought, as he watched his wife's small, tense face.

The longer he delayed, the more frightened she would become.

He said in a gentle voice, "Why don't you go upstairs and get into your nightdress, Sarah? I will come along in about half an hour."

Her eyes lifted and, for the briefest of moments, met his.

"All right," she said. She got up from the table and straightened her shoulders. Without another glance at him, she walked out of the room.

Her husband sighed again and took a long, reflective drink of his wine.

The duke never thought much about his face, but over the years he had become accustomed to its power. Since the time he was fourteen, and the mother of a school friend whom he had been visiting had seduced him, women had wanted to sleep with him. He had no experience in dealing with a reluctant partner.

He finished his wine and went upstairs to his own dressing room, where his valet was waiting to undress him and help him into his silk dressing gown.

After his disrobing was accomplished, the duke sent his valet away and waited patiently until he heard Sarah come into the bedroom next door. He gave her five minutes and then he opened his dressing room door and entered the bedroom as well.

She was sitting up in the large, heavily carved four-poster bed, with the green satin quilt pulled up all the way to her breasts. Her long hair was loose and lay in shining ribbons over her bare shoulders. Her nightdress was ivory silk and low-cut, and the duke suspected that his aunt was the one who had chosen it.

He approached her slowly and carefully, as a hunter might approach a deer he did not want to startle.

Sarah did not move. She remained perfectly still, watching him out of enormous brown eyes. He sat down on the edge of the bed at a little distance from her, and looked into those eyes. She looked back.

Suddenly she appeared to him extraordinarily fragile and brave as she sat there, upright against her pillows, looking him in the eye.

He said quietly, "Sarah, do you know what is going to happen between us tonight?"

She swallowed, but her eyes did not waver. "Some of the girls at school said things . . . but they cannot be true."

"What did they say?"

She flushed. "I couldn't possibly tell you."

Wonderful, he thought with amused resignation. Someone had undoubtedly explained the act of sex to her and she had been horrified.

She said in a small voice, "I don't mean to be a coward, Anthony, but, you see, I don't know you very well."

For the briefest of moments, he had an insight into how she must be feeling.

"I don't think you are a coward at all," he said. "On the contrary, I think you are very brave."

She bit her lip and gave him a dubious look.

"I'll tell you what," he said. "Why don't we talk for a little while, and I will try to explain to you some of the things you ought to know?"

She looked at him cautiously. "All right."

He glanced around the room and noticed the chaise longue that was set in front of the fireplace. He held out his hand. "Come. Let us sit together in front of the fire."

She gave him a tentative smile. Clearly the idea of getting out of the bed appealed to her.

He led her over to the chaise and drew her down beside him, sliding an arm around her shoulder. He held her lightly but firmly, so that her body lay alongside his.

She was stiff with nervousness.

Slowly, reflectively, he began to talk. He did not once use the word *duty*. Instead he spoke of love, of how a man and a woman were but two halves of one whole, of how in marriage the halves came together and were completed.

He took great care not to become too graphic.

And all the time he was speaking, his hand slowly caressed her bare shoulder.

He felt her begin to relax.

He stopped talking and bent his head to lightly kiss her temple. "I would never harm you, Sarah. Please believe that."

She rested her cheek against his shoulder.

"You are being very patient with me, Anthony. Thank you."

With his free hand he ran his fingers through her loose hair, from below her ear to the shining strands that lay against the swell of her breast. His fingers brushed her earlobe and then her nipple.

"Look," he said softly, and he held up his hand in front of them. A silky tendril of brown hair had wound itself around his wrist.

Sarah stared as if mesmerized at that slender hand and narrow wrist. The sleeve of his dressing gown had fallen back, revealing a hard and muscular forearm. The hair on his arms was golden. His hand moved, cupped her jaw and held it. He bent his head and kissed her mouth.

It was not the gentle friendly kind of kiss that he had given her before. This kiss started tenderly, but then, when he felt her yield, he deepened it. She went still, and then, once again, she yielded. He deepened it further.

When finally he lifted his head, he could feel the soft weight of her lying relaxed against him. The eyes that gazed up at him were filled with wonder.

He whispered in her ear, "Do you think you are ready to go over to the bed with me now?"

The tip of her tongue appeared for a moment to wet her lips. Then she nodded.

He surprised her by lifting her in his arms. She put her own arms around his neck and laughed.

He grinned at her. "You're no heavier than a feather."

She smiled back and shook her head.

Then he was laying her down on the silk sheets and sliding in next to her. He did not give her time to think about what was happening, but began to kiss her once again.

This time her mouth opened immediately under the pressure of his, first yielding, and then, finally, responding. He ran his fingers gently down her body and he felt her tense and then tremble.

"It's all right," he whispered, and kissed her again.

He was a consummately skilled lover and he took his time with his young wife, teaching her the pleasure her body could find in a man's touch. Her response was such a mix of astonishment, wonder, and delight that he was charmed.

No man but me has ever touched her like this before, he found himself thinking. Rather to his surprise, the thought aroused him.

He had stripped off both their garments a while ago, and had been pleased to find that, though small, her body was perfect. Her breasts were exquisitely shaped, her waist narrow, her hips slender but rounded. Her skin glowed golden against the white of the pure linen sheets.

She looked up at him and her eyes were dilated and

her lips parted. He could feel her fingers digging into the muscles of his upper arms. His finger rubbed gently between her legs and he could feel her wetness.

Better let her find her release before I go in, he thought, and continued to move his expert finger exactly where he knew she would want to feel it most. He talked to her softly, encouragingly, the way he would to a young filly he was trying to reassure.

As soon as he felt her begin to convulse, he positioned himself to enter.

"Sarah, this may hurt you a little," he said.

She was staring up at him, and the look on her face was absolutely stunned. He knew suddenly that he couldn't wait any longer.

He lifted her hips and entered her slowly, stopping when he hit the barrier of her virginity. He took a deep breath, then drove through it. She flinched, and her fingers dug into his back, but she didn't try to pull away.

He kissed her and moved inside her wet, tight sheath.

She felt absolutely wonderful.

His heart was pounding and he shut his eyes. He could feel the tenseness in her body and realized that he was hurting her.

Best to get this done with, he thought, and drove. Again and again and again, until he was rocked by the sweet, familiar explosion of his own release.

He wanted to collapse on her, to gather her close, to stay inside, but he was afraid that he was hurting her. He made a heroic effort to pull himself together and withdraw.

Then her arms came up to encircle him.

"It's all right, Anthony," she said. "I'm all right."

"Are you sure?"

Her lips touched his cheek in a feathery kiss. "Very sure."

He shut his eyes, relieved that he was not being forced out of paradise quite yet.

A little later, when they were lying side by side, with Sarah's head pillowed on the duke's shoulder, she said, "Do you know, Anthony, that that is exactly what the girls at school said happened? But I didn't believe it."

He chuckled.

"The way you explained it makes it sound much nicer . . . makes it sound more like it really is."

How did I explain it? he thought. And then he remembered his tactful speech about a husband and wife being but two parts of one whole.

He picked up Sarah's hand and held it to his lips. "I'm glad you think so," he said.

CHAPTER
Twelve

THE DUKE LAY ON HIS BACK, HIS HANDS CLASPED behind his head, and stared up at the gold-embroidered green canopy that covered the four-poster. Sarah was asleep next to him in the bed.

He was going to have to stay awake for the rest of the night, and he wasn't sure if he could do it. His body felt so languid, so satisfied. He thought with profound surprise that he had never dreamed his wedding night would bring him such intense pleasure.

He looked down at his sleeping wife. As he always slept with the windows uncovered, and moonlight was streaming into the room, he could see her quite clearly.

Sarah had turned onto her side, and her long brown hair streamed over the satin quilt and the bare shoulder that protruded above it. Long hair was no longer fashionable, but the duke was glad that Sarah had not cut hers. It was so pretty when it was loose.

She was pretty. She was brave. He thought she was going to be passionate.

What luck, he thought in wonder. *What incredible luck, to have got a girl like this.*

He thought of what he might have got, and shuddered.

Then he yawned.

Damn. I can't fall asleep.

He lowered his arms and pushed himself up until he was in a sitting position, his back braced against his pillows.

I never thought about the house having only one bedroom, he thought disgustedly. *Stupid of me. I was so focused on the damn marriage settlement. . . . I could have told Max to check out the bedroom situation, but I just didn't think of it.*

He never would have accepted the loan of Hamilton Hall if he had known there was only one bedroom.

No one, not even Max, knew about the nightmares, and he had every intention of keeping it that way. In order to do that, however, he was going to have to stay awake.

He finally resorted to the strategy that had seen him through many lonely nights at school, as well as through a very unpleasant hospital stay after Salamanca; he re-created in his head every inch of Cheviot Castle, his boyhood home. From the Great Hall to the nursery, in his mind he walked around the castle, imagining each individual room, its furniture, its pictures, its rugs, its ornaments. Then he started on the grounds.

This familiar exercise kept him occupied for the greater part of the night. He did not fall asleep until shortly before dawn.

Sarah awoke to find the sun pouring in through the bedroom window. Anthony was asleep next to her in the bed. She turned her head to look at him.

He was sleeping on his stomach, his face toward her, one arm stretched over his head, the other one lightly fisted on top of the pillow. His hair had fallen across his brow and his long lashes lay against his sculpted cheek-bones. The quilt was pulled up to his waist.

Sarah's eyes focused on the expanse of bare masculine back that was revealed by the merciless sunlight. He was far more muscular than he appeared when he was dressed, but what her eyes were resting on was the long, heavily ridged scar that marred what was otherwise an expanse of flawless white skin.

The scar, which she had felt with her fingertips last night, ran from the top of his right shoulder to beneath his right arm.

It must have been a horrific wound, she thought.

Her gaze moved back to his face, and this time his eyes were open. He was watching her.

Very lightly, she touched the scar.

"Waterloo?" she asked.

"No. Salamanca," he replied.

"You're lucky you didn't lose the use of your arm."

Something flickered in his eyes. "I know."

She smiled. "I won't pursue the subject, Anthony. I know you don't like to talk about it."

He smiled back ruefully and rolled over on his back. "I wish my relatives were as perceptive as you."

He reached for her hand.

Sarah felt her pulse throb at his touch.

She had been stunned last night by the way he had made her feel. He had done such things to her . . . and she had let him do them, and not even been embarrassed!

"Lay down next to me," he said.

The throbbing in her pulse moved to the place between her legs.

What is happening to me? she thought with a mixture of amazement and apprehension.

She slid down in the bed so that they were lying face-to-face, looking into each other's eyes.

"How do you feel?" he asked softly. "Are you too sore?"

She was feeling that she wanted him to touch her again.

She bit her lip and gazed at him out of huge eyes. "No," she whispered.

He smiled. "How nice," and he lifted himself so that he was leaning over her, supporting himself on his hands. He began to kiss her and, instinctively, Sarah raised her arms to hold him close.

For Sarah, the rest of the day passed as if in a dream. They walked around the property of Hamilton Hall, exploring the gardens, the pond, and an old water mill that lay on a small local river not far from the house.

At the water mill, Sarah had felt a brief stab of regret that she did not have her paints with her. The mill and the river would have made such perfect subjects for a landscape.

Later in the day, the duke took her for a drive around the immediate neighborhood. Sarah, with her painter's eye, noticed everything: the green meadows dappled gold with cowslips; the orchards with their blossoms of frothy white and delicate pink; the white lambs in the green fields; the blackbirds pecking in the tall grass at the river's edge.

Being surrounded by such beauty was balm to her soul.

"Have you ever read Wordsworth, Anthony?" she asked as they drove along a narrow country lane, with planted fields stretching away on either side of them. The smell of the manure used as fertilizer floated in the air.

"Certainly I have read him," the duke said. "He is so

very English that I found him a great comfort during the years that I was away."

Sarah tilted her head and thought about this reply. "I can understand that," she said.

The duke spoke softly to the horse directly in front of him, who had thrown up his head in fear when a rabbit ran across the road in front of his hooves, then said to Sarah, "I must say that I prefer Coleridge to Wordsworth, however."

She found this an interesting comment. "Oh? And do you have a favorite poem by Mr. Coleridge?"

For a moment she did not think that he was going to answer. Then he said soberly, "I find "The Rime of the Ancient Mariner" to be absolutely soul-shattering."

Soul-shattering? Sarah thought in surprise, and made a mental vow to reread the poem.

His tone changed from sober to teasing. "Don't tell me you prefer Wordsworth to Byron. I thought all young ladies were mad about Byron."

"I *much* prefer Wordsworth to Byron," she replied emphatically. "Byron can be awfully silly."

The duke chuckled. "I won't disagree with you about that."

A strand of hair had come loose from Sarah's chignon, and she reached up to tuck it back. "Wordsworth is my favorite poet of all," she said. "I would like to paint the way he writes."

He looked intrigued. "And how is that?"

In a low voice, Sarah quoted some of her favorite lines from "Lines composed a few miles above Tintern Abbey":

"The sounding cataract
Haunted me like a passion: the tall rock,

The mountain, and the deep and gloomy wood,
Their colours and their forms, were then to me
An appetite; a feeling and a love
That had no need of a remoter charm,
By thought supplied, nor any interest
Unborrowed from the eye."

The duke said nothing, just allowed the words to hang in the air between them.

"He has such *feeling* for nature," Sarah said. "That is what I love about him, and that is what a good landscape should convey—feelings like the 'aching joy' and 'dizzy rapture' he writes about."

Still silent, the duke nodded in understanding.

Sarah let out a small sigh of pure satisfaction. It was such a pleasure to be able to talk about painting with someone who actually understood what she meant.

He said, "Before we left London, I made some inquiries and I discovered that Sir John Trainor lives close by here. He is a fairly well known art collector and he has in his possession two very fine Ruisdaels. I made arrangements for us to go and see them tomorrow."

Sarah sat bolt upright in her seat.

"Did you really, Anthony?"

"Yes, I did really. Sir John assured my secretary that he would be delighted to entertain us to afternoon tea and to show us his paintings."

The soft spring breeze stirred the hair on his brow and the sun reflected off the shining black coats of the two carriage horses. Sarah glanced upward at the deep blue sky, and said sincerely, "I am very glad that you convinced me to marry you, Anthony. It was the luckiest thing that could have happened to me."

He shot her a glance and grinned. "I have been feeling

rather lucky myself, my darling. I think I am going to very much like having a wife."

Something in his tone brought a faint blush to Sarah's cheeks and a faint humming to her blood.

He had called her *darling*. She liked that very much.

The duke was indeed pleased with his marriage. In fact, he found himself looking forward to the oncoming evening with an anticipation that surprised him.

Making love to Sarah had been unexpectedly sweet. She had none of the skills or arts of the women he was accustomed to, but he was astonished and moved by her capacity to trust. She freely gave him her joy, and was boundlessly generous in her desire to please him as much as he pleased her.

Her innocence called forth from him a feeling of protectiveness and possessiveness that he had never before felt for a woman.

She belonged to him. She had never belonged to anyone else. She was his wife. She would be the mother of his children. When he thought about Sarah, six centuries of dynastic instinct stirred in his blood.

The visit to Sir John Trainor the following day went very well. Their host turned out to be an urbane man in his mid-fifties, whose wife was dead and who lived alone in a small, elegant house nestled in a pretty valley in the Sussex Weald. Sir John was an art lover who had acquired a few fine pictures during the recent upheavals in France, and he was thrilled to have the opportunity to show off his collection to such notables as the Duke and Duchess of Cheviot.

The duke enjoyed looking at the paintings, but he enjoyed watching Sarah even more.

When she looked at a painting, she really looked, he thought with a mixture of respect and amusement, as he watched her closely examine the vigorous, impasted brushwork of one of Sir John's Ruisdaels.

She remained for a full half-hour in front of Ruisdael's picture of Bentheim Castle, just looking. Both he and Sir John had stood in front of the painting also, and neither of them had said a word to distract her from the profound attention she was paying to the picture.

After Sarah was finally satisfied, they had tea with their host, who regaled them with his tales of how he had acquired his paintings. By the time they set off for home, it was much later than the duke had planned, and clouds had rolled in to cover the sun.

"I hope it doesn't rain before we reach Hamilton Hall," the duke commented as he glanced up at the dark gray sky. "If I had realized that the weather had changed, I would have insisted that we start earlier."

Sarah disagreed. "It would have been rude to leave sooner. Sir John was so generous and kind. We had to spend some time with him and allow him to tell us his stories."

The duke raised his hands and the blacks trotted faster. "I don't want you to get wet."

"Nonsense," Sarah said briskly. "If I do get wet, I promise you that I won't melt away."

He frowned, but did not reply. He increased their speed some more.

The rain began when they were still five miles from home.

"I'll canter the horses, if you won't be afraid," the duke said.

"There is absolutely no need to canter them," Sarah

said. "They might slip on the wet road. I don't mind getting wet. In fact, I rather like the rain."

He shot her an incredulous look. She was sitting with her face upturned to the sky, like a thirsty flower soaking up the moisture it needed to keep its bloom.

There were drops on her lashes and she blinked to clear them. Then she took off her hat.

The duke actually laughed. "I was going to offer you my coat."

"I don't want it," she returned. "We don't have very far to go, so you don't have to worry about my getting chilled." She inhaled deeply. "Doesn't the spring air smell wonderful when it rains? When I was a child and I lived with my parents, my mother used to take me out onto the back portico when it rained and we would smell the air."

"Wait until you smell the air in Northumberland," he said.

"I got caught in the rain once with Neville," she confided. "He was so miserable! He kept saying he was going to take a chill."

The duke thought of the rain and the mud he had survived in the Peninsula. "I won't take a chill if you promise me you won't."

"I never get sick," Sarah returned complacently. "I have the constitution of an ox."

He thought of the fragility of her bones and smiled with amusement.

"You would have made a good soldier's wife," he said.

"I take that as a compliment," she returned smartly.

"It is," he said. "It is."

They remained at Hamilton Hall for three nights, and it was on the last night of their stay that the duke gave himself away. He was weary from lack of sleep and he drifted off soon after Sarah did, tumbling deeply into the blackness of profound exhaustion.

There were two separate nightmares that disrupted his sleep, and tonight he dreamed the one about his arm.

He was in the hospital tent at Salamanca. He knew he was conscious because he could hear the voices around him and could feel the vicious pain that had made the entire right side of his body an agony. But he could not seem to open his eyes or move his lips to speak.

A deep, infinitely weary voice said from the darkness, "That arm will have to come off."

He knew instantly that the doctor was talking about him.

No! he screamed in his mind. *No, you can't take my arm!*

Then came the voice of reason, the voice of salvation, Max's voice: "Do you know who this is, Clements? This is the Earl of Alnwick, heir to the Duke of Cheviot. You cannot possibly remove his arm."

"I don't care who he is," the deep voice replied impatiently. "The wound is too massive. If that arm doesn't come off, it will become infected and he will die. Better to be a one-armed duke than a dead one."

No! No! No! Not my arm! Max, don't let them take my arm!

The duke thrashed restlessly in his sleep. Sweat dampened the hair on his forehead. His heart was pounding.

Max's voice came again, "Why can't you just sew it up and see if it will mend?"

"Do you know how unsafe these field conditions are?" the doctor demanded. "It is impossible to give him the kind of care he would need. No, the arm must come off."

The duke threw his head back and forth in anguished denial.

Then a new voice entered the dream, one that he had never heard before.

"Anthony! Anthony! Wake up, Anthony. It's all right. You are all right. Wake up."

He felt a hand on his shoulder, shaking him.

His eyes opened and he bolted upright, shaking, sweating, his heart thundering in his chest. He looked for a brief, startled moment into the worried face of his wife. Then he shut his own eyes and rested his wet forehead on his updrawn knees.

"Christ!" he said, then was silent. His whole body was heaving with the force of his breathing.

Slowly, reflexively, he opened and closed his right hand, the way he always did when he first awoke, to make certain it was still there.

The only noise in the silent room was the sound of his harsh breathing, but he could feel her there beside him. Finally, reluctantly, he raised his head and forced himself to look at her.

She said quietly, "Was it the war?"

"Yes," he said, and clenched his teeth.

"Would you like to tell me about it? You don't have to if you don't want to."

He started to say that he would never talk about it to anyone, but then he thought that she was owed some sort of explanation. It must be quite a shock to discover that she was married to a man who had nightmares. He supposed she deserved to hear the whole sorry tale.

He rested his forehead once more on his knees, shut his eyes, and in a flat, expressionless voice, he began to describe the dream.

She was silent for a long time after he had finished. He

opened his eyes and turned his head to look at her, prepared to find disgust and horror on her face.

She looked thoughtful. "When I saw the scar," she
said, "I thought that it was nothing short of a miracle that
you did not lose the arm."

"It was Max who saved it," he said. "He was a lieutenant in my regiment. First he saved my life by carrying
me off the field, and then he saved my arm by absolutely
refusing to let the surgeon cut it off. He made him sew the
wound up, and then Max took care of me himself. I was
very lucky that the wound healed so cleanly."

"I've never noticed any impairment," she said. "Did
you get the whole use of it back?"

"Yes. I had to work at it a bit, but eventually I did."

"You were fortunate to have had a friend like Max."

He nodded. His heart had finally quieted and the sweat
had dried on his skin. His breathing was normal once
more. He said, "I'm sorry I disturbed your sleep, Sarah.
It won't happen again."

"There is nothing to be sorry about," she said. "I am
quite certain that you are not the only ex-soldier whose
sleep is troubled by bad dreams."

Perhaps, he thought bitterly. *But other ex-soldiers are
not a Selbourne of Cheviot.*

He said with assumed carelessness. "Do you think so?"

"I don't think it's normal to go through a war and *not*
have nightmares about it," she returned.

He tried to reassure her that she was not married to a
total madman. "They are getting better. I used to have one
almost every night, but now it's only once or twice a
week."

She pushed her hair off of her face. "I'm sure it will
continue to get better. You must just give it time. Some-

times wounds to the mind take longer to heal than wounds to the body."

He rubbed his eyes. "Perhaps you are right."

She leaned forward, and he felt her lips touch the scar on his back. "I don't like to think about you being hurt," she whispered.

Her gentle kiss ignited something primitive inside of him that he had not known existed, and he turned sharply toward her. He knew that the desire he was feeling must be stamped on his face. His innocent bride looked back. And smiled.

"Would you like to kiss me?" she asked softly.

He didn't answer with words. Instead he pushed her back onto the bed and followed her, his mouth hard and hungry, his hands urgent as they pushed her nightdress out of his way.

He had not felt this kind of mindless need since he was sixteen years old. All he knew was that he wanted her, that he needed her, that she was so soft under him, that she was such a bliss of release. . . .

He lay with his face buried in her shoulder, his heart thundering, his breath coming hard. Sarah's arms encircled him and held him close.

"It's all right, Anthony," she said. "Go back to sleep. I'll keep you safe, I promise."

He shut his eyes. He was so weary, so very very weary. . . .

He fell asleep in his wife's arms.

Sarah lay awake for a long time, feeling the heavy weight of her husband's body on hers, and cherishing it.

She had never dreamed that it was possible to feel this close to another human being. And it was not just the physical excitement of sex that so astonished her; it was the feeling of completion, of oneness.

She felt so loved. When he held her, and caressed her, and emptied his seed into her shuddering body, she felt loved. Yet he had done this with so many other women, had held them, and caressed them, and loved them with his body, that she knew she was placing more importance on what happened between them than was warranted.

I must not fall in love with him, she thought. *That way lays only heartache.*

That dream of his . . . She had struggled not to show him how appalled she was by it. He was so self-contained, so assured, that she had not even begun to suspect the depths of pain that lurked below that flawless surface.

The dream humiliated him. She had seen that immediately. He thought it was a weakness in him that he could not put the incident behind him.

But . . . dear God . . . for a young man to face the loss of his arm. And not just any young man, but that perfect young man. . . .

Thank God for this Max, she thought.

Anthony stirred and Sarah looked at him anxiously, ready to wake him if the nightmare should be returning. But his lashes were peaceful on his cheeks; his weight against her was relaxed.

Sarah cradled her husband and wondered if she would ever be able to touch him the way he had touched her.

CHAPTER
Thirteen

SARAH WOULD HAVE BEEN PERFECTLY HAPPY TO REmain at Hamilton Hall for a fortnight, but the duke had business he needed to attend to in London. So, late on a sharp, bright spring morning, she and her husband drove away from the charming house where they had spent their too-brief honeymoon.

Sarah was considerably more relaxed on the drive back to London than she had been on the drive into Sussex three days before. She sat beside Anthony on the high seat of the phaeton and thought about the apprehensions that had beset her on that previous journey, and she smiled.

As they drew closer to London, however, a different kind of anxiety descended upon her. Once they reached Selbourne House, she would be expected to step into her role as Duchess of Cheviot. It was a role for which she had neither training nor inclination.

Before her marriage, she had not worried about whether or not she would make a successful duchess. She felt differently now. Now she found in herself a fervent desire to be a credit to Anthony.

Fortunately, the duke was still in a state of official

mourning, so she would not be required to attend any large social functions. Nor did Anthony mean to remain long in London. Once he had attended to the most pressing of his business affairs, they would leave for the north.

Clouds had come in to cover the sun by the time they drew up in front of Selbourne House, which was situated in the aristocratic neighborhood of Berkeley Square. The duke's town residence was a tall, narrow stone edifice, which Sarah thought did not look very different from the house her grandfather lived in. One difference was the pretty garden in the center of the square, which was filled with brightly colored spring flowers.

Almost as soon as the duke stopped his phaeton in front of Number 10, the door opened and an elderly servant came stiffly down the front steps to welcome them.

The duke lifted Sarah down from the carriage and then kept her hand reassuringly in his as they approached the old man.

"My dear," he said, "may I present Woodly, who has been our butler since I was a child."

Woodly smiled benignly at the duke, then bowed stiffly to Sarah. "On behalf of the staff, may I welcome you to Selbourne House, Your Grace?"

"Thank you, Woodly," Sarah said. "You are very kind."

"The carriage with Holmes, Currier, and Her Grace's maid is following close behind us, Woodly," the duke said. "Keep a lookout for it, will you?"

"Of course, Your Grace."

The duke moved his hand to Sarah's elbow. "Come along inside," he said.

Together they walked up the stairs and through the front door, which was placed on the left side of the house and was topped by a very attractive fanlight.

The inside of the house did not look at all like Mr. Patterson's. The front hall was floored with black and white marble, and had niches filled with Greek statues along one wall, and Grecian columns along the other.

A thin woman with gray-blond hair awaited them in the middle of the floor.

The duke said easily, "Ah, Mrs. Crabtree, there you are."

The woman's worn face glowed with sudden radiance as she gazed into her employer's face. The duke said to Sarah, "My dear, may I present your housekeeper, Mrs. Crabtree."

"How do you do, Mrs. Crabtree," Sarah said quietly.

"Welcome to Selbourne House, Your Grace," the woman replied, dropping into a curtsey.

At that moment, a tall, well-built man came into the hall from the back of the house.

"Max!" the duke said with obvious pleasure. "Come here and let me present you to my wife."

Sarah looked with curiosity at the dark-haired man with the erect, military bearing as he crossed the floor in her direction.

Her husband said, "Sarah, allow me to present my secretary and friend, Maxwell Scott."

Sarah bestowed a luminous smile upon the man who had saved Anthony. "How do you do, Mr. Scott. I am so glad to meet you."

The face that looked back at her was strongly boned, with dark eyes that were set unusually widely apart.

Max did not smile back, but bowed and said in a deep voice, "Thank you, Duchess. I am honored to meet you."

The wide-set eyes turned immediately back to the duke. "I hope you found Hamilton Hall to your satisfaction, Anthony."

Sarah felt a shock of surprise at hearing her husband's Christian name on his secretary's lips.

"It was delightful," the duke replied readily. "You were right when you told me that it would be perfect."

Max's face softened. "I am glad."

The duke said to the housekeeper, "Why don't you take Her Grace upstairs, Mrs. Crabtree, and show her to her rooms?"

Sarah almost blurted, *Aren't you coming, too?* but she caught herself in time.

The duke smiled at her and said, "Go along with Mrs. Crabtree, my dear. I'm sure you're tired and would like a little rest."

"Yes," Sarah said slowly. "I would."

"After dinner I will show you the Claudes," he promised.

"That will be lovely," she said.

"This way, Your Grace," the housekeeper said.

As Sarah followed Mrs. Crabtree from the hall, she heard the duke saying to his secretary, "Come along with me to the library, Max, and you can tell me what has been happening here in my absence."

The apartment belonging to the duchess was on the second floor, in a wing at the back of the house. This wing extension was something that Mr. Patterson's house did not have. Not only did the wing give Selbourne House more space, but, since it was only as wide as half the house, the rooms it contained were able to have windows on one side. Mr. Patterson's house, like most London residences, was so close to its neighbors on either side that windows were possible only in the front and in the back.

Once upstairs, Mrs. Crabtree escorted Sarah through

an anteroom, then through two drawing rooms of fairly equal size. One of them was used exclusively by the family, the housekeeper informed her, and one of them was designated as the music room. After the family drawing room, they passed into the wing. The first room in the extension was a very large and elegant drawing room. This room, Mrs. Crabtree told Sarah, was the one used by the family when they held balls and other kinds of entertainments.

A door from the drawing room led into the next room in the wing, which was a woman's dressing room. The gender of the occupant was unmistakable: The walls were covered in pale pink silk and the writing desk and dressing table were dainty pieces of obviously French origin. The room also contained a pier glass and two tapestry-covered occasional chairs.

The housekeeper went to the large wardrobe that stood along one of the pink walls, and opened the door. Inside, neatly arranged, was the bridal wardrobe that Sarah and Lady Linford had bought.

Obviously, this was to be Sarah's own dressing room. She looked around at the pink walls and managed to utter, "Very nice, Mrs. Crabtree."

"The bedroom is through here, Your Grace."

Obediently, Sarah followed the housekeeper through a narrow door and into a large bedroom, which was highly unusual for London in that it had windows on two of its sides. The walls of the bedroom were covered in the same pink silk as the dressing room, and the draperies at the window were of pink silk as well. The hangings on the four-poster, which was larger than the one Sarah had shared with her husband at Hamilton Hall, were a pale rose-colored gauze. Bowls of pink roses were placed on the room's three tables.

Sarah thought faintly that the previous duchess had obviously been extremely fond of pink.

The only other door in the room, besides the one they had come in, was situated on the left wall and had to lead to a passageway. Sarah frowned in bewilderment and asked the housekeeper, "Doesn't His Grace have a dressing room as well?"

"His Grace's bedroom and dressing room are directly below these, on the first floor," Mrs. Crabtree replied. "If you would like, Your Grace, I will be happy to show you around the house."

Sarah fought to keep consternation from showing on her face.

Downstairs? she thought. *Anthony is going to sleep downstairs and leave me alone up here?*

She waited a moment, until she was certain that her voice was under control, and then she said, "I would very much like to see the rest of the house, Mrs. Crabtree. Thank you."

They went back through the second-floor drawing rooms and down the grand staircase to the front hall. Mrs. Crabtree began her tour with the small anteroom that was set off from the hall by the columns that Sarah had noticed when she came in. Behind the anteroom, a large drawing room, decorated in blue and gold, extended to the rear of the original house.

The first room in the wing addition was a large, extremely elegant dining room, with a magnificent crystal chandelier and an impressive display of silver on the sideboard. "Some of that silver has been in the family for hundreds of years, Your Grace," Mrs. Crabtree said.

"It is lovely," Sarah replied.

"The next room is the library." The housekeeper gave Sarah a questioning look.

Sarah answered the look. "I believe the duke is in the library and I do not wish to disturb him. I can see the room some other time."

Mrs. Crabtree's expression changed to one of approval. "This way, then, Your Grace," she said, and led the way into a narrow passageway which took them past the library to another door, which the housekeeper opened.

It was the duke's dressing room, an identical replica of the duchess's upstairs. The bedroom was also the same. There were two major differences between the duke's apartment and Sarah's, however. His was painted pale yellow, and the furniture was heavy and carved, not delicate and feminine.

The housekeeper then took Sarah up to the third floor of the house, which contained ten bedrooms for the use of family and guests. The top floor contained the nursery as well as other bedrooms for the servants.

The whole while they had been touring the rooms, Sarah had deliberately refrained from looking at any of the paintings. She was determined to wait for Anthony to show them to her.

By the time they finished their tour, Sarah's maid had arrived. As Anthony was still closeted in the library with his secretary, Sarah went back up to her bedroom and allowed her maid to undress her and put her into a robe so that she could rest.

She stretched out on the pink chaise longue in her bedroom with a book in her hands, but her mind could not concentrate on the words in front of her.

She found herself wishing desperately that she and Anthony were back at Hamilton Hall.

*   *   *

Dinner at Selbourne House was served at the fashionable hour of eight. At seven forty-five, Sarah, dressed in an evening gown of primrose-colored silk, went quietly down the stairs to the first floor, where the dining room was located.

Woodly was waiting for her at the bottom of the stairs. "His Grace is in the drawing room," the elderly butler informed her, and Sarah smiled and thanked him and allowed him to show her the way.

The first-floor drawing room was decorated in the classical style made popular by Robert Adam. The gilt-and-wood chairs had boldly curved backs and front legs with lion feet at their tips. The two blue silk sofas were supported by legs which sported winged paw feet, and the cabinets were of dark wood with brass lion mask mountings. The draperies on the front windows were of heavy blue silk. The picture above the fireplace was a portrait of a man dressed as a cavalier, and paintings lined the long, windowless wall opposite the door.

The duke was standing in front of the alabaster fireplace talking to another man, but when Sarah came in, both men immediately turned to her.

"Here you are, Sarah," the duke said. He held out his hand to her. "I have persuaded Max to have dinner with us tonight. I think it would be nice for the two of you to get to know each other."

Sarah felt a twinge of disappointment that she was not going to have her husband to herself, but she smiled as she crossed the floor and said, "How lovely."

The duke took her hand in his and raised it to his lips. His eyes met hers. "Did you have a nice rest?"

"Yes," Sarah said. She looked back into his eyes as if she were mesmerized.

He smiled faintly. "Good."

Sarah knew that tone of voice, and she felt a flush rise to her cheeks. She shot a quick look at Max to see if he had noticed.

He was looking at the duke, not at her. There was the faintest of lines between his well-marked brows.

Anthony gently squeezed her hand before he released it.

"Did you two accomplish your business this afternoon?" Sarah asked, trying to speak normally.

"Indeed we did, Your Grace," Max replied in his deep voice.

"Max is my right-hand man," the duke said. "I couldn't function without him."

Sarah remembered how he had saved her husband's life and thought that Max was, in truth, Anthony's right-hand man. Her eyes warmed as she looked into the face of her husband's best friend.

Max's widely set dark eyes looked back at her. They were perfectly expressionless. Sarah felt the faintest twinge of unease.

Max did not appear to be overly friendly.

He doesn't know me, Sarah told herself. *I am well disposed toward him because I know what he did for Anthony. All he knows about me is that Anthony had to marry me to save himself from going bankrupt. It will take a little time for us to become friends.*

Dinner was more comfortable than Sarah had feared it would be, chiefly because Anthony was in such good spirits that they spilled over onto the other two.

The dinner was served by four liveried footmen, which privately Sarah thought a trifle excessive for the three of them. The variety of food was excessive, too, with many of the side dishes going back to the kitchen barely touched.

The meal was delicious, though, particularly the Westphalia Ham à l'Essence.

As the dishes from the main course were being removed, Sarah commented upon the excellence of the food.

The duke smiled with pleasure. "Gaston is a superlative chef. When I was living in Paris, I managed to lure him away from the Princess de Liéve. It took quite a lot of talking to get him to accompany me to England, but I succeeded."

Sarah stared at her husband in astonishment. The man had been virtually bankrupt, but he had brought his chef all the way from Paris. And he had his meals served by four footmen, all of whom must be on his payroll!

Would she ever understand him?

After dessert had been finished, Max excused himself gracefully. Instead of remaining to drink port in splendid isolation, the duke took his wife around the house and showed her his paintings.

There were a large number of portraits of his ancestors and their friends, which Sarah found interesting, but it was the two Claudes that held her attention. They were both landscapes of the Italian countryside, one done in the early morning and the other in late afternoon. The hazy, luminous atmosphere of the times of day caused the space to seem to expand and the forms to melt and almost lose their material solidity. Sarah was enthralled.

They were served a light supper in the upstairs family drawing room, which was furnished in a considerably less elegant and more comfortable fashion than the two large drawing rooms were.

Sarah drank tea and nibbled on a biscuit. In an effort not to insult the chef; she had eaten more dinner than she was accustomed to and she was not at all hungry.

At last Anthony put down his own teacup and said softly, "I do believe it is time to go to bed."

Sarah looked at him out of troubled eyes and did not reply.

He frowned very faintly. "What is wrong?"

"Our bedrooms aren't on the same floor," she said.

His frown lifted. "Oh." He was sitting next to her on an elderly-looking blue velvet sofa, and now he leaned over and kissed the tip of her nose.

"There's a private staircase," he said, looking into her eyes.

Sarah made an effort and replied humorously, "How convenient."

"Yes, isn't it?"

He extended his hand and helped her to her feet. "I'll show you," he said.

They went next door into the large drawing room, but instead of continuing on into her dressing room, the Duke went to a small second door, which was situated on the left wall of the drawing room. He opened the door and Sarah found herself in the passageway she had suspected must be there.

"See?" the duke said, as he showed her the narrow staircase that connected the first and the second floors.

"I do indeed," Sarah said.

"This door is your bedroom," he said, and pushed it open.

Sarah looked into the expanse of pinkness that was revealed to her. "So it is."

He dropped a light kiss on her forehead. "I'll be with you in half an hour," he said.

At those words, she smiled.

CHAPTER
Fourteen

A S THE DUKE CLIMBED THE STAIRCASE THAT WOULD bring him to his wife, he allowed himself to savor the taste of success. The millions that had been transferred into his bank account upon his marriage had begun to work their magic. Max had shown him the list of his father's gambling debts that had been paid in the last few days, and the knowledge that he no longer owed money to his peers was an enormous burden lifted from his shoulders.

Four million pounds, and he had not had to pay a price for it! That thought still astounded him. Not only had he got the huge sum of money that he needed, but he had got a wife whom he genuinely liked.

And now that he had his own bedroom back, he could look forward to sleeping once more at night.

He was smiling as he opened the door to Sarah's bedroom. His eyes went immediately to the large four-poster that dominated the room, but, although the covers were neatly turned down, it was empty. He found her standing in front of the window that looked out upon the small back garden. She wore only her nightdress and her feet were bare.

"You will take cold if you stand there too long," he said. "Where is your robe and your slippers?"

"Anthony." She turned to face him. She was wearing the same nightdress she had worn on their wedding night. Her shoulders were bare, her breasts thinly veiled, her slim legs outlined against the thin silk. He thought that she was so slender and so perfectly in proportion that she did not appear to be as small as she really was.

He looked at her bare feet and frowned.

"Come," he said, crossing the room to her. "Let me put you back to bed."

"I am perfectly capable of getting into bed by myself," she replied a little irritably.

He paid no attention to her protest, but scooped her up into his arms. She weighed scarcely more than a child. He looked down at the swell of breast that was revealed by her nightgown. But she was not a child, he thought with satisfaction. She was a woman, and she was his wife.

He deposited her on the bed and straightened up.

She scrambled into a sitting position.

"I went to look out the window because I could not bear to look one more moment at these dreadful pink walls," she said.

He glanced around the room. "Good heavens. I see what you mean."

"Even the water closet is painted pink."

He said reasonably, "If you don't like pink, then have the rooms redone in a color that you do like."

She frowned. "That would be very expensive."

He went around to the other side of the bed and began to untie the sash of his dressing gown.

"The money doesn't matter," he said. "I want you to be comfortable."

He slid the dressing gown off his shoulders and got into the bed next to her.

She regarded him somberly out of large, shadowed eyes.

"What is it, Sarah?" he asked. "Is something else disturbing you besides the pink walls?"

She managed a tremulous smile. "It is just the newness of everything, I expect."

Her hair was so pretty when it was loose. It shimmered like soft silk in the light of the bedside lamp.

"Don't ever cut your hair," he said.

She looked startled. "I wasn't planning to."

He reached out his hand and buried his fingers in the shining strands that streamed over her shoulders. "I love your hair when it is free like this." He tugged on it gently. "Come here."

For the briefest of moments, he was surprised to feel resistance. Then she sighed, and melted, and was in his arms.

The duke lay on his stomach, his right hand resting just below his wife's breast, his left arm pillowing his head. His whole body felt lazy and replete with the delicious lassitude of sexual satisfaction.

It was so comfortable next to her in this bed. He wished he didn't have to leave.

Sleepily, he opened his eyes. "I am a lucky man," he said.

"Are you?" Her voice was very soft.

"Mm."

He felt himself drifting off and, with a huge effort of will, he swam back to consciousness.

"It's late and you're tired," he said. "I'll leave you so that you can get a good night's sleep."

Under his hand, he felt her body stiffen.

He pushed himself up until he was kneeling over her. "Is something wrong?"

The small, delicate face looking up at him seemed to be all huge brown eyes. "I was just wondering . . ." She stopped and took a deep, steadying breath. "Does anyone else sleep on this floor, Anthony, or am I all alone?"

He stared at her.

"Are you afraid to be alone?" he asked slowly.

Her eyes slid away from his and she plucked at the quilt. "You see, it is that I am accustomed to having someone close by. At school I had the other girls, and at home Grandpapa's room was close to mine."

He had never once thought that there might be a problem with the bedroom arrangement at Selbourne House.

"Perhaps we could get one of the maids to sleep in your dressing room," he said.

"No!" Now she looked anxious. "I didn't mean to sound like a baby, Anthony. I don't want to disturb the household. I will be fine."

It was perfectly clear to him that she was not fine. He thought that she looked very young as she lay there against her pillows, with her hair hanging over her shoulders and in her eyes the expression of a frightened child.

He said carefully, "I would stay with you myself, Sarah, but I don't want to disturb you with my nightmares."

Hope flickered in her eyes. "Oh, Anthony, I don't care about your nightmares! I will sleep far more soundly with you and your nightmares than I would sleep if I am left alone."

He found that he didn't have the heart to desert her.

Besides, if the truth be told, he wanted to stay.

Strange, he thought. *I have never wanted to stay the night with a woman before.*

The duke was a deeply private person, and once he had taken and given the pleasure of sex, he had always desired to return to the solitude of his own bed. But he could not deny to himself that he would be perfectly content to remain snugly in bed with his wife.

"Are you certain?" he asked.

"I'm certain!"

Poor little girl, he thought tenderly. *She really is afraid of being left alone.*

"All right," he said. "But if I am to sleep in this room, the pink will definitely have to go."

He was fascinated by the way her smile could light her small face to beauty. "Thank you, Anthony," she said with fervor.

He noticed the way her nipples were outlined by the sheer fabric of her nightdress. Her breasts were lovely, high and round and firm, just the way he liked them.

His eyes narrowed. "Of course, I might demand a payment for my continued presence."

She looked bewildered; then, as she looked into his suddenly concentrated eyes, understanding dawned.

He watched her assume an expression of mock severity. "That sounds like blackmail to me."

"Yes," he replied with pleasure. "That is exactly what it is."

The elusive dimple that sometimes came and went in her cheek suddenly appeared. "Oh well, I suppose I shall be forced to submit."

"A wise decision," he said, and slid down in the bed to join her.

*   *   *

Once more he was at the siege of Badajoz, standing in front of the place where Wellington's forces had first breached the walls of the castle. In front of him lay a heap of fifteen hundred British soldiers, the dead mixed with the desperately wounded. In the pile the burned and blackened corpses of those who had perished in the explosions were mixed with those that were torn to pieces by round shot or grape or musketry. Stiffening in the gore, the piled bodies were intertwined into one hideous mass of carnage. The smell of burning flesh was strong and disgusting.

On top of the pile he saw a hand move. Someone was alive. Gritting his teeth, he waded into the bloody heap of men.

"Anthony! Anthony, wake up!"

He struggled to hold on to the voice, to escape from the nightmare.

Someone shook him.

He muttered a curse in Spanish and opened his eyes, and looked up into his wife's concerned face. It took a moment for him to realize where he was, to understand that he was not standing thigh-deep in a mound of burned and bloody corpses.

His chest was heaving, his heart was pounding, and he was covered in sweat. He felt like the miserable, puling coward that he was.

When he spoke, his voice was bitter. "Well, you can't say I didn't warn you."

She leaned down and gently kissed his cheek. "I'm glad I was here. That is the sort of dream you need to be woken out of."

He shut his eyes so he did not have to see the sympathy in hers. He should have gone back to his own bed and got her maid to sleep in her dressing room.

Even though his eyes were shut, he could feel her looking at him. His mouth tightened.

She said, "I can understand that you would be upset by such nightmares. What I cannot understand, however, is why you should feel humiliated by them."

He opened his eyes and stared up at the canopy that covered the bed. Of course she couldn't understand, he thought angrily. She was not the descendant of a line of warriors.

He said coldly, "It is not the most attractive of afflictions."

Her voice was troubled as she replied, "But there is no reason to feel humiliated, Anthony. As I told you before, I am quite certain that you are not the only man whose war memories haunt his sleep."

I am the only Selbourne, he thought.

He flung a shielding arm across his eyes and answered with careful indifference, "I am sure that you are right."

There was a very long silence. He was about to say that he had better go back to his own room when she dumbfounded him by saying, "Don't you think that the Selbourne who fought at Agincourt probably had nightmares, too?"

He stared at her. "Of course he didn't."

She shrugged her lovely bare shoulders. "The battle of Agincourt might sound quite thrilling when one reads about it in Shakespeare, but in reality it was fought in a sea of mud and thousands of men were hacked to death. I cannot believe that a man who lived through that would not have nightmares."

He shook his head in sharp disagreement. He was quite certain that the previous earls and dukes of his line, who had fought so bravely in England's many battles, were not the sort of men to be troubled by childish nightmares.

His wife said, "Well, you are wrong. I'll bet that your ancestors who fought at Crécy and at Flodden and at whatever other god-awful battle you can name . . . I'll bet that they saw dead men in their sleep just like you do." She leaned forward, pinioned him with her eyes, and demanded sternly, "Will you tell your son that you have nightmares, Anthony?"

He stared up at her as if she were insane. "Of course I won't."

"And has it never occurred to you that your ancestors probably kept their mouths closed about *their* nightmares, too?"

Silence fell as they looked into each other's eyes. Then he said gruffly, "Nonsense."

But he was beginning to think about what she was saying.

She waved her hand in an exasperated gesture. "Look at what happened to Macbeth after he killed Duncan! I think that any man who is not totally insensitive would be troubled by the horrors he has witnessed in war."

A line from the play she had cited came into his head: *Macbeth hath murdered sleep.*

She was going on, "It is bad enough that you have to endure these terrible dreams, but to blame yourself for having them! I can't bear it." She leaned a little closer. "You are a normal man, Anthony, and it is nothing short of arrogance to think that you should be different from everyone else."

She looked and sounded so fierce that he almost smiled. "All right, Sarah." His voice was mild. "You have made your point."

Her face relaxed and she gently smoothed his hair back from his forehead. "I'm sure it will get better, Anthony. Time is a great healer."

"So they say."

He liked the feel of her hand stroking his hair. He didn't want her to stop.

"They say it because it is true," she informed him. Her hand continued its caressing motion. "Meanwhile, you had better sleep with me so that I can wake you up when you start tossing around. Why go through the whole wretched thing if you don't have to?"

He opened his mouth to reply, but before he could speak she laid a finger over his lips.

"Do not tell me that you don't wish to disturb me. I am very good at going right back to sleep if I awake in the middle of the night. I just conjure up the picture of a landscape in my mind, and I'm gone."

He spoke against her finger. "All right. Prove it to me. Let me see you do it."

She took away her hand, bit her lip, and looked at him indecisively. "You won't sneak away while I'm asleep?"

"No, I promise I won't do that."

"Well . . . all right."

He watched her curl up on her side like a kitten. After a minute, her eyes drifted closed.

It was chilly in the room and he pulled the quilt up over her shoulders.

She smiled but did not open her eyes.

He waited, watching her. At the end of ten minutes, she was asleep.

She had made him feel better about the nightmares. He would never feel good about them, but he definitely felt better. He thought that perhaps she was right about those other earls and dukes of his line. Not all, but some of them at least, might have had bad dreams. Yet they had gone down in history as doughty and indefatigable warriors.

Of course they wouldn't want anyone to know about their dreams, he thought. *I certainly don't.*

He looked at his sleeping wife. How had she known what he was feeling? And, perhaps even more amazing, why didn't he mind?

CHAPTER
Fifteen

WILLIAM PATTERSON WAS A MAN WHO WAS AC-
customed to winning, and even though he was
pleased with the marriage he had made for his
granddaughter, still he had the niggling feeling that
Cheviot had bested him in the marriage negotiations.
Once the marriage had actually been accomplished, Patterson devoted many hours to the study of how he might
turn the tables on his aristocratic grandson-in-law.

It did not take him long to come up with a plan of action, and on the day after the ducal couple's return to
London, the merchant paid them a visit.

The duke's elderly butler showed him into the front
drawing room and said that he would inform Her Grace
that Mr. Patterson had arrived.

Her Grace, Mr. Patterson thought with delight. That
was *his* granddaughter. Her Grace.

Patterson said genially, "You do that. And tell the duke
that I wish to see him as well."

The butler looked down his long nose. "Very good,
sir," he said stiffly.

Mr. Patterson snorted as the servant went out into the
hall.

He passed the time he spent waiting for Sarah and the duke by perusing the furniture in the room. He did not at all care for the slender, classical style of the chairs and sofas.

Hah. Looks like they would break if you sat in them too hard, he thought scornfully, comparing them unfavorably to the substantial furniture that decorated his drawing room at home.

"Grandpapa!" He turned to see Sarah coming through the door. She was dressed in a morning dress of sprig muslin that made her look very young.

"How lovely to see you," she said, and stood on her toes to kiss his cheek.

"Let me take a look at you, girl," he said, catching her chin in hard fingers and turning her face up to his.

It didn't take but one look to see that the duke had done his duty by Sarah. His granddaughter looked radiant, he thought. Damme, she looked almost beautiful. As Patterson had suspected, the duke obviously knew how to handle a woman.

"You're looking well, Sarah," he said.

"Thank you, Grandpapa. Will you sit down?"

She gestured toward a sofa, and he sat down gingerly, not trusting the delicate frame to hold him. It did, however, and he was conversing genially with his granddaughter when the door opened again and this time the duke came in.

Mr. Patterson heaved himself to his feet to shake hands with his grandson-in-law.

"How kind of you to call upon us so soon," the duke said courteously as he gestured Mr. Patterson to resume his seat. The duke himself sat next to his wife on the room's other sofa.

"Well, I wanted to see how Sarah was doing, and it's

plain as a pike that she's doing very well," Patterson returned heartily.

Color flushed into Sarah's cheeks.

"I am glad you think so," the duke said, sounding amused.

"I also have a matter of business that I wanted to talk to you both about," Patterson went on. "It relates to Sarah's inheritance."

The duke merely looked courteously interested. "Yes?"

Mr. Patterson waited, relishing the moment. Then he said to his granddaughter, "I suppose you know all about the trust fund Cheviot set up for you, Sarah."

She looked surprised. "No, Grandpapa." She glanced at her husband, but his expression of polite interest told her nothing. "I know nothing about a trust fund," she said.

The merchant was surprised that the duke had not told her about the fund. He had always assumed that the reason Cheviot had set it up was to buy Sarah's goodwill.

Patterson proceeded to explain the matter to his granddaughter. "Out of the marriage settlement, Cheviot set up a trust fund of a quarter of a million pounds for you. You will have the use of the income for the rest of your life. It should be enough to keep you very comfortable, my girl."

Sarah's eyes enlarged noticeably and she shot her husband another questioning look. "Oh," she said.

Patterson moved his piercing blue eyes to the duke. "Since Sarah has been provided for by the trust fund, I have been turning my mind to the disposition of the rest of my fortune, Your Grace."

The duke continued to look politely interested. "Yes?" he repeated.

Mr. Patterson prepared to blast that courteous look off his grandson-in-law's face.

"It seems to me, Your Grace, that the marriage settlement we worked out is more than ample for your needs as well as Sarah's. Consequently I have decided that when I die I want the remainder of my fortune"—he paused to rub in some salt—"which numbers some eighteen million pounds, to be applied to the expansion of my business. Patterson Cotton has been my life and I want it to live on as my monument after I am gone."

The serenely interested expression on the duke's face did not alter. "Are you telling us that you will not be leaving the remainder of your money to Sarah?"

"Aye," the merchant said with satisfaction. His eyes were riveted on his grandson-in-law's face. "That is exactly what I'm telling you."

The duke said, "You have every right to leave your money as you choose, sir. Thanks to your very generous settlement, I am perfectly capable of providing for my wife. You need have no fears about her future welfare."

Mr. Patterson scowled. This was not the reaction he had expected. He had expected the duke to try to talk him into leaving the money to Sarah.

"Well, the marriage settlement is all you're going to get out of me," he said bluntly. "I just wanted to make that clear."

"You have made it perfectly clear," the duke replied. "Now, may we offer you some refreshment?"

Patterson stared at his grandson-in-law, frustration written all over his face.

Damme, but the boy looked perfectly calm. He certainly didn't look as if he'd just been cheated out of eighteen million pounds!

"I'll order tea, shall I, Grandpapa?" Sarah said.

"No," the merchant said. He was sure he heard the skinny sofa creak as he heaved himself to his feet. "I have to be on my way. Business in the city."

"I see." The duke also rose to his feet, followed more slowly by Sarah.

"It has been a pleasure seeing you again, sir," the duke said. He held out his hand. "You must dine with us one night soon. We will be leaving for Northumberland very shortly, you know."

"Hmmph," said Mr. Patterson.

He took his grandson-in-law's slender, elegant, manicured, surprisingly muscular hand into his own large paw. Then he turned to his granddaughter.

"Take care of yourself, my girl. And remember—I'll be looking forward to a grandson soon."

The chit actually exchanged a glance with her husband. Then she said docilely, "Yes, Grandpapa."

"We will do our best, sir," the duke said gravely.

"Hmmph," the merchant said again. Then, as the duke made to accompany him out of the room, "No, no. I can see myself out."

The duke did not falter. "Of course I will see you out," he said courteously.

Damme, Mr. Patterson thought bitterly as he accompanied his grandson-in-law to the front door. *Does nothing ever shake the boy's composure?*

After the men had left the room, Sarah sat down again upon the sofa and thought about what had just transpired.

Why on earth does Grandpapa feel the need to tell us that he has cut me out of his will? she thought in bewilderment.

As always, her grandfather's motives were an enigma to her.

Her husband came back into the room, but he did not sit down beside her again. Instead he stood with his back against the fireplace and regarded her somberly.

"I am sorry, Sarah," he said. "It is because of me that your grandfather has taken this action."

"I don't understand any of this, Anthony," she said, her mystification showing clearly in her eyes.

Patterson's motive was not an enigma to the duke.

"Your grandfather thinks that I screwed him out of too much money and this is his revenge," he explained. "He is cutting you out of his will in order to get back at me, but you are the one who is being hurt. I am sorry, but I'm afraid there is little I can do about it. His pride has been wounded and it will take time for him to get over it."

Sarah sat for a few moments in silence, thinking about what she had just heard. Then she sighed. "Grandpapa will never understand that it is possible for people to have enough money. He thinks they must always want more."

The duke's light eyes were steady on her face. "I hope you feel that you have enough money, my dear, because, unless your grandfather changes his mind, it might be all that you are going to get."

Sarah said, "I didn't think that I had *any* money. What is this trust fund that Grandpapa was talking about?"

"I was going to have Max explain it to you," the duke said. "It is quite simple, really. I took a quarter of a million pounds out of the money your grandfather settled on me and put it into a trust fund for you. It is totally yours, Sarah. I cannot touch it. No matter what may happen, you will always have that money."

She returned his steady gaze. "Is that a customary thing to do when a man and a woman marry?"

He replied easily, "It is certainly customary to settle a sum of money on the woman as a jointure."

"But the trust fund is different from a jointure?"

"A little. The money has been invested and the income from those investments will come to you for the duration of your life."

Sarah looked down at her hands, which were folded in her lap, then back up to her husband. "What made you decide on a trust fund?"

He shrugged casually. "I thought that it was important for you to have your own money. If you wish to buy a painting, you will be able to do so without applying to me. If you wish to go to Paris, and I won't take you, you will have the funds to go by yourself. It is security for you, my dear. It means that you are not completely dependent upon me."

"I see," Sarah said gravely.

He smiled at her. "I will set up an appointment for you to talk to Max, and he will go over the figures with you."

Her hands moved nervously in her lap. "I don't know anything about handling money, Anthony," she said. "All I have ever had is an allowance. A quarter of a million pounds is too much."

He explained patiently, "You won't have the entire principal, you will have the income from it. If you don't wish to spend it all, you can reinvest it."

Sarah didn't reply, but there was a line between her brows.

"You won't have to do anything," he assured her. "Max will take care of it for you."

The line between her brows did not smooth out. "So what Grandpapa meant was that I will be taken care of by the trust fund, therefore he has no need to leave me any more money?"

"That is right. I am very sorry, Sarah. I never anticipated this reaction when I insisted upon setting up the trust for you."

"I don't care about the money, Anthony," she said impatiently.

He smiled wryly. "Eighteen million pounds is a lot of money not to care about, Sarah."

She shook her head. "All I care about is having the freedom to paint. And you have given that to me."

He gave her his most beautiful smile.

"You are a pearl among women, my wife," he said lightly. He stepped away from the fireplace. "Now, if you will excuse me, I have an appointment with my banker."

"Of course," Sarah said.

She sat alone for another half hour in the drawing room, pondering the thought that while she didn't care about the loss of eighteen million pounds, perhaps Anthony did.

Neville Harvey came to call on Sarah that afternoon.

Unlike William Patterson, the younger man recognized the elegance and the expensiveness of the furnishings in the drawing room to which he had been shown.

Hard to believe that the duke was nearly bankrupt when he has a house like this, he thought, as he regarded his exquisite surroundings. *It probably never even occurred to him that he could have sold this house for a fortune.*

He was examining a Chinese vase that had to be worth a packet when Sarah came into the room.

He turned to greet her and was immediately struck by the same thing that Mr. Patterson had seen. Sarah looked radiant.

For a moment, Neville was struck dumb. He had always thought that Sarah was pretty, but now . . .

He had not expected this. If anything, he had expected just the opposite. He remembered her reaction to his own kiss, and his warning to her about the horror of having to go to bed with a man she scarcely knew.

Obviously, she had enjoyed the experience very much.

Of course she enjoyed it, he thought resentfully. *A man like that, who knows women as he does . . . he would know just how to put her under his spell.*

"Neville!" she said, coming forward with an extended hand. "How good of you to come to see me."

He took her hand and looked down into her great brown eyes. There was an expression in those eyes that he had never seen before. The girlish innocence was gone. It was a woman who was looking back at him today.

Pain, sudden and acute, struck Neville's heart. He had been in love with Sarah since she was ten years old. And now . . . to see her like this . . . and he was not the one who had done it. It was not for him that she wore that luminous glow.

He said with difficulty, "No need to ask you how you're doing. You look wonderful."

Faint color stained her cheeks. "Thank you, Neville. I have always loved the country."

It isn't the country that's made you look like this, he thought bitterly.

He remained with her for a half an hour, talking about the things they had always talked about: his business, his future plans for expanding his business, his employee problems, and the state of the cotton market in general.

As he was standing with Sarah near the door, preparing to depart, the duke came into the room.

Sarah's face lit like a candle.

"I beg your pardon, my dear," the duke said in his soft voice. "I did not realize that you had company."

"You know Neville Harvey, don't you, Anthony?" Sarah asked.

"We have met," the duke replied. He nodded to Neville and said pleasantly, "How are you, Harvey?"

Neville looked into the beautiful face of Sarah's husband and felt hatred sear his heart.

"I am very well, Your Grace," he replied woodenly.

The duke turned back to his wife. "I was wondering if you would like to go driving in the park at five, Sarah. I should be free by then."

Sarah said, "I should love to go for a drive with you."

Neville averted his eyes from the expression on her face.

"I'll have them bring the phaeton around at five, then," the duke said.

"I'll be ready," she promised. "I wouldn't dare keep your precious horses standing."

The duke flashed her a quick grin.

Then he looked once more at Neville and said, "Nice to see you again, Harvey."

"Thank you, Your Grace," Neville replied.

All the muscles in his face felt frozen.

He managed to extricate himself from the house without betraying his feelings to Sarah. Not that she would have noticed if he had dropped down dead in front of her, he thought bitterly. He had been her best friend for fourteen years, but now the only person who existed for her was that good-looking fop she had married.

He would hurt her, Neville thought. A man like that was not capable of remaining faithful to any one woman, and infidelity would kill Sarah.

When that happens, he thought resolutely, *I will be the one standing by to pick up the pieces.*

The following morning, Sarah was late for her appointment with Max. This was because her husband had succeeded in convincing her that his need was more urgent than the need of his secretary to meet with her.

As soon as Sarah walked into the library, Max knew what had detained her.

Enjoying your new plaything, are you, Anthony? he thought to himself with carefully concealed amusement.

Sarah smiled as she reached the desk and apologized for her lateness. She made no attempt to explain what had kept her, and Max thought that she probably didn't realize the languid look in her eyes gave her away.

She said, "I understand that His Grace has given you the unenviable task of trying to explain this trust fund to me, Mr. Scott. I hope I am not too slow a pupil."

He returned a pleasant reply, and invited her to take the chair that he had placed beside the desk. Then he sat behind the desk and allowed himself to take a closer look at Anthony's new duchess.

He had not been impressed when first he met Sarah, and he was not impressed now. When she smiled she was a pretty enough little thing, he supposed, but she was insignificant compared to some of the great beauties who had loved the duke in the past. Anthony would soon tire of her. He always did.

Max had lived with jealousy almost from the first day he had met Anthony, but his jealousy had never been directed toward the duke's women. He had never begrudged Anthony his sexual pleasure, not with the highborn Spanish women he had bedded in the Peninsula, nor with the elegant French ladies who had swarmed all over him in Paris.

Max's jealousy had been directed toward any of Anthony's friends who appeared to be close to him. Most of all, he had been jealous of Anthony's peers, that small, tight-knit circle of young aristocrats who had been at school with him. Their easy banter, the careless lack of ceremony with which they treated the duke, their attitude of belonging to an exclusive club from which outsiders like Max must always be excluded—all of these things had nearly driven Max insane with jealousy.

What had enabled Max to keep a semblance of balance was the knowledge that it was he who had carried Anthony off the battlefield at Salamanca; it was he who had refused to let the surgeon cut off Anthony's arm; it was he to whom Anthony turned when he needed advice; it was he whom Anthony addressed as *my friend*.

Close as he was to the duke, however, he yearned to be closer still. No matter how friendly Anthony might be to him, Max was always conscious of the space that the duke kept around himself, a space into which no one dared step—not his lovers, not his boyhood friends, not even Max.

It was part of Anthony's great fascination—that space. The greatest desire of Max's life was to be the person who breached it. He had not done so yet, but at least he had the consolation of knowing that no one else had come any closer to Anthony than he had.

It never once occurred to him, as he sat with the young duchess in the library on this sunny spring morning, that in Sarah he might have found his most formidable rival for Anthony's love.

CHAPTER
Sixteen

AFTER TWO WEEKS IN LONDON, ANTHONY HAD FINished his business and was ready to leave for Northumberland. The traveling chaise that had belonged to his father took Sarah and the duke, and Max and the servants followed in a series of carriages that also contained mounds of luggage.

Sarah had hoped she could go in the phaeton, but her husband gently informed her that it would not be proper for her to travel in an open carriage on the public turnpikes. He drove the phaeton himself for a portion of each day, but the rest of the time he spent inside the chaise with Sarah, trying to keep her entertained so she would not feel too sick.

It was the company of her husband that made the long journey tolerable for Sarah. As always, the motion of the carriage did not agree with her stomach, but she found Anthony's concern for her welfare infinitely sweet.

He beguiled much of the tedious travel time by talking about Cheviot Castle, and in doing so, he revealed his own deep love for his ancestral home.

The castle, he informed his wife, was built between 1313 and 1316, as the stronghold of Henry Selbourne, first Earl of Cheviot. Unfortunately, the first earl had had little time to enjoy his castle, for he was executed only six years after it was completed, following his defeat by Edward II at the Battle of Boroughbridge.

The period of the castle's greatest fame occurred later in the century, when it became one of England's mainstays against Scots raids from across the border. It was at this time that the first Selbourne was named Warden of the Scottish Marches, an honor the family had continued to hold until it was inherited by Anthony himself.

One of the skirmishes between the English and the Scots during this period had become the subject of what was perhaps England's most famous and beloved ballad: "The Hunting of Cheviot."

"The battle took place on August 13, 1388," the duke told Sarah. "A small force of Scots under the Earl of Douglas were heading back home after a pillaging session in England when my ancestor, Thomas Selbourne, Earl of Cheviot, fell on them and demolished them, killing the Earl of Douglas in the process." He cocked an eyebrow. "The ballad itself is hardly history, however. It has been greatly embellished to glorify the English, and most especially, I must confess, the House of Selbourne."

Sarah was familiar with the famous ballad and she laughed at his comment and quoted a few lines to him:

> " 'Noe, Douglas! quote Earl Cheviot then,
> 'Thy profer I doe scorne;
> I will not yeelde to any Scot
> That ever yett was borne!' "

He smiled wryly. "Killing men sounds quite noble when you hear about it in ballads. It is not so pleasant in the actual doing, however."

Sarah knew a sudden, urgent desire to reach out to him. She restrained it, however, clasping her fingers together tightly in her lap and staring straight ahead. She had come to know him well enough to realize that he would not welcome her sympathy.

After a moment's silence, he again took up the tale of the castle's history.

"Cheviot's defenses were put to the test during the Wars of the Roses, when it was besieged by the Lancastrian forces in 1462 and 1464. The last attack against its walls actually came during the Civil War, when Cheviot held out for King Charles against a siege by Cromwell."

"It isn't still a real castle, is it?" Sarah asked. "I mean, with walls and towers and battlements."

"Oh, it's still a real castle," he assured her. "The curtain wall is almost perfectly intact, and so are the towers built into it. I think you will find the walls rather impressive—they enclose a little over eleven acres."

A vision of a stark medieval keep surrounded by a series of open baileys connected by intimidating drawbridges rose before Sarah's mind's eye. She swallowed.

"I'm sure the living quarters have been updated since the fourteenth century," she ventured.

"Somewhat," he returned carelessly. "We did have water closets installed a few years ago."

Sarah struggled to hide her dismay as she envisioned a residence whose walls were composed of cold gray stone, whose furniture was all made out of hard oak, and whose main decorations were suits of armor and swords.

But Anthony loved it. She could tell that from his voice.

I suppose I shall grow accustomed to it, she thought bravely. Then, *Thank God it has water closets.*

They stayed overnight at inns along the way and, to Sarah's infinite satisfaction. Anthony did not once have a nightmare.

Finally, three days after they had set out from London, they reached the Northumberland border.

The duke, who had just come into the chaise to join Sarah, said wryly, "I don't know which feeling is uppermost in my mind—happiness at the thought of seeing Cheviot again, or dread at the thought of meeting my stepmother."

It was the first mention he had made of the dowager duchess. All his lavish talk of Cheviot had been about its past inhabitants; of his stepmother and his brothers he had said nothing.

"Is she really such a horror?" Sarah asked.

His reply was brief but certain. "Yes."

Sarah did not question him further, but instead peered out the window at the sky, which was a deep blue interspersed with high white clouds. It looked different from the sky in the south, Sarah thought. It was higher . . . more dramatic, somehow.

She commented on this to the duke, who looked pleased. "You will notice that everything looks different in the north," he said. "The light is different here. You'll find it interesting, I think."

On either side of the road, low stone walls separated the fields. Sarah noticed campion and toadflax growing in the crevices between the stones, and in the grass along the verge, wild thyme and yellow cinquefoil grew in profusion.

They made a brief stop at Newcastle to rest the horses, and then proceeded directly north. Shortly after Alnwick, they turned off the main road onto a smaller road that ran east, in the direction of the sea.

Pastureland stretched along the sides of the road, dotted with sheep and scattered farmhouses. The duke informed Sarah that the farms all belonged to Cheviot Castle.

The windows of the carriage were always left open to allow Sarah to have fresh air, and the duke said, "Put your head out the window for a moment and look straight ahead."

She did so, and there in the distance, towering above the flat pastureland from its perch on a rugged basalt cliff, loomed the gray stone towers and walls of a great medieval castle. From each of the towers flew the scarlet flag bearing the gold wildcat that Sarah recognized as the arms of the House of Selbourne. The whole was spectacularly outlined against the dramatic, deep blue Northumberland sky.

It was a view to stop the heart.

"I must paint that," Sarah breathed.

From beside her Anthony said, "I thought you would like it."

"Like it?" She turned to him, her eyes glowing. "It is marvelous!"

The duke inhaled the faintly salt-tinged air that was pouring in through the open carriage windows. "I think it is, too."

The chaise passed into a small wood, leaving behind the pastureland and the sheep. After a short drive, it came out into the open once more, and Sarah looked around in wonder.

They were driving through an elegant park that reminded her very much of the park at Hartford Court.

"My grandfather, the sixth duke, is responsible for

this," the duke said, waving his hand to indicate the grounds. "He wanted to 'civilize' the castle, and so he imported Capability Brown to create a park."

"It is beautiful," Sarah said faintly, as she looked at the sweep of open lawn around a large man-made pool, upon which two swans regally floated.

The contrast between this elegant scene and the towering battlemented stone walls that rose above it was startling.

The duke said, "The lawn needs to be cut."

It was true that the grass was high, Sarah thought, but the scene was still lovely.

The drive reached the bottom of the hill upon which the castle was built, and the horses slowed as they began the upward pull.

Sarah glanced at Anthony and then averted her eyes to give him privacy.

They reached the top and the chaise began to approach the immense stone curtain wall of the castle. Sarah imagined the courage it must have taken for men to hurl themselves against such seemingly impregnable defenses, and shuddered.

She peered out of the window once more and saw that they had almost reached the open gate, which was guarded on either side by two massive towers.

In front of one of the towers stood an elderly man, dressed in the gold and scarlet livery of Cheviot.

He would have looked more at home wearing chain mail, Sarah thought.

The carriage drew alongside the man, who was beaming all over his face, and Sarah said softly, "Anthony, here is someone who wishes to greet you."

"Good heavens," the duke said, noticing the old man for the first time. "I believe that is Norton."

He called to the coachman to stop the chaise and the old man came over to the window.

"Oh, Your Grace," he said in a trembling voice. "Welcome home!"

"Norton," the duke said with his charming smile. "How wonderful to see you still at your post."

The lined old face was bathed in radiance. "Thank ye, Your Grace. I remember ye well from when you was a small boy. It is good to have ye back wi' us."

He bowed again and stepped back from the window. The coachman started the horses again, and Sarah found herself within the grim walls of Anthony's beloved Cheviot Castle.

The main castle building looked exactly as she had expected it to look: like a massive Norman-style keep with three projecting towers rising to a battlemented skyline.

But . . .

In front of the castle, there were several grand baroque terraces which had been blasted out of the rock. These terraces fell away gracefully to a vast expanse of lawn.

Sarah looked around. The entire area enclosed by the grim, forbidding walls was filled with spreading green lawns and flower gardens.

"Good heavens," Sarah said in surprise.

At that moment, the chaise stopped. Sarah looked out to see that they were parked in front of the wide flight of steps that had been built to lead up to the castle's front door. The steps were filled with a mass of people, all of whom were dressed in the uniforms of various kinds of servants.

"Who are all those people, Anthony?" she asked faintly.

The duke's eyebrows lifted in surprise as he regarded the picture before him. "I did not think that my stepmother would bother to acknowledge my arrival in such a formal fashion," he said.

He turned to Sarah to explain. "It is an official greeting party. That is the entire staff of the castle lined up on the front steps." At her look of alarm, he added reassuringly, "Don't worry. You have only to smile and look gracious. Nothing else is expected of you."

"I suppose I can manage that," she returned, trying not to look as overwhelmed as she felt.

A stately male figure, dressed in formal black, came forward to open the carriage door. A footman dressed in scarlet and gold was right behind him to set the steps.

The duke alighted first, then he turned to hold out his hand to Sarah. Once she was standing beside him, he said to the elderly man in black, "How splendid to see you again, Jarvis. It has been a long time."

"Too long, Your Grace," the man returned as he bowed reverently. "May I say how happy we all are to have you safely home."

"Thank you," the duke replied. He turned to Sarah, "My dear, this is Jarvis, who has been butler here since I was a child."

Sarah smiled and said how do you do and wondered if all of Anthony's servants were of such venerable years.

She felt his hand—which was resting on her arm just above her elbow—tense, and she looked with him toward the three people who formed the first line of the welcoming party.

"Anthony," said the woman, who was dressed in a black silk mourning gown. Her voice was cold and flat. "How nice to see you again."

"Thank you, ma'am," the duke replied, his own voice quiet and steady. "It is good to be home."

At his use of the word *home,* Sarah saw the dowager's lips tighten.

She was a thin woman, of medium height, with hair that had once been blue-black but was now streaked with gray. Her eyes were dark blue and very hard.

"You will scarcely know your brothers, they have grown so since you last saw them," she said. She gestured to the figure beside her. "This is Lawrence."

Lord Lawrence Selbourne was a tall, black-haired young man with an eagle's beak of a nose and burning blue eyes. He held out his hand to Anthony, but he did not smile. "Welcome home, Cheviot," he said.

Sarah felt a chill in her bones. The expression on Lawrence's face was in direct contrast to his words.

"And here is Patrick," the Dowager said next.

Lord Patrick was a youngster of thirteen, with the same black hair as his mother and his elder brother. His still-childish face was less stark-looking than Lawrence's, however, and his expression was shy and defensive.

"How do you do," he said stiffly to his eldest brother.

As the duke introduced her to his family, Sarah tried to hide her consternation.

No wonder Anthony had never wanted to come home!

His reception from the servants massed on the front steps was far warmer than the one he had received from his family. Many of the older servants appeared to remember him with great fondness, and a number of them confided that they had prayed for his safety while he was in the Peninsula.

The duke was charming. Sarah was friendly. Then, at last, they were able to go into the house.

As soon as she stepped inside the front door, Sarah felt as if she had passed into another world. The entrance hall, instead of being the great echoing stone chamber filled with the suits of armor that she had expected, was instead a magnificent eighteenth-century creation, soaring to a high ceiling upon which was painted what Sarah recognized as a replica of Veronese's *Apotheosis of Venice.*

Sarah's mouth dropped open as she stared at the classically beautiful room before her. Then she turned accusingly to her husband. "You did it on purpose! You deliberately led me to think that I was coming to live in a pile of medieval stone!"

He grinned, looking astonishingly like a small boy who has just done something exceedingly clever.

"I can assure you, Duchess, that Cheviot Castle is far from a pile of medieval stone," the dowager said in her cold, precise voice. "I believe I may say with perfect truth that it can stand beside any great house in the country."

As if to demonstrate the truth of this statement, the dowager insisted upon taking Sarah and the duke on a short house tour. It was evident, from the condescending way she pointed out and identified the various sets of rich English, French, and Italian furniture, that she thought the new duchess must be little more than an ignorant parvenu.

As they walked through the series of staterooms on the first floor, with their gilded tables and tapestried chairs, the duke several times asked his stepmother what had happened to a certain Chinese vase, or French porcelain figure, or painting by Rubens or Van Dyck.

After the sixth time that the dowager had replied, "Your father sold it," the duke stopped asking.

Even though Sarah could see that there were empty spaces on the walls and on the tables, still the overwhelming impression she received was that the house was magnificent.

The most spectacular room of all was the state bedroom, which the dowager told her was still reserved for the visits of royalty.

"Several kings have slept in that bed," she announced grandly.

At this point, Anthony made one of his few comments. "I remember that my grandfather, who was not a king but a prince, used to sleep in this room when he came to visit. I thought it was a great treat when he let me get into the bed with him in the morning."

The dowager scowled, clearly not liking to be reminded of her stepson's royal blood.

Sarah looked around the chamber in wonder. The entire bedroom was decorated with a profusion of seventeenth-century gilt. The canopied state bed was adorned with rich red hangings and gilt cresting, and, in the style of the French court, it was separated from the rest of the room by a finely carved balustrade.

The furniture in the room was covered in velvet, the ceiling was painted, and rich tapestries hung upon all the walls. It was the sort of chamber that Sarah would have expected to see at the Versailles of Louis XIV.

She thought fervently, as she regarded the opulence around her, *Thank God I don't have to sleep in here*.

The room Sarah actually liked the best was a beautiful T-shaped long gallery on the second floor, which the dowager informed her was the only surviving Elizabethan interior. The gallery walls were hung with rather boring family portraits, but the delicate ceiling plasterwork was lovely, featuring young trees and tendrils of foliage, and the long walls were decorated with an array of lovely silver sconces.

After she had shown Sarah two of the drawing rooms on the second floor, the dowager announced frigidly, "I have, of course, vacated the ducal apartment for your use. If you will follow me, I will show it to you now."

Abruptly, Sarah decided that she did not want to see her private rooms in the company of her stepmother-in-law.

"Thank you, Duchess," she said pleasantly, "but Anthony can show me the apartment. I have trespassed on your time long enough."

The dowager's blue eyes shot daggers at Sarah. "It is no trouble," she said with determination.

Sarah glanced at her husband. His face was perfectly expressionless. A feeling of protectiveness she had never known before welled up in her.

She turned to the dowager and said, "To be truthful, I am rather tired and would like to rest. I hope you do not mind."

The dowager frowned forbiddingly.

"I will take care of my wife, ma'am," the duke said quietly. "When the carriages with the rest of our staff arrive, please let me know."

The dowager set her mouth, nodded, and stalked away.

"Your bedroom is this way," the duke said, and Sarah followed him first into a small sitting room, and then through another door into what was obviously a woman's dressing room. The duke did not stop to give her time to look around, however, but strode across the floor to open the door that led into the bedroom. Sarah followed more slowly.

Once inside, she turned to her husband and said with something like awe, "Anthony, she is *horrible*."

He didn't reply.

Sarah regarded him worriedly. His face was the same unreadable mask that it had been ever since he had encountered his family. She had the feeling that he was very far away.

"Do you know who she reminds me of?" she inquired.

He shook his head.

"Lady Macbeth."

A flicker of expression crossed his face. "Lady Macbeth?"

"Yes. I kept thinking of that speech she makes when she first learns that the king is coming to visit her."

He frowned slightly, clearly trying to focus his attention on what she was saying.

Sarah said, "*You* know. The one where she calls on the evil spirits to take away her femininity and fill her 'top-full of direst cruelty.'"

He still looked puzzled.

Sarah said, "It appears to me as if the spirits have answered the dowager's plea."

For what seemed to be a very long moment, Anthony just stared at her. Then his face splintered into laughter.

He laughed so hard that he actually had to sit down in one of the upholstered silk chairs. Sarah smiled as she watched him.

When finally he had regained his breath, he stretched out a hand and said, "Come here."

She crossed the floor and he drew her down to sit upon his lap. His arms encircled her and she rested her head trustingly against his shoulder.

"I have hated her for nearly all my life," he said. "She did everything she could to make me feel like an intruder in my own home. Finally she succeeded in driving me away."

"I knew she was fiendlike," Sarah murmured. "She

has the coldest eyes of anyone I have ever met. How on earth did your father come to marry her?"

"She was very beautiful when she was young," he said. "Like many people, my father was incapable of seeing beyond the outer facade." Once again his voice held that expressionless note that she found so distressing.

After a minute, she said, "A lot of landscape painters are like that, too. They only see the prettiness on the surface; they never see into the heart of things."

She heard him chuckle and then his lips touched her temple. "Why did I suspect that painting would come up somewhere in this discussion?"

She smiled and closed her eyes and felt the faintly scratchy wool of his coat under her cheek. Finally she said, "What paintings did your father sell?"

She heard the bitterness he was trying to hide. "Everything that had value. We had some splendid pictures that I wanted to show you, but . . . they appear to be gone."

Sarah stirred, glancing upward from his shoulder to his face. "Anthony, does she have to live here with us?"

"Good God, no." He sounded horrified at the thought. "I have every intention of replacing her jointure, which was one of the many things that my father gambled away. Part of the jointure settlement was for her to have the house in Newcastle to live in for the duration of her life, and that is where she shall go."

"And your brothers?"

He was silent for a long moment. Then he said, "They did not appear very glad to see me, did they?"

"No, they didn't."

He sighed. "I suppose I can't blame them. According to my Aunt Linford, my stepmother has been assuring them for years that I would be killed in the war and that

Lawrence would be the next duke. It must have been quite a shock for them to learn that I had survived."

Sarah felt a shiver run up and down her spine.

"I'm sure they don't wish you dead, Anthony."

Once more she felt his lips touch her temple. "I'm glad you're here, Sarah," he said.

She felt as if he had given her a gift.

CHAPTER
Seventeen

SARAH REALLY WAS FATIGUED FROM THE JOURNEY, AND the duke left her in her bedroom to rest and returned downstairs by himself.

In the front hall he encountered his secretary, who had just arrived. "Max!" he said with undisguised relief. "How glad I am to see you."

Maxwell Scott came forward, amusement in his widely spaced dark eyes. "Surely it can't be that bad, Anthony."

The duke smiled ruefully. "The duchess compared my stepmother to Lady Macbeth, and I must say that there is a noticeable likeness."

At that moment, the dowager's chill voice floated across the hall to their ears. "Jarvis has informed me that one of your servants has arrived, Anthony."

The duke turned. "Not a servant, ma'am," he said. "Allow me to present my personal secretary, Captain Maxwell Scott."

The dowager swept across the green marble floor, her black silk skirts rustling. "Your secretary?" she said, managing to look down her thin, high-boned nose at Max even though he was considerably taller than she.

"My secretary, and my friend," the duke replied.

The dowager's nose quivered, as if she smelled something unpleasant.

"How do you do, Captain Scott," she said frigidly.

Max bowed. "Duchess. I am Mr. Scott nowadays, however. I resigned from the army soon after Waterloo."

The dowager looked supremely uninterested in this piece of information. She said to the duke, "I will have one of the housemaids show Mr. Scott to his room."

"What room have you given him, ma'am?" the duke asked.

The dowager looked amazed at such a question. "He may have one of the bedrooms on the fourth floor."

"I would like you to give Mr. Scott the yellow bedroom," the duke said pleasantly. "It will be more comfortable for him."

"The yellow . . ." The dowager's blue eyes looked like twin glaciers. "Anthony, the yellow bedroom is one of our best guest chambers."

"I know it is. That is why I wish Mr. Scott to have it."

The duke's voice was at its softest. He put a hand on Max's arm, both in affection and command. "Come along with me, Max, and I'll take you upstairs myself." Over his shoulder he said to his stepmother, "You may have one of the footmen bring Mr. Scott's luggage to the yellow bedroom, ma'am."

The dowager looked absolutely furious.

The duke steered Max to the stairs and began to ask him about his journey.

Before he changed for dinner, the duke took a walk down to the stables, which were located in the same place they had occupied since the Middle Ages, along the curtain wall to the south of the keep.

Even though the stables were in their original location,

they had been completely redone by the duke's grandfather. The sixth duke had also been responsible for the addition of the park, as well as the improvements made to the staterooms of the castle.

Unfortunately, all of these renovations had cost a great deal of money, and, since he had made some very unwise investments, the sixth duke had been forced to pay for them out of the principal of the family fortune.

As Lady Linford had told Mr. Patterson, both her father and her brother bore the responsibility for the financial wreck of the House of Selbourne.

Anthony walked down the path that led to the stables, and watched the seagulls circling in the air on the far side of the castle walls. He inhaled the cool, damp, salt-smelling air, and felt his heart lift.

He was home. Cheviot was finally his.

This time, it was his stepmother who would have to leave.

The original medieval stables had been built right along the south wall, but when they had been redone, the building had been moved away from the wall to lessen the damp. The stable building itself was constructed of brick, not stone, and it looked to the duke as if all the doors and windows had been given a recent coat of paint.

The first people the duke saw when he walked into the stableyard were his two brothers standing in front of one of the box stalls. The upper part of the stall door was open, and the two youngsters were looking in at the box's resident.

As the duke approached the stall, he saw that the box held Rodrigo, the dark bay thoroughbred colt he had bought two years ago. The colt was standing halfway back in his box, regarding his two young admirers with the haughty arrogance that only thoroughbreds can muster.

His whole demeanor said, *I am a superior being and you are peasants*.

The duke gave a soft whistle.

The horse's perfect ears pricked and he gracefully stepped forward to the front of the box.

"How are you, fellow?" the duke said.

The colt blew softly through his nose. Now that his head was clearly illuminated, its beautiful shape was evident. His face was slightly dished, showing his Arab ancestry; he had a white star on his forehead; and his intelligent eyes watched the duke closely.

Anthony took a piece of carrot from his pocket and offered it to the colt. With infinite graciousness, Rodrigo extended his proud neck and accepted his tribute.

He then retired to the rear of his box.

"God, what a beauty," Lawrence said. His admiration was enthusiastic and wholehearted.

"He certainly thinks so," the duke said with amusement.

"What do you do with him?" Lawrence asked. He was speaking with his eyes still glued to the colt.

"Actually, I have raced him. In France. He is very fast."

At that, Lawrence turned to stare at his brother. "You've raced him? How did he do?"

"He won."

Lawrence's blue eyes gleamed. "How old is he?"

"He is four."

Lawrence's blue eyes flared. He turned back to look at Rodrigo and said, "Will you race him in England?"

"I doubt that I shall have the time this year," the duke said.

Silence fell as the three of them contemplated the gleaming dark horse, who turned his sleekly muscled back on them and began to nibble on a loose strand of hay.

Finally Lawrence said gruffly, his eyes still on the colt, "Your wife . . . according to Aunt Linford, you have married a girl with money, Cheviot. Is that true?"

"Yes," the duke said evenly. "It is true."

"Well, that is something, at least," Lawrence said tersely. "I'm sure you have been told that the situation here is dire. Papa ran through everything. If you are wondering why the stables are so empty, it is because Papa sold all of the horses, except for my hack and Patrick's pony and a few old nags to pull the carriage for my mother."

At last Lawrence turned to look at his elder brother. "There are mortgages on everything," he said bitterly. "If Cheviot itself had not been entailed, Papa would probably have mortgaged the castle as well."

"I have paid off the mortgages," the duke said.

A look of incredulity flashed across Lawrence's dark face.

"*All* of them?"

"All of them."

"Even the mortgages on the farms?"

"Yes. Some of the property that goes with the other houses had already been sold, but the farms that are attached to Cheviot are now clear."

Lawrence looked dazed. "Your wife must have a great deal of money."

The duke did not reply.

Lawrence flushed. "I beg your pardon. I suppose that your finances are none of my business."

Now that the humans were no longer paying homage to

him, Rodrigo decided to come to the stall door to see what was happening. Patrick reached out and tentatively stroked his soft nose. Regally, the colt allowed it.

Lawrence said, "A warning, Cheviot. When you go around the property you will see that the farms are in terrible shape. I did what I could, but Papa let me have precious little money. The land has been neglected and the houses all need new roofs, not to mention other major repairs."

The duke regarded his brother thoughtfully. "I thought Williams was the steward for Cheviot."

Lawrence scowled. "Williams is an old woman. He was incapable of standing up to Papa."

Patrick said passionately, "Lawrence has worked like a Trojan for Cheviot while you have been away, Anthony. If it weren't for him constantly pushing the few servants that we have, the grounds and stables would have become as decayed as the farms."

Patrick's face was pale and tight. It was quite obvious to the duke that he thought it was unfair for his eldest brother to have what Lawrence had labored so hard to save.

"I see," the duke said quietly. He turned to Lawrence. "You and I must sit down and you can tell me what you think are the immediate needs. I have already talked to Williams, of course, but apparently you are the one who has his finger on the heart of things here."

For the first time, Lawrence looked less hostile. "I can give you an earful, Cheviot," he said.

The duke nodded. "Perhaps we can meet sometime tomorrow."

At this moment, the stable clock began to sound the hour.

"Good God," Lawrence said. "Look at the time! My mother will be furious if we are late to dinner."

The duke frowned. "It is only five o'clock."

"We eat at six," Patrick informed him.

"We don't keep town hours at Cheviot," Lawrence said, and the hostility was back in his voice. "Of course, you can change that if you want. You can do anything you want here now. You're the duke."

"I think I will leave the dinner hour up to my wife," his brother returned tranquilly. "If we are indeed dining within the hour tonight, however, we had better return to the castle and change."

Lawrence grunted an affirmative reply.

The duke said to Patrick, "Tomorrow I should like to see your pony."

"Tucker is too small for Patrick now, but Papa wouldn't get him a new horse," Lawrence said.

"I don't want a new horse," Patrick said stubbornly. "I want Tucker."

The three brothers headed for the stable path together.

"Why aren't you at school, Patrick?" the duke asked. Term was not yet over.

"Couldn't afford it," came the laconic reply. "I am studying with the local rector."

The duke's brows drew together. He looked at Lawrence. "But you went to school, Lawrence."

"I went for a few years, then the money ran out and I had to come home. You are the only one of us who had the benefit of a full education, Cheviot."

Silence fell as the three of them proceeded up the inclined graveled path that led to the house.

At last the duke said mildly, "Your mother would have sold her wedding ring if necessary to get me away from Cheviot."

At that, the heads of both his younger brothers jerked around in an identical, startled gesture.

"You didn't like it here," Patrick said. "You never even came home when you were wounded."

"I wasn't invited," said the duke.

Patrick's hazel eyes enlarged and he looked troubled.

"You didn't need to be invited," he said. "This is your home."

"Thank you, Patrick," the duke said. "That is nice to hear."

Dinner was not pleasant. It started with the dowager saying to Sarah in an ominous voice that she hoped the new duchess would not object if Patrick ate with the family.

Sarah was startled. "Of course Lord Patrick must eat with us," she said. "He is not a baby."

The duke had invited Max to join the dinner party as well, and the dowager was not as gracious about his inclusion as Sarah was about Patrick's. When his stepmother queried him in the drawing room, the duke replied in the soft, gracious voice that managed to convey complete authority, that he expected his secretary to be a regular part of the family dinner.

The dowager's usual frozen expression had grown even icier, but she had not dared to object further.

They ate in the state dining room, Sarah presiding at one end of the enormously long table, the duke at the other.

Sarah looked up at the two huge crystal chandeliers that illuminated the extended table. The gold walls were hung with the ubiquitous family portraits and over the white marble fireplace hung a magnificent French gilt mirror.

Sarah wondered how the mirror had escaped being sold by the last duke.

The polished wood floor was bare. Sarah had a suspicion that the rug that had once covered it had not been as fortunate as the mirror.

No fire had been laid in the fireplace and the room was cold.

Sarah looked at the people, who were seated so incongruously far apart from each other, and repressed a shudder. If she had to dine like this every night, she wouldn't be able to eat.

She looked down the long length of the table toward her husband, and found him watching her.

When he saw her looking at him, he winked.

Sarah stared at him in stunned surprise.

Anthony winked at me, she thought.

The elusive dimple flashed in her cheek and she turned to address a remark to Lawrence with more aplomb than she had thought she could muster.

The dinner seemed interminable to Sarah. She actually found herself feeling grateful that the duke had brought his immensely expensive chef north with him, because the food served up by the castle cook was not good. Her stomach was still feeling uneasy from the long journey, and she found the smell of the boiled brussels sprouts and the overcooked lamb to be nauseating.

The duke's brothers ate with the concentrated single-mindedness of hungry youngsters.

The dowager's cold voice drifted down the table from her place beside the duke, "Are you not hungry, Duchess?"

"Not very," Sarah confessed. "I am still feeling a trifle unwell from the long journey."

"I never suffer any ill effects from travel," the dowager stated.

She made it sound as if travel sickness were a moral flaw.

"How fortunate for you," Sarah murmured.

"My sons take after me," the dowager went on. "They have scarcely been ill a day in their lives."

"How fortunate for them," Sarah said.

"How do you like our dining room? Is it not magnificent?"

"Very magnificent," Sarah returned. "It is, however, a trifle overwhelming for a family dinner. Is there no other, smaller, room where we might take our meals?"

"There is a smaller dining room," Anthony said quietly. "I shall tell the staff that we will eat there from now on."

"We usually do eat in the small dining room," Patrick piped up. "We haven't used this room in donkey's years."

The dowager glared at her youngest son. "I chose this room because I thought it was appropriate for the occasion."

Patrick opened his mouth to reply, shot a quick, startled look at Lawrence, closed his mouth, and said nothing.

Sarah had a suspicion that Lawrence had kicked him under the table.

"The chandeliers are particularly fine, Your Grace," Max said to the dowager.

She turned to him with a chilly smile, grateful for an ally, even if it was only Anthony's pushy secretary.

Sarah retired to bed early.

The ducal apartment consisted of two separate bedrooms with dressing rooms attached. There was also a private sitting room for the duchess and a private library-cum-office for the duke.

Sarah sat upright in her lonely bed, with the coverlet pulled up to her chin for warmth, and contemplated the splendor of her bedchamber.

The walls were lined with a series of magnificent tapestries. Before she had got into bed, Sarah had looked at them closely and seen that they depicted a forest with all sorts of things happening in it—a stag hunt, farmworkers collecting the harvest, a unicorn, and a goddess with her court.

At any other time she would have been delighted by the beauty of the tapestries, but tonight they only made her feel lonely and depressed.

For the first time since Anthony had made love to her, Sarah wished she had not married him.

How could she bear to live with that awful woman?

Would Anthony expect her to exert her rightful authority over her predecessor?

Sarah thought about trying to give orders to the dowager's servants and shuddered. She wanted peace and quiet so that she could paint; she did not want to find herself fighting a domestic war.

The rest of the household was scarcely better than the dowager.

The duke's brothers were sullen and hostile.

His secretary seemed pleasant enough, but for some reason Sarah did not think that he liked her.

The only person she could talk to in this dreadful place was her husband, and he was going to sleep in a separate room. She would probably only see him in the company of other people, or when he stopped by her bedchamber to assert his marital rights.

Tears welled into Sarah's eyes.

Stop this, she told herself. *You are acting like a baby.*

But the tears continued to fall. She was homesick. She actually thought she would be glad to see her grandfather. At least she understood him. How could she hope to understand these aristocrats among whom she now lived?

She gave in and had a good cry, in the process thoroughly dampening her pillow. Then she blew her nose and washed her face and got back into bed and turned out her light. She was actually drifting off to sleep when the door that led to the duke's bedroom opened and candlelight flickered.

Sarah opened her eyes and watched as Anthony crossed the floor, opened the drapes that the maid had pulled shut across the window, then came to place his candle on the bedside table. He untied the sash of his dressing gown, let it drop to the floor, and got into the bed beside her.

She said in a low voice, "What time is it?"

"You should not still be awake," he returned. "It is after midnight." He yawned. "Go to sleep. You'll feel better in the morning."

He punched his pillow into the shape that he liked, pulled the coverlet up over his bare shoulder, and settled down beside her.

Miraculously, Sarah's loneliness fled. She snuggled deep into the bed and went to sleep.

When she awoke the next morning, Anthony was still sleeping.

Five nights in a row with no nightmares, she thought exultantly.

He was lying on his stomach, his short hair fanned out on the white pillow, and just looking at him made her shiver.

I love him, she thought.

The thought frightened her. Love had not been in the bargain the two of them had made. That bargain had been made very clear by the both of them: He had wanted her grandfather's money and she had wanted the freedom to paint. They had agreed to marry so that they could each have what they needed.

But she had fallen in love with him.

How could she not? she thought. He was the only person, other than her teachers, who understood her.

And he had awakened her sexual passions.

She looked at the back of his neck and felt desire stab through her.

She drew a long, uneven breath, sat up, and rested her chin on her updrawn knees.

Shame on you, Sarah, she thought.

But she could not deny what she was feeling between her legs.

A soft voice said, "Good morning."

She looked down into her husband's eyes. "Good morning," she returned, trying to sound brisk and cheerful.

"Did you sleep well?"

"Very well, thank you," she said.

There was the faintest stubble of a beard on his cheeks and chin. For some reason, it made him seem even more attractive.

"Lie down here beside me," he said.

She wanted to so much that it frightened her.

Slowly, she lay back down in the bed.

He slid his leg over hers, his fingers caressed her nipple, and his mouth came down on top of hers.

Sarah shuddered and gave herself up to him.

Later, when he was putting on his robe and preparing

to retreat to his dressing room, she said, "You have turned me into a wanton woman, Anthony."

His fingers, which had been tying a knot in his sash, stilled. "Wanton? You think you are wanton?"

"Aren't I?"

He began to laugh.

Sarah glared at him. She was a little insulted.

He came back to the bed, kissed her forehead, and said, "Don't ever change, my darling. Please."

He was still laughing softly as he went out of the room.

CHAPTER
Eighteen

MAX PACED IMPATIENTLY BACK AND FORTH ACROSS the library floor. He was waiting for the duke, who was uncharacteristically late. They had an appointment to meet at nine to ride around the estate together in order to inspect the farms, and it was now nine-thirty.

When Anthony had still not appeared at nine-fifty, Max asked one of the servants if the duke had come down to breakfast yet.

He was informed that His Grace had only just made an appearance in the family dining room.

Max left the library and went along to the room where he himself had breakfasted over an hour and a half ago.

He found the duke and his wife at the table. The duchess was eating a muffin and the duke was working his way through a heaped plate of shirred eggs.

They looked up when he came in.

"Ah, Max," the duke said. "Join us for breakfast."

"Thank you, Anthony, I have already breakfasted," Max returned with dignity. "Have you forgot that we were to ride about the estate this morning?"

"Heavens, I had forgot." The duke gave his secretary

the smile that always made Max's heart turn over. "Forgive me, my friend. I was more tired than I realized from the long journey."

It wasn't fatigue that had detained him, Max thought, regarding the duke's face with knowledgeable eyes. Those slightly heavy eyelids were a dead giveaway of what Anthony had been doing.

Max thought bitterly, *Now that he's finished with her, perhaps he can spare a little time for me.*

"Shall I order the horses for a half an hour from now?" he asked stiffly.

"No," Anthony replied. "I have changed my mind. I am going to take Her Grace around the castle walls this morning. You and I can go over the estate later this afternoon."

Max felt his hands curl into fists at his sides and he forced them to relax. "Very well," he said with slow, deliberate calm. "I shall be in the library. You may send for me when you need me."

As he turned to leave, he heard the duke say to his wife, "The views of the sea are wonderful from the walls. I shouldn't be surprised if you found something that you wanted to paint."

"Well, if you would just finish eating that enormous breakfast, we would be able to go and see them," the duchess retorted.

The duke put some more eggs on his fork and shook his head in bemused wonderment. "I cannot imagine why I am so hungry this morning."

It was not Anthony's words that caught Max by the throat; it was the note of intimacy that sounded in his voice.

Max had never heard that tone from the duke before.

The secretary's head came up and his nostrils flared, like a wild creature who has scented danger.

After breakfast, the duke escorted Sarah across the north lawn toward the stairs that led to the walkway on top of the walls, where once the castle's defenders had been posted. The steps that led up to the wall were too narrow for two to go up them side by side, and the duke gestured for his wife to go first.

"So I can catch you if you trip," he said gravely.

She wrinkled her nose at him, lifted her skirts, and whisked herself nimbly upward.

When she stepped onto the wall, the North Sea lay spread before her in a stunning vista of turbulent gray water dappled with white-foamed waves. Wide-eyed, she crossed the fifteen feet of stone that formed the width of the curtain wall, and looked downward.

Beneath her, a cliff a hundred feet high fell sheer to the waves that crashed on the rocks below. The salty wind was strong enough to blow a few strands of hair loose from her chignon, and the seagulls screamed as they rose and fell in the air over the rocks. The whole untamed scene was incredibly powerful and beautiful.

Her husband's soft voice said next to her ear, "What do you think?"

She looked at the gray sea, the white waves, the intense blue sky with the white seagulls outlined against it, and shook her head, speechless.

He put an arm around her shoulders and she leaned against him, her eyes still fixed on the seascape she was going to paint.

Max fretted in the library until at last he received the long-desired summons from Anthony. Eagerly he strode down to the stableyard, only to find the duke in the company of Lawrence and Patrick.

Frustration stabbed through Max. He had been looking forward to having Anthony to himself, and now it appeared they were to be saddled with his two ill-mannered louts of brothers as well.

"I have asked Lord Lawrence and Lord Patrick to accompany us," the duke said, sublimely ignorant of Max's bitter disappointment. "Apparently, Lord Lawrence has been acting more of the steward here than Williams."

"Very well," Max said tightly. Then he scowled, as a stableboy brought up beside him the elegant chestnut gelding the duke always rode.

"No, no," he began to say impatiently, but the duke cut him off.

"You are riding Sam today, Max."

Max stared. "And who will you be riding, Anthony?"

"Rodrigo," came the light reply.

"*Rodrigo!*" Max said, appalled.

"I am afraid that we don't have an extra riding horse for you, Mr. Scott," Lord Patrick explained.

"Rodrigo is a racehorse, not a hack," Max told the duke. Anthony was an excellent rider, but Max did not like the idea of him riding the excitable thoroughbred around unfamiliar roads.

"He will be fine," the duke said carelessly, and Max folded his lips to keep himself from protesting further.

Lawrence was riding a big-boned bay gelding and Patrick a sturdy pony whose gray coat had long since turned white. The duke's three companions mounted without incident, but as Anthony swung up into the saddle, Rodrigo decided that he did not like the look of a stable boy carrying a water bucket, and he leaped into the air, kicking out at the hapless boy with his iron-shod feet.

Anthony, who had not yet picked up his other stirrup when the colt erupted, kept his seat with ease, laughed, and patted the thoroughbred's sleek mahogany shoulder.

Rodrigo tossed his head, but quieted.

As they turned to leave the stableyard, the duke remarked, "I see that one of the first things I shall have to do is buy some horses."

At those words, Lawrence perked up. "A friend of mine has a very nice hunter for sale."

He then proceeded to talk about this horse in great, and, to Max's mind, tedious detail. Even though Max had been in the cavalry, he was basically uninterested in horses.

The duke listened to his brother with friendly attention. For the entire time that they were riding through the park toward the patchwork of farms that stretched away to the Cheviot Hills, Lawrence talked about his friend's hunter.

Max, who knew how choosy the duke was about his horses, doubted very much that he would be interested in this animal Lawrence was describing in such boring detail. But he understood what the duke was doing by giving Lawrence so much attention. He was trying to win over his younger brother.

He is too tolerant, Max thought disapprovingly, a judgment he had made many times before. *He thinks he can make everyone his friend.*

The farmland that was attached to the Cheviot estate was extensive, but, as Lawrence had warned, the buildings were in poor repair. Max looked at everything with a shrewd eye and calculated that it would take a great deal of money to restore the property to what it must once have been.

Of course, thanks to Mr. Patterson, Anthony was in possession of a great deal of money.

Lawrence was greeted with respect and pleasure by all of the Cheviot tenants. In fact, Max thought resentfully, Anthony's brother seemed to take upon himself the role that by rights belonged to Anthony himself.

However, no hint that he found Lawrence's popularity disturbing ever appeared on the duke's perfect face. Instead, he smiled, and shook hands with all of his tenants, who regarded him with varying degrees of dazed wonder. Several of them commented on how much he looked like his mother.

All of the tenants managed to say, in one way or another, that Lord Lawrence had done his best for the farms.

"I am glad to hear that," the duke invariably replied. "He will be able to advise me as to what repairs are needed most immediately."

At these magic words, faces had brightened dramatically.

Rodrigo sidled and danced for practically the entire afternoon, behavior which the duke calmly ignored. Max had several times thought that the stallion was going to explode, but somehow Anthony managed to keep him under control.

When finally they reached the castle park again, the duke asked Lawrence, "Is the ride around the perimeter still in good repair? It's not overgrown?"

"It is ridable, if that's what you mean," said Lawrence coolly.

"Good," Anthony said with satisfaction. "Rodrigo needs to stretch his legs."

And he turned the colt around on the path and let him go.

"My God," Lawrence said reverently, as they watched Rodrigo disappear down the ride. "He really *is* fast."

"He won the French equivalent of the Derby last year," Max informed Anthony's oafish brother.

"How did Anthony acquire him?" Lord Patrick asked.

"His uncle, the Prince of Varonne, gave Rodrigo to him when the colt was a yearling," Max returned.

There was a noticeably hostile silence from the Selbourne brothers at the mention of the Prince of Varonne.

The silence continued as the three of them waited for Anthony. When finally he reappeared, having made the full round of the park, he had color in his cheeks and his bright hair was disordered.

He looked happy.

He is so perfect, Max thought achingly. *Why does he trouble himself with these boorish brothers of his?*

Lawrence said, as if the words were forced out of him, "You are a decent rider, Cheviot."

"Thank you," the duke replied tranquilly.

Rodrigo was sweating and he walked quite like a gentleman for the rest of the way home.

As May gave way to June, and the weather turned warmer, the lives of the various members of the Cheviot household began to settle into a pattern.

The duke worked on setting his estate in order, and Sarah set up her painting studio.

The location she chose was the Margaret Tower, the tower in the southeast corner of the curtain wall that had taken its name from the long-ago duchess who had been forced to give birth in its protective heights during the siege of the castle by Oliver Cromwell. Once the studio was arranged to her satisfaction, Sarah began to work on a painting of the sea.

To their secret surprise and mutual delight, Anthony and Sarah found that they were immensely happy. After so many years of exile, he was back at the home of his childhood, working hard to make it what he wanted it to be. And she had a magnificent view to paint, with uninterrupted time to paint it in. In the evening, each found in the other an interested and sympathetic listener to whom they could recount the day's achievements. And at night, they came together with tenderness and passion in the big four-poster in Sarah's room.

The duke and the duchess were quite content with their lives. Unfortunately, their peaceful state of mind was not shared by the other members of the Cheviot household.

The dowager could not accept the fact that she was now the dowager duchess and must always come second to Anthony's wife. Even though Sarah continued to leave most of the running of the household in the dowager's hands, still the fact that whenever the young duchess expressed the slightest desire for something, everyone leaped to serve her, irked her-stepmother-in-law unbearably.

It annoyed her that all of the household staff so obviously adored the new duchess. As the dowager did not believe in being sympathetic or friendly to one's servants, she thought that Sarah's behavior toward the castle underlings was regrettably bourgeois. Servants were there to serve; they were not there to have their opinions consulted as to what color they would like to have their dining hall painted.

Nor did the dowager think it was at all necessary for Sarah to purchase two dozen new mattresses for the servants' beds. The ones that had been on those beds had been there for decades; they had been good enough for the servants in the past, there was no reason why they weren't good enough for the servants of the present.

And every night, when Sarah presided at the head of

the table, or retired to the ducal apartment, the dowager ground her teeth. She had no appreciation at all for the fact that Sarah was obviously trying to get along with her; in fact, she rather despised the young duchess for being so accommodating.

She did everything she could think of to make life difficult for her stepson's wife, and hated it that Sarah seemed happy.

Lawrence's nerves were also growing increasingly ragged. He was happy to know that his beloved Cheviot was finally going to get the attention it so desperately needed, but he hated it that it was Anthony who was bringing about the improvements. He hated it that Anthony was ingratiating himself with Cheviot's tenants. He hated it that Anthony was the duke and he was not.

For years, Lawrence had expected to hear that his brother had been killed in the war. His mother had practically assured him that this would happen.

For years, Lawrence had fully expected that he, not Anthony, would be the next duke.

The reality of what had actually happened was a bitter pill for him to swallow.

Patrick was torn. He loved Lawrence, and he thought it was dreadfully unfair that Anthony should have stepped into the position that they had all fully expected Lawrence to inherit. But Patrick was also finding that he liked Anthony. It was increasingly difficult for him to wish that his brother had been killed in the war.

This division of loyalties made Patrick very uncomfortable. He felt he was betraying Lawrence by liking Anthony, but he also felt that it wasn't fair to blame Anthony just because he had been born first. And Patrick was beginning to suspect that Anthony had not been treated very well by Patrick's mother.

He had asked the dowager why Anthony had not come home when he was injured so badly at Salamanca, and the dowager had replied that Anthony had always disliked Cheviot.

This wasn't true. Patrick could see that Anthony loved Cheviot. He was going to spend a great deal of money to bring the estate back to what it once was. Patrick remembered Anthony's words that he had not returned to Cheviot because he had not been invited, and he worried.

Patrick was in the unhappy position of one whose picture of the world is being wrenched apart before his eyes.

By far the most unhappy person at Cheviot, however, was Max.

He had looked forward to going to Northumberland with such high hopes. He had pictured himself constantly at Anthony's side, advising him, helping him, being to him what he had been when the duke had first come out to the Peninsula.

It had not happened that way.

For one thing, Anthony seemed determined to include his brother in almost everything he did. Whenever they rode about the estate, Lawrence accompanied them. Even when the duke and Max sat together to work on finances, Lawrence was there.

Max understood what Anthony was trying to do, but he felt it was a futile and demeaning exercise. Lawrence was nothing but a sullen, moody, ungrateful boy, and Anthony was never going to change him.

While Lawrence's ubiquitous presence certainly irritated Max, he did not really regard the young man as a rival. Anthony's feelings for his brother came from his sense of duty, not from his heart. Lawrence might be a competitor for Anthony's attention; he could never be a competitor for Anthony's love.

The duchess, however, was something else.

Never had Max seen Anthony so bewitched by a woman. His secretary found it unfathomable that the fastidious duke could be so fascinated by a girl who wore dreadful old clothes and invariably had paint stains on her fingers.

Max had previously managed to hold his possessive jealousy of Anthony in check because he had never before scented a serious rival for the duke's love. He had tolerated the duke's friends because he had seen that none of them possessed that inner part of the duke which Max craved for himself.

What Max wanted was quite simple. He wanted to be the most important person in Anthony's life.

The thought of anyone else filling that place roused him to anguished fury.

As the days went by, and he saw how close Anthony was growing to his wife, Max's feelings for the duchess began to change from dislike to hatred.

It was only a matter of time before the boiling cauldron of Max's emotions was bound to erupt, precipitating the inhabitants of Cheviot into a volcano of fear, suspicion, and turmoil.

CHAPTER
Nineteen

SARAH STARTED HER NEW PAINTING IN HER USUAL WAY, by doing a preliminary oil sketch. In order to capture the early morning light breaking over the sea, she set up her easel on the curtain wall, and for a week she began work promptly at seven o'clock in the morning.

Max broodingly watched that small figure perched on top of the battlements, and his curiosity about her talent grew until it had reached the point of obsession. It tormented him that Anthony appeared to regard his wife's painting with such respect. The secretary kept assuring himself that the duke's deference was just another example of his misplaced generosity, but Max very badly wanted to see Sarah's work so he could reassure himself as to its mediocrity.

His opportunity came on a morning when the sky was filled with great towering white clouds and the air was heavy with the humidity of a coming storm. Max was leaving the castle by the back door, when he saw Sarah approaching from the garden.

He waited, holding the door for her.

"Good morning, Your Grace," he said as she reached

him. She was wearing a paint-stained dress and several wisps of long hair hung untidily around her neck.

How can Anthony bear her? Max thought with a shudder of disgust.

She smiled at him. "Good morning, Mr. Scott."

"Working hard again, I see," he returned.

"Yes." Her brown eyes were luminous and there was the bloom of a faint golden tan on her forehead and cheeks. "I told His Grace that I would have breakfast with him, however."

The snake of jealousy twisted inside Max. The duke and duchess had taken to having breakfast served in the duchess's sitting room upstairs, another sign of intimacy which Max held against this small girl who had become Anthony's wife.

Once Sarah had disappeared into the castle, Max turned his steps toward the Margaret Tower. With Sarah out of the way for a while, he thought he would pay a visit to her studio and take a look at her work.

Luck was with him and there was no one around as he approached the door of the tower and ducked inside. He stood still for a moment, allowing his eyes to grow accustomed to the dark. The only light in the tower came through the narrow arrow-slit holes that had been pierced into the thick stone walls. The air outside had been hot and laden with humidity, but inside the tower it was cool and damp.

When his vision had adjusted, Max climbed the steep spiral stone staircase, careful to place his toes on the widest part of each of the narrow steps. When he arrived at the upper landing, he saw that there were two doors that opened off of it. He pushed open the one nearest to the top of the stairs.

The first thing he saw was the easel set up by the large

light-filled window. Originally the window had been
open to the gales of the North Sea, but Sarah had had it
glazed. The floors had also been scrubbed, and the stone
walls cleaned. A charcoal brazier had been brought in to
give heat.

The room was stark and businesslike. Canvases were
stacked along the wall and a long table held a collection
of paints and brushes.

Max felt a pang of unease. This did not look like the
workplace of a lady amateur.

Slowly, almost reluctantly, he approached the easel and
looked at the canvas that was resting upon it.

The painting was barely started. She had just begun to
fill in the sky and the sea with streaks of blue and gray.

Max frowned with annoyance, and then his eye was
caught by a second, smaller painting that was propped on
a chair next to the easel. It was the oil sketch that Sarah
had done from the castle walls, which she was using as a
model.

Max looked at the sketch, which was well illuminated
by the light coming in the window.

The painter's quick, skilled brushstrokes had brilliantly caught the atmospheric effect of the changing light
in the morning sky. Max could almost see the movement
of the clouds and the crashing of the sea as it hurled itself
upon the rocks.

The potent reality of the little sketch was overpower-
ing.

Fear and fury and, above all, an all-consuming hatred
roared through Max with all the relentless force of the
surging sea Sarah had painted. For a moment he felt
dizzy, and the very air in front of him seemed to turn a
hazy red.

She could paint.

Unbidden, words that Anthony had spoken to him weeks before came back to his mind. *She is a person,* the duke had said about Sarah Patterson.

Fool that he was, Max had not understood the danger implied by those simple words. He heard again the soft intimacy of the duke's voice when he spoke to his wife, and he literally shook with rage.

For all these long years, *he* had been the one to stand by Anthony's side, always there to help him, to guide him, to love him. He, Max, had been the one to save Anthony's life at Salamanca, to save his arm! And for what? To be cast aside for a stupid woman, a *merchant's daughter.*

Max had left the studio door open when he entered the room, and now, through the roaring in his ears, came the distinct sound of the heavy door to the tower being opened below.

Max froze. He did not want to be caught in Sarah's studio.

His breath was coming in heaving gasps, but he moved on quiet feet to the door. Whoever had entered the tower was coming up the stairs.

Quickly, Max darted into the room next door.

This room was much smaller than the studio, and even though it had been cleaned up, it was empty except for a few tins of paint cleaner and a pile of paint-stained cloths.

Max stood with his ear pressed against the door, listening intently.

After a few moments, he thought he heard the studio door click closed.

The duchess must be going back to work, he thought. Now was the time for him to make his escape.

Slowly and cautiously, he opened the door of his hiding place, and went rigid with shock.

Sarah was standing at the top of the spiral staircase, her back toward Max. She had a canvas in her hands, which she was in the process of shifting from one arm to the other.

For a moment he stood frozen, like a deer caught in the unexpected flare of a lantern.

And then, before he even realized what he was going to do, Max darted out from behind the door, reached out his hand, and shoved Anthony's wife down the stairs.

She cried out sharply and dropped the canvas as she grabbed at the wall to try to save herself. The canvas bounced down the stairs, and then she herself tumbled after it, disappearing from Max's view around the curve of the spiral. He heard her body thudding as it hit against the wall and steps on its way down.

Max stood stiffly at the top of the stairs, breathing heavily. His heart was pounding so hard he could hear it in his head. He was covered in sweat.

My God, what have I done?

He listened, but there was no sound from below.

Have I killed her?

He waited for what seemed to him an eternity, but no sound came from the duchess. Max started to descend the stairs.

He found her halfway down, lying flung across the width of the staircase, her head crammed up against the stone wall. She was perfectly still.

Moving very deliberately, Max bent and peered into her face. Her eyes were closed, but in the dim light let in by the arrow slits below, he thought he could see that she was breathing. He straightened and stepped over her recumbent body to pick up the canvas that had come to rest just below her.

It was a sketch of Rodrigo. The colt was drawn so accurately that he was instantly recognizable.

Max's jaw clenched as he opened his fingers and allowed the small picture to drop once more to the stairs. Then, without another glance at Sarah, he went quickly downward.

He circled the tower at the bottom, peering out through the arrow slits to make sure no one was in the vicinity. Then, very carefully, he opened the door and stepped out into the stifling, humid air.

Moving as quickly as he could without running, Max headed for the stables.

Half an hour later, a traveling chaise stopped in front of the wide front steps of Cheviot Castle, and Neville Harvey got out. He told his coachman to wait and walked up the stairs to lift the great knocker on the castle's front door. He informed the tall footman who opened the door of his name, and requested to be announced to the duchess.

He was shown into a drawing room filled with gilt French furniture and was requested to wait. After ten minutes, Sarah's husband came in.

"My dear Harvey," the duke said. "What a delightful surprise."

He sounded perfectly courteous; there was not a trace of sarcasm to be found in that soft, cultivated voice.

"I was in Newcastle on business and thought that, since I was so far north, I would stop to say hello to Sarah," Neville said defensively.

He had worked very hard to manufacture business in Newcastle, but he certainly wasn't going to tell that to the duke.

"She is out at her studio," the duke replied. "I have sent

someone to tell her that you are here. She will be delighted to see such an old friend." He gestured to an elegant gilt chair with yellow satin upholstery. "Please, sit down. I have had one of our servants show your coachman to the stables, so you need not be concerned for your horses."

Neville sat down.

He had forgotten just how good-looking the duke was.

"Your home is very impressive, Your Grace," he said stiffly. Privately, he could not imagine how anyone could wish to live in such a huge pile of stone.

"Thank you," the duke replied. "May I offer you some refreshment? A glass of wine, perhaps?"

Neville looked horrified. Did this fellow drink wine at ten-thirty in the morning?

"No, thank you," Neville said. "I am perfectly fine."

The duke sat down on a delicate-looking sofa. "How was your journey?"

Neville wished he would go away. He did not want to meet Sarah in the company of her husband.

"Long," he said baldly. "The roads north leave something to be desired."

"They are far better than they used to be," the duke replied.

Did Neville detect a trace of amusement in the man's voice?

He was in the process of directing a hostile blue glare at the duke when a strapping looking footman came running into the room. "Your Grace! Your Grace! The duchess has been hurt!"

The duke was on his feet. "Where is she?"

"In the Margaret Tower, Your Grace. Sim found her lying on the stairs. She must have fallen."

Before the servant had finished speaking, the duke was out of the room. Neville ran after him.

In the hall he caught a glimpse of Cheviot disappearing toward the back of the house, and, without hesitation, Neville followed. When he erupted from the back door of the castle, he saw the duke racing across the lawn in the direction of one of the stone towers. Neville stretched his own sturdy legs and ran as fast as he could to try to catch up.

He developed a stitch in his side, but he kept on going.

The duke disappeared inside the tower and, half a minute later, Neville entered it himself. The first thing he heard was Cheviot's urgent voice.

"Sarah! Sarah, my love! Are you all right? Can you hear me?"

Breathlessly, Neville raced up the stairs. He found the duke just around the first turn, sitting on the stairs beside his wife, holding her wrist in his hand, his fingers on her pulse. He looked up for a moment and his eyes went to a spot beyond Neville's head.

"Send for the doctor," he said. His face was grim.

"I've already done that, Your Grace," came the voice of the footman who had been with them in the drawing room.

Neville said, "For God's sake, lift her head, Cheviot! It is all pushed up against the wall."

"I am not moving her until I am certain that she has not injured her back or her neck," the duke replied. He bent once more so that his lips were close to his wife's ear. "Sarah!"

Neville saw her head move slightly.

"Don't move yet," the duke said sharply. "Stay perfectly still. Can you hear me, Sarah?"

"I . . ." Her lashes fluttered. "Anthony?"

"Yes. Can you look at me, Sarah? No, don't move your head yet. Just open your eyes and look at me."

Sarah's eyes opened and fixed on her husband's face.

"Anthony," she said faintly. "Someone . . . someone pushed me."

Neville inhaled audibly.

"Pushed you?" the duke said.

"Yes." Her eyes looked like great bruised pools in her pinched white face. "My head hurts."

The duke said matter-of-factly, "Let us discover if you have broken anything. Try to move your legs."

There was a little silence, and then she said, "I can move them."

"Good. Now move your head. Slowly."

She gave a little hiccup of pain, and Neville swore under his breath. "I can move it." Neville saw her flex her fingers. "My hands are all right, too, thank God."

"Good girl," the duke said. "All right, I am going to pick you up and carry you back to the castle. The doctor is coming. I think you probably have a concussion, and I'm sure you're bruised all over, but you don't seem to have broken any bones."

Neville frowned at the slender-looking duke. "Cheviot, perhaps you had better have that strapping footman carry Sarah."

"No," Sarah said. "I want Anthony."

"Put your arms around my neck," the duke said, and he bent to slide his own arms under her knees and shoulders. Then, with seemingly no effort at all, he rose to his feet.

The stairs were narrow and treacherous, but he went down them as if they were as wide as the castle walls.

Then they were outside in the humid daylight. Sarah winced and turned her face into her husband's shoulder.

They crossed the wide expanse of lawn, the duke carrying Sarah with ease. Once they were inside the castle, the duke said to the servants who were lined up at the door, "Bring some ice to Her Grace's bedchamber."

Three servants ran.

The duke began to walk toward the grand staircase. Neville followed.

The duke said over his shoulder, "Wait in the drawing room, Harvey. I will let you know how she does."

Then he carried Sarah up the stairs, out of Neville's view.

Slowly and reluctantly, Neville went into the room where he had been sitting only half an hour before. His mind was in a whirl, but three words kept repeating themselves over and over in his brain.

Someone pushed me, Sarah had said.

It took the doctor another twenty minutes to arrive, and then he was upstairs with Sarah for half an hour. During the whole of this time, Neville sat and thought about what had just happened to Sarah.

The conclusion he came to was as bloodcurdling as it was inevitable. Someone had tried to kill her.

Once he had made that judgment, it did not take Neville very long to decide upon the guilty party.

Neville knew all about the change in Mr. Patterson's will. He knew that the duke had gotten all the money out of Sarah that he was going to get.

In fact, at the moment, Neville deduced that Sarah was actually worth more money to Cheviot dead than she was alive. With his wife dead, he would have the use of the quarter of a million pounds in Sarah's trust fund. And he would be free to marry another heiress.

In Neville Harvey's perception of the world, everything always came down to money. And as far as he could see, the only person who stood to gain monetarily from Sarah's death was her husband.

"My God, my God," Neville muttered to himself as he paced up and down the polished wood floor of the duke's elegant drawing room. "I must convince Sarah that she is in danger. I must convince her to come away with me. It is the only way to keep her safe."

CHAPTER
Twenty

SARAH WAS UNABLE TO TELL THE DOCTOR HOW MANY fingers he was holding up, and he agreed with the duke's diagnosis of a concussion. Her shoulders were badly bruised, as were her ribs and her back. Nothing was broken, however.

"You were very fortunate, Your Grace," said Dr. Seton, an elderly man who spoke with a distinct Scots accent. "A fall such as that could have killed you."

"Yes," Sarah said vaguely.

"The best medicine for you right now is sleep," the doctor recommended.

She smiled wanly. "My head hurts so much that I don't think I shall be able to sleep."

"I will leave you some laudanum," Dr. Seton said. "That will help you to sleep."

"Thank you, Doctor," returned Sarah gratefully.

The duke saw the doctor out of the room and when he returned he had some packets in his hand.

"Will you mix the laudanum for me, Anthony?" Sarah said a little thickly.

He frowned, lifted her chin, and looked into her eyes. They were not able to focus on him.

"No," he said decisively. "I'm dreadfully sorry, my dear, but laudanum on top of a concussion is dangerous."

Sarah frowned. "But the doctor—"

"The army doctors saw many more head injuries than Dr. Seton ever has, and they knew that it is not safe to take laudanum with a concussion. I am very sorry that you must suffer, but I am not going to give you this drug."

Sarah stared at him, trying to see his face clearly. Her lips quivered and she pressed them together to steady them. After a minute she said in a small voice, "All right."

"That's my brave girl." He bent to drop a feather-light kiss upon her hair. "I think you will fall asleep, you know."

She sniffed. "And feel better in the morning?"

He replied cautiously, "I hope so."

She said fretfully, "Everything is so blurry!"

"I know. Try to go to sleep, Sarah."

She closed her eyes and settled herself carefully against her pillow. "All right."

The pain pounded in her head. Sarah thought of the awful wound that had almost cost Anthony his arm and told herself, *Stop being such a baby. This headache is nothing compared to what Anthony had to endure.*

She heard the soft sound of the door closing as her husband left the room.

In twenty minutes, she was asleep.

The duke went down the grand staircase, a sharp furrow of concern between his brows.

She was not going to feel better in the morning, he knew. Her head might hurt less, but the bruises would feel much worse. He was enormously relieved, however, that her injuries had not been worse.

As Dr. Seton had said, such a fall might have killed her.

His mind shied away from such a dreadful thought, and he shifted his attention to what Sarah had said about someone pushing her.

She must be mistaken, he thought. *It's the concussion that made her fancy that she was pushed.*

He went into the drawing room to report to Neville Harvey, and found not only Harvey, but his stepmother and his two brothers awaiting him.

They all got to their feet when he came in, the dowager more slowly than the others. The four of them were reflected back at him by the great gilt mirror, making it seem as if he were facing two of each of them.

"How is she?" Harvey demanded.

He sounded almost belligerent, and the duke looked at him in surprise. He had not been pleased to see Neville Harvey this morning. He thought that the merchant's presence in his home was a distinct imposition, but he replied with impeccable courtesy, "The duchess has a concussion and bruises. The doctor said that the best thing for her right now is rest."

"What happened, Anthony?" the dowager asked imperiously. "According to this . . . gentleman"—she glanced at Neville as if he were a piece of tarred driftwood that had somehow washed up in her elegant home—"Sarah fell down the stairs in the Margaret Tower."

"That is what happened, ma'am," the duke replied. "She must have missed her step. Those stairs are very narrow."

"But this man said that she was pushed!" Patrick said.

The duke looked at his young brother's small, tight

face, and said gently, "That is what Sarah thought, but she must be mistaken, Patrick. No one would do such a dreadful thing."

"Someone might if he had reason enough," Harvey said. The belligerence in his voice was very pronounced.

The duke looked at the young merchant and for the first time irritation showed on his face. "What reason could anyone have for harming my wife?"

"*You* might have a reason, Your Grace," Harvey returned grimly. "In point of fact, you are the only person I can think of who would actually profit from Sarah's death."

The duke stared at the merchant as if he were insane.

"Good heavens, man!" Lawrence cried. "You can't be serious. Sarah represents a great deal of money to Cheviot. He wouldn't hurt her."

"Thank you, Lawrence," the duke said with irony.

"He likes Sarah," Patrick said. "We all like Sarah. She's nice."

The dowager turned a little, so she could look at the merchant. "Precisely how would Cheviot profit from Sarah's death, Mr. Harvey?"

Harvey thrust his head forward, a posture that made him look rather like a pink-cheeked blond bull.

"Her trust fund would come to him, Your Grace," he said. "And that fund represents a quarter of a million pounds."

The duke raised one elegant eyebrow. "Perhaps you don't realize that I was the one who created that trust fund, Mr. Harvey," he said. "And I created it out of the money that Mr. Patterson settled on me. If that quarter of a million pounds was so important to me, I would simply have kept it in the first place."

"You set up that trust fund to curry favor with Sarah's

grandfather," Harvey cried. "And you gave away the money when you still thought that Sarah would inherit all of Patterson's millions when he died."

A very still look came over the duke's face. "What are you implying?" he asked softly.

"I am *saying* that I know Patterson told you he is not leaving his money to Sarah. All those millions, which I'm sure you were counting on, are to go to his business, not his granddaughter." Harvey swung around to look at Lawrence. "So you see, Lord Lawrence, Sarah does not represent a great deal of money to Cheviot. He has already received all of the money he is going to get from this particular marriage. On the other hand, if Sarah dies, he will be free to marry another heiress."

There was stunned silence in the room.

Patrick spoke first, in incredulous tones. "Do you think that Anthony is trying to *kill* Sarah?"

"Someone pushed her," Harvey said. "Sarah is not the kind of girl to make up stories. Someone pushed her, and I think that someone is her husband."

"That's ridiculous," said Lawrence.

But there was doubt in his voice.

The duke was standing behind one of the sofas with his hand resting lightly on its curved back. Harvey, Lawrence, Patrick, and the dowager were standing opposite him, almost in a row. For a brief moment, he knew what it must feel like to be a prisoner in the dock.

Then the dowager said, "I believe that war can make a man very callous. Life loses its value to someone who has seen so much death."

"On the contrary," the duke returned grimly. "War makes life seem more valuable." He looked at Harvey and his eyes were as cold as the sea that ringed Cheviot Castle. "As for you, sir, let me say that I do not appreciate your accusations and I am certain we will both be happier if you leave Cheviot immediately."

His tone of voice was different from anything any of them in the room had ever heard from him before. They recognized it immediately, however, as the voice of a man who had commanded a regiment of men in wartime.

It took a great deal of courage for Neville Harvey to say, "I am not leaving here while I think Sarah is in danger."

The dowager put her hand on the young merchant's arm. "Of course you may remain at Cheviot, Mr. Harvey. I am certain that dear Sarah will welcome the presence of a friend."

There was a catastrophic silence. Patrick stared at the floor, Lawrence looked at the ring on his hand, and the dowager and the duke looked at each other.

Finally the duke said, "Very well, ma'am. If that is what you wish."

And, swinging around with his inborn gracefulness, he left the room.

It was midafternoon when Max finally returned to the house. He had made a round of the farms, making certain to talk to someone at each place he stopped so that they would remember he had been there.

He let himself into the castle by the side entrance and slowly made his way to the library. When he walked into the large, high-ceilinged, book-lined room, he saw the duke standing in front of one of the windows, looking out. There was a rigidity about his figure that told Max something was very wrong.

Christ. Did I kill her?

It was a moment before he felt sufficiently collected to say, "Good afternoon, Anthony."

The duke turned slowly. "Max," he said, and fell silent.

Max assumed an expression of concern. "You don't look well. Is something wrong?"

"Haven't you heard?"

Max swallowed. "I've been out at the farms all day. I've heard nothing."

The duke was still as a statue. He said, "The duchess fell down the stairs of the Margaret Tower."

"Dear God," said Max. He came farther into the room. "Is she all right?"

"Yes," said the duke.

Max didn't know if the jolt of feeling that went through him was disappointment or relief.

The duke went on, "She has a concussion and is bruised all over, but she will be all right."

"I am very glad to hear that."

The duke stood in motionless silence, his figure framed between the crimson velvet drapes that adorned the library window. He looked like a painting, Max thought. An impossibly beautiful painting.

The duke said, "The duchess thinks that someone pushed her."

Max's heartbeat accelerated.

"Pushed her?" he croaked.

The duke nodded gravely.

"But who would do such a thing?"

The duke's eyes met his. They looked more green than gray, always a sign that he was distressed. He said, "According to Mr. Neville Harvey, I would."

This time Max's surprise was genuine. *"You?"* He frowned. "The man must be insane to say such a thing."

"Actually," said the duke in a cool, disinterested voice, "he makes a great deal of sense."

"You are being ridiculous, Anthony," Max said impatiently. "You just married the girl. Why on earth should you want to do away with her?"

"Because her grandfather has cut her out of his will and therefore she isn't worth any more money to me."

"What?"

For the first time since he had turned to face Max, the duke moved. He lifted his hand and rubbed his forehead as if it ached. "You heard me correctly," he said. "When we came back from our honeymoon, Mr. Patterson met with both the duchess and me and told us that he was not leaving his fortune to her. I thought he was angry because I had managed to squeeze so much money out of him in the marriage settlement, and that this was his way of getting back at me."

"It probably was," Max said grimly. "You raked him over the coals, Anthony."

"Yes, well, apparently Patterson's action has given me a reason to wish my wife dead."

"I still don't understand," Max said. "Why should Patterson's cutting the duchess out of his will make you want to kill her?"

The duke said flatly, "According to Harvey, so that I may then marry another heiress. Not to mention the fact that her trust fund will come to me as well."

Max felt a surge of healthy anger sweep through him. "Do you mean to tell me that Harvey actually had the nerve to accuse you of these things?"

"In my own drawing room, in front of my stepmother and my brothers—who, I might add, seemed to think that he might be right."

He looked so bleak that Max longed to go to him. But he knew the duke well enough to realize that he could not be the one to make the first move.

"Get rid of him, Anthony," Max said forcefully. "Kick the man out of the house."

"I tried that, but my stepmother invited him to stay."

Max scowled. "This isn't her house, it's yours. He can't stay here if you don't want him."

"Perhaps it is better if he does stay for a while," the duke said wearily. "Once he sees that nothing else is going to happen to Sarah, he will realize that her fall was an accident. I really don't want him going back to London and informing Patterson that I am trying to murder his grand-daughter."

"Good God, no."

The duke shrugged. "So, we will leave things as they are for the moment. The most important thing now is for the duchess to get better."

Max looked at his hands.

"Does she really think that someone pushed her?"

"That is what she has said. But she has a bad concussion, Max. I am certain that her memory of what occurred is not clear."

"Of course it isn't," Max said heartily. "It is ridiculous to think of anyone pushing her. Why, everyone in the castle is quite fond of her, I believe."

"Yes, I believe they are."

Max looked long and hard at the face he had loved for seven long years. He said, "Don't let it upset you that your brothers think you capable of such a deed, Anthony. Remember, they don't know you very well. Anyone who knows you knows that you would never harm a hair on the duchess' head."

The duke's eyes began to turn from green to gray. "Do *you* know that, Max?"

Max said, with the utmost sincerity, "Of course I do."

At that, the duke finally moved. He came across the

room, put his hand on Max's shoulder, and said fervently, "Thank God for a friend like you."

Max allowed his own fingers to cover the slender hand resting so generously on his shoulder. "I will always be your friend," he said.

Anthony smiled into his eyes. "And I, yours."

He removed his hand from beneath Max's, and sighed. "Can you imagine what a delightful dinner we are going to be forced to endure this evening?"

Max shuddered eloquently.

Anthony laughed. "I'll tell you what, old friend. Let's you and I drive into Alnwick and have dinner together at the Alnwick Arms."

"That is a wonderful idea," said Max.

"I'll have the phaeton brought 'round at seven."

"Excellent."

The duke began to walk to the door. "I think I will go and check on the duchess. With any luck, she is still sleeping. I'm afraid that when she wakes she is not going to be very comfortable."

"The day after is always the worst for bruises," said Max.

Anthony nodded. "I know." He opened the library door. "I'll see you at seven," he said, and went out.

Max stood for a long time, staring at the doorway, his mind going over all that he had just learned.

The duke had a nightmare that night. He awoke to the sound of his own voice. *No, no, you can't take off my arm!*

He was breathing hard and his body was covered in sweat. The storm that had threatened all day still had not broken, and the air was uncomfortably humid.

He had chosen to sleep in his own bedroom this night so that he wouldn't disturb Sarah, and he realized now how much he missed her, how much he had come to rely on her being there when he had one of his dreams.

She was actually very good at waking him shortly after a nightmare started. He hadn't got this far along in the dream in a long time.

He lay in bed and stared up at the gold tapestry canopy over him and felt very alone.

A rumble of thunder sounded in the distance. The storm was finally coming.

The sky outside his open window lit with lightning. A few moments later, thunder sounded again.

The duke got out of bed and pulled on his dressing gown. He would just go next door to make certain that Sarah was all right.

Softly, he opened the door that connected their bed-rooms.

Thunder boomed again.

Sarah's voice said, "Anthony?"

"Yes, I'm here." He walked to the bed. "I just wanted to make certain that you were all right. Do you want me to close the windows?"

"Why aren't you here in bed with me?" she asked. A lightning flash outside showed him her small, pale face. Her eyes looked as if they took up at least half of it.

"I'm sleeping next door. I didn't want to disturb you," he explained. "You are injured, my dear. You need to rest."

"I can't rest if you're not here," she said fretfully.

His heart leaped. "I'm afraid I might turn over and bump into you."

She moved her head restlessly on her pillow. "I've been waiting and waiting for you. I didn't know you were next door."

"Well . . . I'll get in with you, if that will make you more comfortable."

"Yes."

He went around to the other side of the bed, slid out of his dressing gown and in under the sheets.

He felt her hand touch his.

"I hurt all over," she said.

"I know you do. I am so sorry, love. I wish I could help you."

"Hold my hand until I go to sleep."

"Of course I will."

As the storm continued to rage outside, the duke, with his wife's hand curled safely in his, drifted off into a dreamless sleep.

CHAPTER
Twenty-one

WHEN SHE AWOKE THE NEXT MORNING, SARAH felt terrible. Not only did her head ache, but her entire body hurt anytime she tried to move. She made no objection when Anthony insisted that she remain in bed.

The day after that, she felt a little better. She still had a headache, but it was no longer acutely painful. She insisted on getting out of bed and spending the afternoon in her sitting room.

At three o'clock she received a request from Neville Harvey to pay her a visit.

Sarah was not overjoyed at the prospect of seeing her old friend. She was feeling very low, thinking about all the time she was missing from her painting, and she was not in the mood for company. But poor Neville had come all this long way to see her, and she felt she had to make an effort.

So she smiled when he came in the door, and held out her hand.

"Neville. How lovely to see you. I'm sorry that you came at such a bad time. It was so stupid of me to fall down those stairs."

He crossed the room to where she was lying on the sofa propped by pillows, took her hand into both of his, and looked gravely into her face.

"You have a bruise on your forehead," he said.

"I know. That is what probably gave me the concussion." Gently, she withdrew her hand from his. "Pull up that chair, Neville, so that we may talk."

He did as she suggested, picking up a mahogany shieldback chair and bringing it over next to the sofa.

He sat down.

"Anthony told me that you had business in Newcastle and decided to pay us a visit," Sarah said. "I didn't know you did business in Newcastle, Neville."

"I do, occasionally."

"Oh." She looked at him with perplexity. Neville did not usually ignore the lure of a conversation about his business. She had fully expected to be regaled with all the details of what he had done in Newcastle.

"I was in the drawing room with your husband when word was brought that you had fallen down the tower stairs," he said.

Her mouth quirked into a wry smile. "Oh dear, what a welcome for you, Neville."

He did not smile back. "I followed him to the tower, Sarah, and I heard you say that you were pushed."

She plucked at the light cotton blanket that lay across her lap. The weather had cooled considerably after the storm.

"I thought I was, but I must have been mistaken. I have a concussion, you know. Anthony says it is very unlikely that I would remember the circumstances of my fall."

Neville's face was very somber as he regarded her.

She frowned. "What is the matter, Neville? I am going

to be fine. There is no need for you to look as if you were attending my funeral."

He ran his hand through his hair, leaving a few dark blond strands sticking up.

"Sarah . . . I don't quite know how to tell you this, but I feel I must warn you."

She stared at him with a mixture of alarm and puzzlement. "Warn me? Warn me of what?"

"Suppose someone did push you," he said.

She replied, her voice both gentle and reasonable, "No one has any cause to wish me harm, Neville. I must have imagined that I was pushed."

"There is one person who might wish you harm," he said.

Her delicately drawn brows drew together in bewilderment. "Who?"

"Cheviot."

Sarah's eyes widened with shock. "That is a terrible thing to say."

"I am very serious, Sarah," he replied.

She made a motion as if she would wave him away. "I don't want to listen to this, Neville. If you can't talk about something sensible, then you had better leave."

He leaned toward her. "You *must* listen to me, Sarah. Your very life may depend on it."

"Oh, stop being so melodramatic," she snapped. "I can assure you that Anthony did not push me down the stairs."

"Will you just listen?" Neville leaned forward even more, bringing his face close to hers. The tone of his voice was tense and urgent.

"Think of this," he said. "When Cheviot married you, he had every expectation that one day you would come into your grandfather's fortune. Then, when you returned from your wedding trip, he found out that your grandfather was leaving his money elsewhere. That news must have come as quite a blow to him."

Sarah shook her head impatiently. "Anthony didn't care about that. He got more than enough money from Grandpapa in the marriage settlement."

"I don't know of any man who wouldn't care that he had just lost eighteen million pounds," Neville said grimly.

"Anthony was only upset for me," Sarah said. "He thought that Grandpapa did it to get back at him because he had outwitted Grandpapa on the marriage settlement. He didn't care about the money for himself. He only cared for me."

Neville said, in the same grim voice as before, "That is what he told you."

Color flushed into Sarah's pale cheeks. "That is what he said, and I believe him."

Neville's blue eyes narrowed. "Then think of this," he said. "If something should happen to you, Cheviot would be free to find himself another heiress. *And* he would still have all the money that your grandfather gave him—in addition to your trust fund."

Sarah opened her mouth to refute this angrily, but before she could speak, her husband's voice came from the doorway.

"That is quite enough, Harvey. You may leave the room."

Sarah's eyes swung to the door. When she saw the look on Anthony's face, her throat went dry and her heart started to pound.

Neville had gone very pale. Slowly he rose to his feet. "I felt it was important for Sarah to be put in possession of the facts," he said steadily.

"Get out," Anthony said. At his sides, his hands were slowly opening and closing into fists.

Sarah was terrified by the way Anthony looked. "Do as he says, Neville."

He looked down at her and she saw his uncertainty. She glanced again at Anthony and felt her heart beating all the way up in her throat.

"*Go,*" she said to Neville.

He bit his lip, but he began to walk toward the door. For one dreadful moment, Sarah was afraid that Anthony wasn't going to let him by. At the last minute, however, he stepped aside and allowed Neville to pass unharmed through the doorway.

Then he was gone and they were alone.

Sarah let out her breath. She looked at her husband, who was standing just inside the doorway. He looked back at her. The dangerous look that had so panicked her was gone from his face. His expression now was completely shuttered.

"I'm afraid that poor Neville must be jealous of you, Anthony," she said, trying to find an explanation for her friend's extraordinary accusation. "He thought he was going to marry me himself, you see."

He didn't reply, just stood there, looking at her with that distant expression on his face.

"Anthony?" she said uncertainly. "What is wrong? You can't think I would believe such nonsense?"

His expression never changed. "Don't you?"

All of the emotions Sarah had been experiencing blazed up into sudden anger.

"What kind of an idiot do you think I am? Of course you didn't push me down those stairs! Neville's problem is that he thinks everyone is as concerned about money as he is."

At her words, his face changed. He said her name in a breathless sort of voice, and strode across the room to sit beside her on the sofa. He reached for her hands and held them tightly in his own.

She gazed up at him worriedly. "I can't believe that you let Neville upset you so much," she said. "No one could believe such nonsense."

"You don't believe it," he said. "Max doesn't believe it. But my stepmother and my brothers have their doubts."

Sarah blinked. "The dowager would let herself believe that you roasted babies alive if someone told her that." She frowned and added disapprovingly, "But I should have thought that Lawrence and Patrick would have had more sense."

He looked down at their clasped hands. "Max says it is because they still don't know me very well."

She heard the pain he was trying to hide and her heart ached for him. "Max is right," she said firmly. "No one who knows you would believe you capable of such a terrible thing."

"I have plenty of money," he said tensely. He was still looking at their hands. "I don't need any more."

"I know you don't, Anthony," she said. "Please don't let this upset you. Everyone will shortly see how foolish they have been."

Finally, he looked up. His eyes were very bright. "You always seem to be comforting me," he said.

"Don't you know?" she replied. "That is what a wife is supposed to do."

"Is that so?" She was enormously relieved to see the familiar glint of amusement come into his eyes. "In that case, I am very glad that I have one."

"You should be," she said serenely. "You should be."

*   *   *

A week passed, and Sarah's bruises began to heal. She was still a little stiff, but the worst of the pain was gone and her head was clear. Eight days after her accident, she returned to her studio and once more began to paint.

When she entered the Margaret Tower for the first time, she was surprised to find that a banister had been attached to the stone wall of the spiral staircase. Then she smiled. Obviously Anthony was trying to make certain that she did not fall again.

He had been wonderful to her during the week that she had been confined to the house. She knew how much he loved to be outdoors, yet he had spent several hours every afternoon in her sitting room, reading to her, playing cards with her, and in general trying to keep her entertained.

They had dined together every night in her sitting room as well. He made her laugh by saying that her injuries were a wonderful excuse for them to avoid the doom and gloom of the company in the dining room.

And so, instead of driving them apart, her fall only served to bring them closer together. This caused Max's jealousy to flame up even hotter.

That first night after Sarah's fall, when he and the duke had gone out to dinner together, Max had thought that a new era was starting in their relationship. At last Anthony was beginning to realize that Max was his one true friend, that Max was the only person whom he could completely trust.

And then the duchess had shown that she did not believe Harvey's accusation, and Max's faithfulness had receded into the background. Without a qualm, Anthony had consigned Max to the wintry chill of the dining room, while night after night he dined cozily with the duchess in her sitting room upstairs.

It was bitter gall to Max to be put aside in such a fashion. After all, was he not the man who had facilitated Anthony's career in the army? Without Max to guide him, who knows what mistakes the inexperienced young captain would have made?

Was he not the man who had saved Anthony's life? His arm?

What had the duchess ever done for him, that he should prefer her company to that of his most devoted friend?

Max's jealous resentment came to a head one afternoon when he came into the library and found the duke and duchess sitting together behind the great desk. The duke had a pen in his hand, and the two of them had their heads bent close together over the paper upon which he was writing.

"I beg your pardon," Max said stiffly. "I did not realize that the room was occupied."

The duke and the duchess looked up at him, identically startled expressions on their faces.

"Oh, Max," the duke said. "The duchess and I were just making up a list of the new staff we need to hire."

A chill went through Max. "I thought that was something we were going to do," he said.

The duchess frowned thoughtfully and pointed to the list. "Do you know, Anthony, instead of hiring a head gardener, I think it would be a good idea to give that position to young John Kirkland. He has done a very good job, with very little help, and I think he deserves a promotion."

The duke looked at her with a smile. "You amaze me," he said. "I don't even know who this John Kirkland is."

"It's too bad all your staff aren't horses. I bet you'd know who they were then," the duchess retorted.

The duke started to laugh.

Agony twisted inside of Max.

The space that Anthony always kept between himself and other people wasn't there between him and his wife.

Pain was succeeded by fury.

It didn't matter to Max that Anthony had taken an impecunious army captain and given him an extremely well paid and responsible position as his private secretary. It didn't matter to Max that Anthony had given him power over all his finances. It didn't matter to Max that Anthony, who held one of the highest titles in all of Britain, considered him a friend.

Max wanted more than that.

He remembered how sweet it had been during those two days when he had been the only one to believe in Anthony. He remembered the feel of Anthony's hand on his shoulder, the way he had said, *Thank God I have a friend like you.*

Then the duchess had proven her belief in Anthony as well, and had stolen away Max's place.

Max began to wonder if there wasn't a way he could make it happen that he would be the only one to believe in Anthony again.

Sarah had assumed that, after his confrontation with the duke, Neville would leave Cheviot. The young merchant was determined to remain, however, and Anthony said that it would probably be better for him to see for himself that nothing nefarious was going on at Cheviot.

"We don't want him going to your grandfather and telling him that I am trying to kill you," he said.

"Good heavens," Sarah said faintly. "No, we certainly do not want that."

So Neville remained at Cheviot, making up one of the jolly party that assembled every evening in the dining room.

At least the food is good, Sarah thought, as she sat at the head of the table eating one of Gaston's magical concoctions. She closed her eyes briefly, letting the piece of *Poularde à la Condé* melt in her mouth.

When she opened her eyes again, Patrick was looking at her.

"I say, Sarah, would you like to come and see my tree house tomorrow?" he asked.

Sarah looked into Patrick's hopeful hazel eyes. She had often thought that it was lonely for him, being the only child in the castle. His mother paid little attention to him, and Lawrence was either busy about the estate or off with friends of his own.

So now she smiled and said, "I should love to see your tree house, Patrick. Where is it?"

His face brightened. "In the park. I built it myself this spring."

"*All* by yourself?" Lawrence said teasingly.

"Well, mostly by myself," Patrick amended. "Davey did help me a little bit."

Davey was the very large footman who had brought the news of Sarah's fall.

"Where in the park is this tree house?" Max inquired idly. "I thought I had covered every inch of the woods there."

"It is in that huge ivy tree near the pond," Patrick said. "You probably didn't see it because of all the leaves."

"How does one ascend to this tree house?" the duke inquired.

"I nailed wooden rungs to the tree," Patrick said proudly. "It is just like a ladder."

A faint frown drew the duke's brows together. "Perhaps it is not such a good idea to take Sarah there—given her history with steep stairs."

Patrick looked disappointed. "Of course, Anthony," he said. "I'm sorry, I hadn't thought—"

Sarah interrupted. "Nonsense. I should love to see the tree house. And I can assure you, Anthony, that I am perfectly capable of going up a ladder. When I was at school I used to climb into a neighbor's hayloft all the time to see the kittens."

She smiled at Patrick and suggested, "Perhaps we could take a picnic with us."

The boy's face lit up. "That would be fun!"

"It does sound like fun. I'll come with you," Neville announced.

It was perfectly clear from the expression on Patrick's face that he preferred to have Sarah to himself. "If you like, sir," he said tightly.

Sarah felt sorry for Patrick, but it was impossible to gracefully rid herself of Neville's company.

"That will be very nice," she said, and glanced up to the other end of the table, where her husband was regarding her with a faint frown.

"Don't fall," he said to her.

"I won't," she assured him.

"Anthony," the dowager said in her most imperious voice, "I want to know what you are doing at the Coles'. I drove by there yesterday, and there were workmen all over the place. There is nothing wrong with that farm. I think you might better spend some of your money right here at Cheviot."

This was a song she sang on an almost nightly basis.

With difficulty, Sarah refrained from rolling her eyes. To comfort herself, she took another bite of *Poularde à la Condé*.

*   *   *

It rained overnight, but by morning the sky was blue and the sun was shining. Sarah had the kitchen put together a picnic luncheon which she and Patrick and Neville could eat in the tree house.

They were walking to the park, and instead of taking along a footman, Sarah punished Neville for his intrusion by making him carry the picnic basket.

They went up the drive to the gatehouse, then down the hill that led to the park. All the while they were walking, Sarah ignored Neville and encouraged Patrick to talk.

He told her about his pony. He told her about his studies with the local rector. He told her about how hard Lawrence had worked to keep Cheviot from becoming totally derelict.

"I know that Lawrence hasn't been very nice to Anthony," he said. "Well, perhaps I haven't been very nice to him, either. But somehow it just does not seem fair that he should come and take Lawrence's place—just like that. Not when Lawrence has worked so very, very hard."

"But surely you both knew you had an elder brother," Sarah said gently. "Anthony's return can't have come as such a great shock."

"We knew about Anthony of course, but . . ." Here Patrick broke off and gave her an uneasy look.

"Perhaps you did not expect him to live through the war," said Sarah.

Patrick bit his lip. "In all those years, he never once came to see us."

"No," Sarah agreed.

They walked for a while in silence, Sarah and Patrick side by side, Neville trailing behind them, laden down with the basket. Then Patrick said, "I don't think my mother likes Anthony very much."

"There is certainly no love lost between them," Sarah

said. "I rather think that is why Anthony kept away, you know. It was not that he didn't want to see you and Lawrence, but he did not get along with your mother."

Patrick said in a rush, "I asked him why he did not come home after he was wounded at Salamanca, and he said he had not been invited."

Sarah sighed. "I don't think he got along very well with your father, either, Patrick."

"Lawrence didn't get along with Papa," Patrick said solemnly. "He was always yelling at him for selling the family pictures and things."

"Do you know what I think?" Sarah said. "I think that we all should put the past behind us and go on with the present. I know that Anthony wants to be friends with his brothers. He has been solitary for almost all of his life. He would love to have a family."

"He has you," Patrick said.

Sarah lifted a hand and ruffled his silky hair. "Yes," she said, "he has me."

They reached the tree house at one o'clock, and Sarah regarded with awe the magnificent tree which harbored Patrick's creation.

"See?" Patrick said, pointing to a platform high above them in the branches. "It is not so very high."

"It looks pretty high to me," Sarah said, craning her neck to look upward.

"You're going to go up, aren't you?" Patrick said anxiously.

"Of course I am," she returned.

"May I make a suggestion?" Neville said. It was almost the first time he had spoken since Sarah had loaded him down with the picnic basket. "Why don't we eat down here? I have no desire to try to carry this basket, which is extremely heavy, up into that tree."

"I'll take it, sir," Patrick said mischievously.

"No, you will not," Sarah said. "Neville is right. Besides, I am starving and I don't want to wait another moment for my luncheon."

"I'm hungry, too," Patrick admitted.

Without further ado, Sarah spread the cloth that one of the scullery maids had packed, and began to put out the cold meat and cheese and bread that was to be their meal.

Silence fell as they all ate hungrily.

Finally, realizing that she could delay no longer, Sarah pronounced herself ready to climb the tree.

"Men first," she said firmly.

"Patrick first," said Neville. "He knows what he's doing."

"All right," Patrick said. He put his foot on the first wooden rung he had hammered into the tree, and began to go up.

Neville followed, and then Sarah, who first kilted up her skirt so she wouldn't trip on it.

When she reached the top, Neville extended a hand to help her onto the platform. She straightened her skirt and then looked around.

Patrick's tree house consisted of a large wooden platform, which had been furnished with a small covered tent.

"However did you get all of this wood up here?" Neville asked in wonder, staring at the planks under his feet.

"Davey carried it for me," Patrick admitted. "But I did all the nailing."

"You did a very good job," Sarah said admiringly, and she began to walk toward the tent, which was on the far side of the platform.

Suddenly the wood beneath her feet gave way.

For one incredulous moment, she thought she was going to fall.

Then Neville had her by the arm and was half-pulling, half-lifting her to safety.

She huddled next to him and stared with horror at the hole that had opened up in the platform.

"My God," she said shakily.

"That wood *can't* have given way," Patrick said shrilly. "I've been up here a hundred times. It was perfectly safe, Sarah, I swear it!"

"Just a moment," said Neville. He got down on his hands and knees and crawled to the edge of the hole. Then he swore.

"What is it?" Sarah said in a frightened voice.

He rose to his feet and stood looking down at the yawning hole in the midst of the broken planks. "The rest of the platform is perfectly safe," he said. "The reason this piece collapsed is because the wood has been cut."

CHAPTER
Twenty-two

A S THE THREE OF THEM MADE THEIR WAY HOME, Neville tried to convince Sarah that the duke must be the one responsible for cutting the boards of the tree house.

"I don't believe it," she said quietly

"Well, someone cut those boards," he returned angrily. "And I don't think it was Lord Patrick."

"Any one of the three of us could have fallen through that hole," Sarah pointed out. "It was just chance that I was the one who happened to step on the boards first."

"That is true," Patrick said.

He was walking close beside her and both his face and voice were very troubled. Sarah put her arm around his thin shoulders and gave him a brief, reassuring hug.

"Life is cheap to a man like Cheviot," Neville said grimly. "It was worth his taking a chance it would be you."

"I don't want to hear any more, Neville," Sarah warned.

Suddenly Neville moved in front of Sarah and Patrick, blocking the path and forcing them to halt.

"You *must* listen to me, Sarah. You are in great danger.

I want you to leave this place and come back to London with me. Don't you understand? You must get away from him before it's too late."

Neville's frantic urgency made an impression on Patrick.

"Perhaps Mr. Harvey is right, Sarah," he said. "Perhaps you should leave—just for a little while, you know. Until things are sorted out."

Sarah looked into Patrick's worried face.

"I will think about it," she said tensely.

They arrived home to find the dowager duchess sewing in the upstairs drawing room. When Neville asked where the others were, she responded that Anthony and Lawrence were in the office with Max.

"I think we had better send for them, Your Grace," Neville said grimly. "Something has happened that must be discussed."

First the dowager tried to discover what had happened, but when it became clear that she would have to wait until the others arrived, she sent a servant to the office to fetch her stepson and her son.

Max had been on edge all afternoon, waiting to hear what had happened at the tree house. He had gone out to the park at four in the morning, when the sky was just beginning to brighten, and made the necessary cuts in the wood. He knew those planks wouldn't hold anyone for more than a second.

Something had to have happened.

When the footman came to the office and requested the presence of the duke and Lawrence in the drawing room, Max knew the time of reckoning had come.

Without asking permission, he followed the brothers out of the office. Lawrence strode ahead of them, not realizing that Max was coming as well, and the duke, who saw him, said nothing.

When Max entered the room after the other two, he saw that Sarah was sitting in a chair by the window, with Patrick sitting on an ottoman at her feet. The dowager and Neville Harvey were sitting on the sofa in front of the fire, and Neville rose to his feet when the newcomers came into the room.

No one was hurt, Max thought, as his eyes went from Sarah to Patrick to Neville.

It mattered not at all to him if anyone had been hurt or not. What was important was that everyone else should suspect Anthony of trying to arrange an accident.

In a hard, angry voice, Neville Harvey was relating the tale of what had happened in the tree house.

"The boards were cut, Your Grace," he said emphatically. "I looked at them carefully, and Lord Patrick looked at them as well. There can be no doubt about it. Someone tampered with the boards in the hope that one of us would fall."

"My God," said the dowager. "How dastardly."

"Another accident to Sarah?" said Lawrence. "This is getting to be awfully suspicious."

"Yes," said Harvey. "If I hadn't been close enough to grab her, she would have crashed to the ground. That tree house is very high. She could easily have been killed."

Three pairs of eyes looked at Anthony.

"Are you all right?" he said to his wife.

"Yes," she returned quietly. "I am perfectly fine."

"I wonder how those boards came to be cut, Your Grace," Harvey commented.

Anthony did not reply.

Max stepped protectively to his side. "I hope you are

not implying that His Grace had anything to do with this prank," he said to Neville Harvey.

"*Prank?*" Harvey returned incredulously. "I would rather call it an attempt at murder."

Max stepped even closer to Anthony, silently assuring him that he was on his side.

Anthony said, his voice sounding as if it were coming from very far away, "I will have the servants questioned to see if one of them might have seen someone go near the tree house."

"As if they would inform on their employer," Neville said scornfully.

Max glanced at Anthony, whose shuttered face gave nothing away. He said, in the same distant voice with which he had spoken before, "Contrary to popular belief, I had nothing to do with damaging the tree house."

"Of course you did not," Max said fiercely.

For the first time since they had come into the room, Anthony looked at his secretary. "Thank you, Max," he said quietly.

Sarah got slowly to her feet. "I have a headache. If you will excuse me, I will go to my room and rest."

"Of course," the dowager said. She could scarcely disguise the note of triumph in her voice.

Without another word, Sarah turned and went through the door that led into the next drawing room.

The duke said, "I will see about having the servants questioned. Max, perhaps you would assist me."

"Of course I will, Anthony."

She has turned her back on him, Max thought triumphantly, as he followed the duke out of the room. *Now he will know which one of us really loves him.*

Sarah sat in the window seat of her bedroom, looking out at the topiary garden below. John Kirkland, the young gardener, was trimming one of the hedges.

He will do very well as head gardener, Sarah thought. *He is a very conscientious young man.*

She rubbed her eyes. The scent of the yellow roses that were in a bowl on a nearby table came drifting to her nostrils.

I must try to understand what is going on here, she told herself. *I have to think about it.*

She didn't want to think about it. She started to shake every time she remembered how close she had come to falling that afternoon. If it hadn't been for Neville . . .

Neville thought that Anthony was trying to kill her.

I can't believe it, Sarah thought. *I won't believe it.*

She stared blindly at the formal hedges that stretched out below her and thought that, after all, she had not been wrong about her fall down the tower steps. Someone *had* tried to push her.

She remembered vividly the feel of a hand between her shoulder blades. It was a memory she **had** tried to repress. She had tried to tell herself that Anthony was right, that the memory was just part of her concussion.

She didn't think that any longer.

Who else in this house would want to hurt me? she thought in bewilderment.

She could come up with no answer.

She turned her head away from the window and looked at her bed. She thought of Anthony's tenderness, of his passion. She simply could not believe that the man who could make love to her like that would wish her ill.

Yes, and you know so much about men and about sex, Sarah, she told herself mockingly. *How many other women has Anthony embraced and loved the way he embraces and loves you? Dozens, at least.*

The thought was pure pain.

She turned back to the window, leaned her forehead against the glass, and watched John Kirkland carefully trim the yew hedge to a perfect roundness.

Her heart told her that her husband would never hurt her, but her brain kept saying, *If it isn't Anthony, then who?*

She had told Neville that money wasn't important to the duke. But he had married her for her money. She mustn't forget that little fact. He had not married her for love, he had married her for money. And he had fully expected that when her grandfather died, even more money would come pouring into his coffers.

She knew how much he loved Cheviot. It would take a huge amount of money to restore his precious estate to what it once had been. She knew the lavish way he lived—his servants, his French cook, the horses that he wanted to buy. That, too, required a great deal of money.

Could Neville be right?

"No," she whispered in anguish. "No. I won't believe it."

She heard the sound of a door opening and turned to see her husband come in from his own bedroom. He did not move away from the doorway, just stood there, one hand raised to touch the door molding, looking at her.

"None of the servants saw anyone go near the tree house," he said.

His face was so reserved, so distant. His eyes looked gray and bleak.

All of a sudden, some lines from "Rime of the Ancient Mariner," the poem that Anthony had once called 'soul-shattering,' came into Sarah's mind:

> Alone, alone, all, all alone,
> Alone on a wide wide sea!
> And never a saint took pity on
> My soul in agony.

She thought of the rest of that poem, of how appalled she had been by its images of death, isolation, and despair. It had frightened her that this was the poem that spoke to Anthony's soul.

She thought of his nightmares, of the horror he still felt at the many deaths he had seen.

Quite suddenly she knew, beyond the shadow of a doubt, that he was not responsible for these accidents. In fact, he was being victimized by them almost as much as she.

Her eyes widened as a thought struck her.

"Anthony," she breathed. "What if someone is trying to hurt me in order to get at you?"

His expression didn't change. "What do you mean?"

"Think about it." She leaned a little forward. "These staged accidents are so obvious. First, I was deliberately pushed, a push that I *felt*. Then, today, there was no effort made to disguise the fact that those planks had been sawed."

Her eyes dilated as she realized what was happening. "Someone is trying to make it look as if you are trying to kill me," she said. And shivered.

He said in a strange voice, "Does this mean that you do not think I am the guilty party?"

"Of course you're not guilty," she said. "If you were indeed trying to kill me, you would go about it far more cleverly than this."

At that, he pushed away from the door and crossed the

room to where she sat on the low window seat. He knelt in front of her and buried his face in her lap.

"Thank God," he muttered thickly. "Thank God."

She touched his bright hair with gentle fingers.

"I am so afraid for you," he said, his voice muffled by her skirt. "You must leave Cheviot, Sarah. Go back to your grandfather in London until I can find out what is happening here."

"No," she said. "I am not leaving you."

At that, he lifted his head and looked up into her face. His expression was strained. "Don't you see? Why do you think someone is going to all this trouble to make it look as if I am trying to kill you?"

"I have no idea," she returned helplessly.

"So that, when you do die, I will be arrested for your murder. And once I am out of the way, Lawrence will be the duke."

"Oh no," Sarah breathed. "Do you think that Lawrence . . ."

"Possibly," he returned grimly. "Or it could be my darling stepmother, fighting for her son. Whichever it is, however, you are in danger. And that I cannot allow."

Silence fell as they looked at each other. Then Sarah said slowly, "Do you know, it could even be Neville. He was very upset when he learned that I was going to marry you. Perhaps he is trying to scare me away, so that I will divorce you and marry him."

"That is a possibility," he acknowledged. "It is certainly true that none of these accidents happened until he arrived on the scene."

"We have to find out the truth," Sarah said. She drew a long, unsteady breath. "But how?"

"I was planning to have Lawrence and my stepmother

followed," he said. "Perhaps I should add Harvey to that list."

"But who will follow them? You can't bring in the Runners. If Lawrence and the dowager know they are being followed, they will take care not to be discovered."

"I thought I would employ several of the servants." He gave her a shadowy smile. "You can probably recommend the ones whom we can trust. You know them better than I."

Sarah's brow puckered thoughtfully. She nodded.

He rose to his feet, looked down into her face, and touched the tip of her nose with a gentle finger. "What would I do without you?" he asked softly.

At his words, his look, his touch, all of her overwrought emotions blazed up like dry kindling into a hot bonfire of desire. She stood up, put her arms around his neck, and lifted her face to his.

Their kiss ignited a flame in them both. After a moment, he bent, picked her up, and carried her over to the bed.

He laid her down on her back, bent over her, and kissed her again. She arched up toward him, whimpering deep in her throat, and he said hoarsely, "Wait a minute."

Her heart was hammering as she lay still and watched him strip off his clothes. The shadow of betrayal and death hung over them both, and she wanted him desperately, wanted him between her hands, between her legs, living and breathing and pounding his life into her. He tossed the last of his clothes on the floor, then came over to the bed to undress her. It was not long before he had her naked, and then he moved over her.

She lifted her legs, opening herself to his entry. Their mouths met hungrily as their bodies joined. Her eyes closed as she concentrated on the feel of him, the smell of him. Her hands moved up and down his back, feeling the smooth skin, the hard muscles, the strong bones. All that strength and power felt so invulnerable, but she knew it was not. She held him tighter.

His voice was in her ear as he drove deeper and deeper inside of her. He felt so good. He began to kiss her again and his hair brushed against her face. Inside she felt herself softening, yielding, trembling as she rose toward climax. She stretched her legs and took him even farther in, closing around him, as if by so doing she could protect him and hold him safe.

He drove her up the bed until her head was pressed against the headboard. Her body convulsed with pleasure just as he flung his head back, crying out his own release with triumph and joy.

They lay together in the wrecked bed, their hot bodies entwined. Sarah's forehead was pressed against his shoulder. She opened her lips and tasted the salt sweat that dampened his skin.

"I love you so much," she said.

She felt his body tense. He lifted her chin so that he could look into her eyes. What he saw there apparently satisfied him, for he returned her head to his shoulder and began to stroke her long loose hair.

He said, "Always before, I was alone. Now there is you."

Her heart leaped at his words. But she said softly, "There are many people who love you, Anthony."

His fingers continued their stroking motion. "There are many people who love the image they have made of me," he said.

It was true, she thought. Anthony was so extremely

beautiful that there were few who were able to see below the dazzling surface to the man who lived beneath.

He said, "And to think, I would never have known you if it weren't for the fact that I needed money."

The note of wonder in his voice brought tears to her eyes.

"And I never would have married you if you hadn't promised to help me be a painter," she said.

"You *are* a painter. I just promised to help you be a better one."

She smiled.

"I still think it would be a good idea for you to go back to London, Sarah," he said. "I am afraid for your safety here."

She pointed out practically, "If I go back to London, the attempts will stop, and we won't be able to find out who is behind them. And if we don't find the culprit, Anthony, neither of us will ever be safe."

There was a long silence. Then he said, "You are probably right."

Another silence fell. Then he said, "I'll let you stay if you will allow me to have someone act as a bodyguard for you."

He spoke in what she thought of as his "command voice."

She sighed. "All right. Are you going to assign one of the servants to me, too?"

"No," he said. "I am going to give the assignment to someone I know I can trust. I will give it to Max."

CHAPTER
Twenty-three

SARAH AND THE DUKE CAME DOWN TO DINNER AND, TO everyone's astonishment, behaved as if nothing at all had happened that afternoon. After dinner, the duke joined his wife in the music room, sitting contentedly on the sofa with his eyes closed while she played Mozart to him.

The few times they spoke to each other, their voices were soft and intimate.

This display of marital unity had varying effects upon the rest of the household.

It convinced Neville that the duke was a master of seduction and a grave danger to his wife. Frustrated by Sarah's capitulation to her husband, all Neville could think to do was remain at Cheviot and try his best to keep her safe.

Patrick's reaction had been the opposite of Neville's. As he sat in the music room and watched Anthony listen to Sarah play, he suddenly knew for certain that his brother was not trying to kill his wife.

I think it's that Mr. Harvey, Patrick thought with abrupt enlightenment. *He wants Sarah for himself and he's trying to make her think that Anthony wants to hurt her.*

Patrick's eyes moved to Neville's face and he remembered how the merchant had insisted upon accompanying him and Sarah to the tree house. He remembered how conveniently Neville had been positioned to rescue Sarah when the planks had given way beneath her feet.

I'm going to stay close to Mr. Harvey, Patrick resolved. *I won't let him do anything more to hurt Sarah.*

Lawrence, too, was affected by the obvious harmony between Sarah and Anthony, and, after he retired to bed that night, he did not fall immediately into his usual deep, dreamless sleep. Instead he lay awake, going over again and again in his mind the question of who might be trying to harm Sarah.

His mother was convinced of Cheviot's guilt, but Lawrence was growing less and less certain. His opinion of Cheviot had changed from the days of the duke's first arrival. Quite simply, his brother had not turned out to be the man that Lawrence had expected him to be.

For one thing, it was obvious to anyone with eyes that the duke loved his home. This surprised Lawrence, who had always been told by his mother that Anthony hated Cheviot. But the look in his brother's eyes when he surveyed the castle was unmistakable. And there was also the indisputable fact that he would not be putting so much money and effort into Cheviot if he didn't care about it.

The duke had also shown himself willing to include Lawrence in all of his schemes for the renovation of the estate. In fact, he consulted Lawrence regularly. And he and Lawrence had had some splendid conversations about how to go about building up the stables. Cheviot actually had gone to look at the hunter Lawrence recommended, and he had bought him.

Lawrence also remembered the hot afternoon when they had stripped to their breeches and gone into the sea to cool off, and he had got a look at the scar on his brother's shoulder.

"That must have been nasty," he had said gruffly, as he stood next to Cheviot in the midst of the cold, tumbling North Sea waves.

"Very nasty," the duke had replied serenely. "I was lucky, though, and it healed well."

"How long did it take before you could go back to your regiment?"

"Six months."

"You didn't come home," Lawrence said. "Where did you convalesce?"

"At Hartford Court," Cheviot had answered lightly.

He had gone to his aunt's home, not to the home of his heart. Lawrence thought he knew why.

"I remember you used to fight a lot with Papa," he said.

Anthony's wet face turned grim. "I wanted to horsewhip him for what he was doing to Cheviot."

The duke had stood there, waist deep in foaming seawater, staring up at the huge gray stone castle that was outlined so dramatically against the sky. Lawrence had looked at his brother's surprisingly muscular torso, and thought a little unwillingly, *Anthony is a brother to be proud of.*

"I wanted to horsewhip him, too," Lawrence said.

At that, Cheviot had turned to him and grinned. "Well, now that he is gone, we can make Cheviot into what it should be."

He had said *we.*

So now that Lawrence was faced with what looked like indisputable evidence that someone was trying to kill Sarah, he was finding it difficult to believe his brother would do such a thing.

Besides, he thought, *Cheviot is fond of Sarah. Any fool can see that. If I didn't know for a fact that he married her for her money, I would think that he married her for love.*

He scowled into the darkness.

But if it wasn't Cheviot, then who was it?

It might be Harvey, Lawrence thought.

It was obvious to Lawrence that the young merchant's feelings for Sarah were not disinterested. Lawrence remembered that it was Harvey who had been the first one to accuse the duke. Perhaps he was trying to break up Cheviot's marriage so that he could have Sarah for himself.

I think I had better keep an eye on Harvey, Lawrence thought. Perhaps he would be able to unearth something that would help resolve the mystery of who was behind these frightening accidents.

For Max, the more he saw of the closeness between Anthony and his wife, the greater grew his anguish and his fury. His jealous hatred of Sarah swelled until finally there was room inside him for nothing else.

If she should die, then Anthony will turn to me.

This was the thought that increasingly haunted his twisted mind. When Anthony had asked him to play bodyguard to the duchess, Max had been forced to restrain himself from breaking into wild laughter.

Every time he saw Anthony touch his wife, he wanted to scream in pain.

He was going to have to do something or he would go mad.

Several days went by and John Kirkland, the young gardener whom the duke had assigned to watch Lawrence, reported to his employer that Lord Lawrence appeared to be following Mr. Harvey.

The duke and John were meeting in the estate office, which was located just inside the back entrance to the castle. The duke looked with incredulity at the gardener, who was standing in front of his desk.

"Lord Lawrence is following Mr. Harvey?" he repeated.

"Aye, so it seems, Your Grace."

The duke frowned. "Why do you think this?"

"Everywhere Mr. Harvey goes, Lord Lawrence goes, too," John replied. "I know Lord Lawrence well enough, Your Grace, to know that he is not interested in looking at mills."

The duke's incredulity increased. "Lord Lawrence is looking at *mills*?"

The young gardener nodded his rough black-haired head. "Aye, Your Grace, that he is. He went yesterday with Mr. Harvey into Newcastle to look at a mill, and the day before that he went walking with him in the park. For the whole afternoon, Your Grace."

"Tell one of the footmen to find Lord Lawrence and ask him to come to me here in the office," the duke said.

"Aye, Your Grace." The gardener bowed his way out of the room.

It was half an hour before Lawrence made his appearance in the serviceable, plainly furnished room that served as the estate's office.

"You wanted to see me, Cheviot?" he said as he came in the door.

"Yes," the duke replied. He leaned back in his chair, resting his fingers on the edge of his desk, and regarded Lawrence soberly. "I want to know if it is true that you have been following Mr. Harvey."

Color flushed into Lawrence's dark face.

"Who told you that?"

"I have it on the best authority that you went into New-castle with him yesterday to look at a mill, and that the day before that you spent the entire afternoon walking with him in the park. The only reason I can think of to account for your sudden penchant for Harvey's company is that you are following him."

Lawrence scowled and took a step closer to the desk. "Has it never occurred to you, Cheviot, that Harvey might well be the man who is behind these accidents that keep happening to Sarah?"

There was a moment of silence, then the duke waved a hand to the chair that was set in front of his desk. "Sit down, Lawrence," he said.

Lawrence gave his brother a wary look, but he sat.

"Why would Mr. Harvey want to hurt Sarah?" the duke asked, his tone of voice merely curious.

"I don't know that he really wants to hurt Sarah so much as he wants her to think that *you* are trying to hurt her," Lawrence said. "Sarah once told me that she and Harvey were engaged practically from childhood, and then she jilted him and married you."

He leaned forward and fixed intense blue eyes on the duke's face. "Suppose he is trying to break up your marriage, Cheviot. Suppose he has arranged these accidents in order to throw suspicion on you. You must admit it, if somebody really wants Sarah dead, he is going about it in an extremely clumsy manner. He could have finished her off while she lay helpless on the tower stairs. And he certainly could have fixed the planks on the platform so that it appeared that the nails gave way. He didn't have to cut them."

The duke met his younger brother's blue stare, and his own eyes were very bright. "I thought you suspected me," he said.

At that, Lawrence looked away, down toward the desk. "Well, I did at first. But I have got to know you better, and I really can't picture you trying to kill Sarah." He shifted uncomfortably on his seat. "You seem to be dashed fond of her, in fact."

A faint smile curved the duke's lips. "I *am* dashed fond of her."

"Yes, well, the more I thought about it, the more it appeared to me that Harvey is the culprit. Remember, he arrived on the very day that Sarah fell down those stairs. If that ain't suspicious, I don't know what is."

"Thank you, Lawrence, for believing in me," the duke said in a quiet, steady voice. "Your confidence means a lot."

For some reason, Lawrence suddenly found it difficult to breathe. After a moment, he managed to get out, "I realize I haven't behaved very well toward you, Cheviot, and I'm sorry."

The duke picked up a paperweight from the desk and balanced it in his hands. "You had every reason to resent me," he said. "I always understood that."

Lawrence went on doggedly, "I thought you hated Cheviot, you see, and it was killing me to think that you—not I—were to have control of its destiny." He looked up from his contemplation of the desk. "But that's not true, is it? You love Cheviot."

"Yes," the duke said softly. "I do."

"I caught Patrick following Harvey, too," Lawrence offered next. "He had come to the same conclusion I had. I sent him about his business, though. We don't need Patrick getting himself hurt."

The duke's eyes got even brighter. "Patrick, too?" he said.

Lawrence said gruffly, "I'm sorry I suspected you, Anthony. It was stupid of me."

"Well, I suspected you, too," the duke admitted.

"What?" Lawrence looked so astounded that the duke smiled.

"Yes. I thought perhaps you were trying to cast suspicion on me so that when Sarah actually died, I would be convicted of her murder."

Lawrence's mouth was hanging open. "But why would I do that?"

"So that you could be the next duke," Anthony said dryly.

"Good God."

The duke replaced the paperweight on the desk.

"So you see," he said, "I must beg your pardon as well, Lawrence."

Suddenly Lawrence laughed. "It seems the only people we have not suspected are Patrick and my mother."

The duke replied blandly, "That is so."

The gentlemen remained in the dining room for an inordinately long time after dinner that evening. The duke had the port bottle in front of him, and he and Lawrence partook freely while they discussed the various means by which they were going to add horses to the stables.

"We could get some mares and breed them to Rodrigo," Lawrence suggested as he downed another glass of port.

"That is so," Anthony replied, and he and Lawrence launched into a long and intricate discussion of what kind of mare would make a good match for Rodrigo.

Max sat on Anthony's other side, nursed his single glass of port, and listened idly to the conversation, which he found excessively boring. Neville Harvey sat next to him, casting disapproving looks at the duke and his brother.

As the evening wore on and the port was passed between Anthony and Lawrence, their schemes grew grander and grander. In desperation, Max turned to Neville and began a conversation about the government.

Then someone touched his sleeve. Max turned his head and looked directly into Anthony's brilliant eyes. The brightness of those eyes and the flush of color along his cheekbones were the only signs he gave that he had been drinking.

He said, "My little brother can't hold his wine."

Max looked across the duke and saw that Lawrence's head was lying on the table. He appeared to be asleep.

"He consumed a great deal," Max said disapprovingly.

"I wanted to get drunk, and he was good company," said the duke.

The perfect clarity of his speech gave him away, Max thought. He did not speak so distinctly when he was sober.

Max pinched his lips together and said nothing.

Anthony looked amused. "You don't approve, do you? Don't you ever get drunk, Max? Are you perfectly righteous and sober all the time?"

"I try to be," Max said.

The duke lifted the second bottle of port that had been placed in front of him, and filled Max's glass to the top.

"Drink," he said.

"Anthony . . ." Max gave him an exasperated look. "I don't really like the taste of port."

The duke said inexorably, "Max. Drink it."

Max shook his head.

Anthony leaned back in his seat and folded his arms.

He said, "I cannot have a man who does not drink port act as my private secretary."

Max stared at him. Anthony stared back. He meant it. For some reason, he was determined that Max join him in a drink.

Max lifted his glass. He held his breath. He drank. He put the glass down and said, "Satisfied?"

"Good man," Anthony said. He sat up, and before Max's horrified eyes, he poured more port into his secretary's glass. Once more he leaned back in his chair and folded his arms. "Go ahead," he said. "Drink some more."

Max sighed. "Only if you will drink with me."

Anthony looked delighted. "Done," he said, and poured himself another glass.

Max was miserable the following morning. He shuddered at the sight of the eggs and bacon and ham that were laid out on the sideboard for breakfast and merely took a cup of coffee.

He was sitting over his coffee, hollow-eyed and nauseated, when Anthony came into the room.

The duke looked perfectly fine.

Max scowled at him. "Doesn't your head hurt?"

"Not really," the duke said. "I have always had a hard head when it comes to wine."

Max groaned.

The duke chuckled and came to lay a brief hand on his secretary's shoulder. "Poor Max. But I needed someone to celebrate with me last night, and who better than my best friend?"

He could always do it, Max thought. He could always find the words to disarm and seduce him.

"What were you celebrating?" he asked.

The duke grinned and did not reply.

Abruptly, Max's sense of danger awoke.

She is having a baby, he thought. *It must be that.*

Panic replaced the nausea in Max's stomach. Once Sarah gave him an heir, her hold on Anthony would be complete.

I can't let that happen, Max thought desperately. *I must do something soon.*

CHAPTER
Twenty-four

SARAH FINISHED HER PAINTING AND DECIDED THAT next she would like to paint a landscape of the Cheviot Hills. Consequently, she and Anthony and Patrick spent several afternoons driving around the area in search of a good view. Finally she picked out a spot on a ridge of high ground that afforded a wonderful vista of the misty green pastures of Northumberland and the distant blue hills of the Cheviots.

She was especially pleased by the way the colors of pasture and hills looked bathed in the hazy afternoon light.

On the day she was to begin working on her preliminary sketch, Anthony asked Max if he would drive the duchess and her painting gear in the gig, and wait for her until she was ready to return to the castle.

"You are the one man I feel safe entrusting with my most precious possession," he said with his heartbreaking smile. "I would take her myself, but the attorney from Newcastle is coming this afternoon to finish up the arrangements for my stepmother's jointure, and I must be here to meet with him."

His most precious possession.

Max nearly ground his teeth.

He said, "Of course I don't mind, Anthony."

"What would I do without you, Max?" the duke said lightly, and went on his way.

It was ten-thirty in the morning by the time Sarah had packed all of her paints and her easel into the gig that Max was to drive. The gig was heavier and more balanced than Anthony's phaeton, as well as affording more storage space.

She joined Max on the front seat and gave him a shy smile. "It is very kind of you to accompany me, Mr. Scott. I am sorry that I must put you out like this, but the duke is adamant that I remain within your eyesight until this unpleasant business has been cleared up."

Max's widely spaced dark eyes glittered.

"Anthony has cause to be concerned, Your Grace," he said.

She sighed. "I know."

They drove between the gate towers and along the path that led through the park. The flowers that bordered the path sported their full profusion of summer color: pink lupines, deep purple larkspur, white peonies, and violet-blue irises. The border itself was weeded and tidy. Sarah made a mental note to compliment John Kirkland on his industry.

She tried to start up a conversation with Max several times, but he was unresponsive, and after a while she gave up and simply enjoyed the views of the countryside.

They had just entered the thick woods that covered the ridge Sarah had chosen when she said a little breathlessly, "Would you mind stopping for a moment, Mr. Scott?"

The road was too steep and narrow to pull over to the

side, so Max stopped the gig right where it was. He looked at Sarah and saw her sitting with her forehead on her knees.

"Are you all right, Your Grace?" he asked.

Her voice was a little muffled as she replied, "Yes. I just felt a little faint all of a sudden. I shall be fine in a moment."

He looked at her bent head. "Are you certain? Perhaps we should return to the castle."

"No. There is no cause for you to be concerned, Mr. Scott." After a few more moments, she lifted her head and drew in a long, deep breath. "It has happened several times recently, but after a moment I am perfectly fine."

She is breeding.

The thought was like a knife to Max's heart.

I knew that must be what Anthony was celebrating the other night.

No wonder he had called her his most precious possession. She was going to give him an heir.

Max couldn't bear it. He couldn't bear it that this small, undistinguished girl should be the one to wake in the morning and find Anthony's face on the pillow beside her. He couldn't bear it that she should be the one to whom Anthony gave his body. He couldn't bear it that she should be the one to whom Anthony gave his love.

Hatred and despair tore through Max like a whirlwind that cannot be controlled.

For weeks, he had been hovering on the edge of a precipice. His suspicion of Sarah's pregnancy was the final thing needed to send him toppling over the edge.

Patrick was bored. There was no one around for him to talk to. Lawrence had gone out somewhere with Neville Harvey, Anthony was locked up in the library with a boring attorney, and his mother was writing letters.

She was always writing letters.

Sarah had gone out to paint.

Patrick sat on the stone bench next to the waterfall in the park and kicked his heels. The day stretched in front of him interminably.

His tree house had been declared off limits since Sarah's accident.

He could always ride his pony, but he had nowhere to go. He thought for a minute of riding into Alnwick to visit a boy he knew, but he decided that would be boring.

He thought that it might not be too boring to spend the afternoon watching Sarah paint.

Patrick liked Sarah. She listened to him as if what he had to say was important. And she seemed to understand how he was feeling, without his having to tell her.

He could always take his pony and follow her. He had been with her and Anthony on the day she had decided where she would set up her easel. He thought he remembered how to get there.

She'll be happy to see me, Patrick told himself. *That stupid old Max is a bore.*

Patrick jumped to his feet, pleased to have determined what he was going to do with his day.

Sarah set up her easel and arranged her oil paints. As was her custom, she would do a sketch in oil to use as the basis for the larger picture she would paint in her studio.

Over an hour went by. Sarah was utterly absorbed in her painting, utterly unaware of Max or what he might be doing. He actually had to repeat himself twice before she heard what he was saying to her:

"Stand up, Duchess, and turn around."

Sarah frowned in annoyance, turned her head, and, to her stunned amazement, saw Max standing six feet away from her, with a gun pointed at her heart.

She stared at him in absolute shock.

He smiled. And then she knew.

It was Max who was responsible for her accidents.

It can't be! she thought wildly. *He is Anthony's best friend.*

She looked once more at Max's face, and knew that it was true.

"Stand up," he said again.

She swallowed. Her heart had begun to slam in her chest.

"What on earth are you doing, Max?" She spoke in what she hoped was a calm, reasonable voice.

"Stand up," he said once more.

Very slowly, she got to her feet and faced him.

He said, "You want to know what I am doing? I am going to kill you, Duchess, that is what I am doing."

His voice was a grim monotone.

Sarah's heart beat harder and faster. "You . . . you can't be serious."

"I am very serious, Duchess."

"But . . ." Sarah's throat was so dry, she could hardly get the words out. "But, why?"

He bared his teeth in a terrifying smile. "It is very simple," he said. "Anthony loves you."

Her pulse was pounding so hard that Sarah's ears were ringing. She had never been so frightened in all her life. Her instinct told her to keep him talking. He wouldn't shoot her if he was talking to her.

"I d-don't understand," she stuttered.

"Of course you don't understand, you stupid bitch,"

Max said, an edge finally enlivening the dead monotone of his voice. His widely set eyes were black and glittering. "And to think I was almost glad when he had to marry you. I never thought I would have anything to fear from a merchant's granddaughter."

His tone was full of contempt as he said the words *merchant's granddaughter.* He stared at her with those terrifying eyes, his brow furrowed in genuine bewilderment. "I will never understand what Anthony sees in you."

Sarah moved her right hand slightly, in the direction of the open jar of green oil paint that was resting behind her on the easel.

"Anthony loves you, too," she said. "You are his dearest friend."

"I *was,* until you came along," Max said. His eyes were glittering like chunks of black obsidian. "I've done everything for him. I was his mentor in the Peninsula. I saved his life at Salamanca. I saved his arm. And this is how he repays me—by spurning me for a little paint-splattered, merchant's granddaughter."

A lightning flash of anger rippled through the massive inertia of Sarah's terror.

"He has repaid you amply," she retorted. "He has made you his private secretary, his financial advisor, his best friend. He has made you a member of his family. What more can you possibly want of him?"

"I want him to love me," Max said.

"He does!"

Max shook his head. "No," he said. "I want him to love only me. No one else. Just me."

His face was cold and set and fanatical. His eyes were frightening.

He is mad, Sarah thought. *Completely mad.*

She slid her hand a little closer to the paint jar.

"You can't possibly hope to get away with this." Her voice was shaking. "Everyone knows you were the one to accompany me today."

His laughter sounded genuinely amused. "I'm the only one whom no one suspects! Isn't that ironic? When I tell Anthony how someone shot me and kidnapped you, he'll believe me. And when they find your body, no one will be more grieved than I."

Keep him talking, Sarah thought.

"Shot you?" she said. "What do you mean?"

She stared into his eyes, holding them, and moved her hand a little closer to the paint.

"A necessary evil, I'm afraid," he replied. "I shall have to shoot myself in the shoulder." He shrugged. "Wounded in the pursuit of my duty. I'm sure Anthony will take good care of me, just like I once took such good care of him."

Sarah wet her lips. "You can't kill me," she said. "Everyone will blame Anthony. Surely you don't want that."

"Ah—but *I* won't blame Anthony," Max said. "I shall stand his staunch friend, the only one who believes in him. Then he will know who really deserves his love."

"But he may be arrested for my murder!" Sarah cried.

"That will never happen," Max said positively. "There is no evidence and he is the Duke of Cheviot. There may be talk, but there will be no arrest."

He clearly believed every word he was speaking.

My God, my God, what am I going to do?

Max jerked the gun. "Step away from that easel. You and I are going to take a little walk together."

Sarah didn't move. "What are you going to do to me?"

He smiled and Sarah tried not to let him see her shudder. "There are several possibilities in these woods. I shall think of something."

A clear, youthful voice that was just beginning to change its register cut through Sarah's terror.

"Sarah! Are you around here? It's me, Patrick!"

Max's head turned involuntarily toward the voice and Sarah picked up the jar of oil paint, threw it toward his face, and ran for the cover of the woods.

Bang.

A bullet scorched her right sleeve. Then she was within the bulwark of the thick trees.

"Patrick!" she shrieked at the top of her lungs. "Run! It's Max! Max is trying to kill me!"

Patrick's voice came back to her, high and shrilly soprano. "Sarah! Where are you?"

She heard the sound of his pony crashing through the trees.

"Get Anthony!" she screamed. "Go!"

All the while she was yelling, she was racing through the woods herself. Holding her skirts up to her knees, she plunged downward, dodging trees and crashing through fallen branches.

Two more shots rang out, but nothing hit her.

Through the sobbing of her breath and the pounding of her heart, she thought she heard the sound of hoofbeats.

Patrick was going for Anthony.

Mindlessly, blindly, Sarah raced on, scrambling through the steep forest of the ridge, climbing down rock outcrops, sliding into wet and muddy gullies. She had to use her hands to hold up her skirt, so she couldn't protect her face from getting scratched by low-hanging branches.

At last she could go no farther. She bent over, her arms

wrapped around her middle, fighting for air. She listened.

Nothing.

Where was Max? Wasn't he following her?

The only sound she heard other than her heaving breath was the long trill of a wood warbler overhead.

Slowly, Sarah backed into a thicket of undergrowth and crouched down on her heels. She would stay here, quietly, until Anthony came.

When Max heard Patrick's voice, he had felt for one dreadful moment like a man suspended over an abyss who hears the crack of the tree branch to which he has been clinging. At any second, he would find himself falling onto the cruel rocks below.

Then the paint had hit him in the face and Sarah had begun to run. Almost reflexively, Max had raised his gun and fired. Then he had fired twice more.

He heard Patrick calling for Sarah. He heard Sarah's words: *Max is trying to kill me! Get Anthony!*

Max dropped his gun on the ground and stared at it blindly.

The boy would get away.

Anthony would know.

Slowly, Max lifted his head and looked out at the view that Sarah had chosen to paint. The stretching green pastures and distant bluish hills were bathed in the light of the hazy afternoon sun.

Max had no doubt about what would happen once Anthony discovered his friend's duplicity.

Anthony would repudiate him, would turn his back on him, would never want to see him again.

Max thought that if he were deprived of the light of Anthony's presence, he would be destroyed as surely as a plant would be destroyed without the life-giving warmth of the sun.

Moving stiffly, like an old man, Max bent and picked up his gun. Then he turned and, slowly and steadily, he began to walk into the forest. Not even the heavy feel of the gun in his hand caused his heart to hurry its heavy rhythm. It plodded dutifully onward—*thump, thump, thump*—not realizing yet that the organism it sought to invigorate was already dead.

Sarah heard the shot, but she did not know what it meant. She remained hunched in the undergrowth, shivering with shock, until a long time later when she heard Anthony's voice calling her name. Then she crawled out of her hiding place and shouted to him. There was a small clearing nearby, and she moved into the opening to wait.

It took him ten minutes to climb down to her. She stood in the clearing, calling to him periodically, aware for the first time that her hair was streaming all around her, her face was scratched and bleeding, and her clothes were torn and ripped. When finally she saw his familiar figure step into the clearing, she ran forward and threw herself into his arms.

He held her tightly.

"Are you all right?"

Her face was pressed into his shoulder, and she nodded.

"Patrick said that . . . that Max . . . was trying to kill you?"

"Yes," she said. She drew a deep breath and pressed her face even harder into the safety of his shoulder. Her arms were clamped around his waist. "He had a gun, An-

thony. When I ran away he tried to shoot me." She raised
her head a little and nodded at her torn sleeve. "Look!"

"Yes," Anthony said. "I see."

For the first time, Sarah registered how strange his
voice sounded. She took a deep breath, loosened her
arms, and stepped away from him.

He was very white, and on his face was the closed
look he wore when he wanted to keep people at a distance.

He patted her shoulder. "Come along," he said. "I'll
have someone drive you back to the castle."

"Wh-what are you going to do?" she asked.

He didn't reply, just turned and began to climb back
the way he had come. Sarah scrambled after him.

There was a group of men waiting at the top of the
ridge. They were all carrying guns.

Anthony had called for a search party.

Patrick was there as well, looking big-eyed and
somber.

"Sarah!" It was Neville who came running toward her.
"Are you all right?"

"Yes," she replied. "I am fine, Neville."

"Your face is all scratched," he said.

She raised her fingers and touched her cheek. "It's
nothing."

The duke said crisply, "Harvey, would you drive the
duchess back to Cheviot? And take Patrick with you."

"Certainly," Neville replied. He put his hand on
Sarah's arm. "Come along, my dear, and I'll take you
home."

Patrick said, "Let me stay and help you, Anthony."

Sarah's eyes went to her husband. His face still wore
the same closed expression. He didn't reply to Patrick,

just looked at him. Patrick flushed and moved toward the gig.

Sarah said again, "What are you going to do?"

The duke replied, "I am going to look for Max."

Then he turned and gestured to the four men who were waiting. "We'll search the woods first. He's on foot. He can't have got very far."

Obediently, the men with the guns fanned out and entered the forest. Without looking again at his wife, the duke, who was the only one unarmed, turned and disappeared among the trees as well.

Sarah stood staring after him, her eyes dry and burning. The grief she felt was too terrible to find a release in tears.

The dowager came into the front hall to meet Sarah.

"What has been going on here?" she said sharply. Then, "Your hair! And your face is all scratched!"

She sounded as if Sarah's lack of grooming was her chief concern.

"We discovered who was trying to kill Sarah, Mama," Patrick explained in a voice that quavered slightly. "It was Mr. Scott."

The dowager's eyes flashed blue fire. "Mr. Scott? That's insane. Whyever would he want to harm Sarah?"

"If you will excuse me, ma'am," Sarah said, "I am going to go to my room."

Neville looked at her worriedly. "Will you be all right?"

"Yes. I just need to lie down for a while."

The dowager said shrilly, "I certainly hope that someone is going to tell me what is going on here!"

"I will tell you, Mama," Patrick said.

Sarah turned her back and went up the stairs.

The rest of the afternoon dragged interminably. At seven o'clock Lawrence returned to the house with the news that Max had been discovered.

"He killed himself," he told Sarah when he met with her in the privacy of her sitting room. "I found his body."

"My God." Sarah shut her eyes.

"Yes. It wasn't a pretty sight. Anthony didn't turn a hair, though. I suppose he's used to seeing worse sights than that."

Lawrence had obviously been shaken.

"Did he shoot himself?" Sarah asked.

Belatedly, Lawrence realized that he shouldn't be talking like this to Sarah.

"Yes," he said cautiously.

"In the head?" Sarah asked.

Lawrence looked a little sick. "Yes."

More nightmares, Sarah thought wearily.

"Where is Anthony now?" she asked.

"He was taking Scott's body into Alnwick. He didn't want to bring it back here."

Sarah bent her head.

"What I don't understand is why Scott should have wanted to kill you," Lawrence said. "He had nothing to gain by your death."

"I think he must have been deranged," Sarah said.

Lawrence scowled, dissatisfied with her answer.

She said, "I really am not feeling very well, Lawrence. If you don't mind, I shall just have some soup in my room and go to bed."

He stood up hastily. "Of course. You've had a terrible experience. I'll leave you to rest."

Sarah did have some soup, but she did not go to bed. Instead, she stood at her window, watching for Anthony's return.

It was nine-thirty when finally she saw Sam coming through the gate, the setting summer sun reflecting off his bright chestnut coat. Anthony did not even glance up at her window, but rode directly to the stables.

Two hours passed. Finally, Sarah allowed her maid to undress her and put her to bed. She did not go to sleep, however, but lay with her eyes open, listening for sounds outside her door.

At midnight, she heard Currier's voice in the room next to hers. Another hour went by, and still Anthony did not come.

He was going to sleep in his own room.

All Sarah could think of was that dreadful closed look she had seen on his face that afternoon.

She was the one responsible for Max's betrayal. Was he going to turn away from her as well?

She couldn't bear it. She couldn't bear to be shut out from him like this. For the first time, she had a dim understanding of how Max must have felt.

She wanted, desperately, to go to him.

I do not want him to bear this alone. He has just lost his closest friend. He cannot be left to bear this alone.

But she could not go to him. If their marriage was to mean anything at all, Anthony had to come to her.

The minutes ticked by. Sarah stared at the small lamp that she had kept burning on her bedside table. She stared at it until her eyes stung with the tears she could not shed.

At two in the morning, the door between their bedrooms opened and Anthony came quietly into the room. He closed the door behind him, glanced first at the still-lit lamp and then at the bed. He said softly, "Sarah? Are you still awake?"

"Yes." She pushed some pillows behind her back and sat up. "I couldn't sleep."

He nodded, walked over to the fireplace, and sat on the edge of a chair. The whole width of the room was between them.

"He is dead," he said in a curiously flat voice. "He killed himself."

"I know, Anthony," she said.

"I liked him more than any man I ever knew," he said, still speaking in that same flat voice. He stared at his perfect bare feet, which protruded from beneath his black silk dressing gown. "He seemed to . . . understand things. He seemed to understand me."

"He loved you," Sarah said.

His short laugh was not pleasant.

"He did," she insisted.

"It wasn't love." His voice was angry now. "No one who loved me would have acted as he did."

"In a strange way, I think I understand him," Sarah said.

His eyes came slowly up. "What do you mean?"

"I mean I can understand what drove him to do this terrible thing. He was jealous, Anthony. He saw that you . . . cared . . . for me, too, and he couldn't bear to share you. Jealousy can make a person do things he would never normally dream of doing."

His eyes were both angry and puzzled.

"By all the saints in heaven, was I to care for no one but Max?"

"I think that is what he wanted." She couldn't bear to look at him and bent her head to smooth the fine cotton sheet that covered her lap. "Mr. Blake once told me about a kind of art collector for whom possession means everything. Such a person cannot enjoy a painting if it belongs to someone else. He must have it for himself. He must own it before he can take any pleasure in it." She looked up from the sheet and met his eyes. "I think that is how Max felt about you. He wanted to possess you. He didn't want any part of you to belong to anyone else."

He stared at her, his eyes very dark. Then, "God!" He buried his face in his hands. "What is wrong with me that I attract such a mutilated kind of love?"

Sarah's heart was wrung with pity for him. She pushed the sheet back, swung her legs out of the bed, and walked barefoot across the carpet until she was standing in front of him. She said softly, "It is because you are so much better, so much more beautiful than everyone else. They idolize you, or envy you, or are jealous of you. It is not your fault."

He reached for her blindly, wrapping his arms around her waist and pressing his face into the hollow between her breasts. "He's dead, Sarah," he said. "He's dead."

He was shivering. She held him close and rested her cheek against his smooth hair. "I know, my love," she whispered. "I know."

She felt something hot and wet soak into her nightgown, and she gathered him even closer. "It was better that he did it himself," she said. "You wouldn't have wanted to prosecute him."

"I would have," he said.

"I know. And it would have torn you in two."

They remained clasped together in silence for quite a long time. Anthony's shoulders were still, but Sarah's nightgown slowly became soaked.

Finally she said, "When you didn't come tonight, I was afraid you had turned away from me. I was afraid that perhaps you blamed me for what Max did."

He lifted his head and looked up at her. His eyelashes

were wet. "I could never turn away from you," he said. "If I did that, the loneliness would be unbearable."

"Anthony," she whispered. Her heart ached for him, but deep within, some part of her was singing.

He closed his eyes and rested his head against her once more. "Hold me, Sarah," he said. "Hold me."

And she did.

EPILOGUE

IT WAS AN AFTERNOON OF PERFECT SUNSHINE AND WARM temperatures when the travel chaise of the Duke and Duchess of Cheviot pulled up to the front steps of the Chateau de Vienne, home of the Comte de Vienne, one of the duke's cousins. The chateau was an elegant Renaissance structure situated in the picturesque countryside outside of Honfleur. During the years of Napoleon's rule it had belonged to one of the emperor's marshals, but after Waterloo, the Comte de Vienne, who had spent the war years in exile in England, had been granted his ancestral home back by the restored French king.

Sarah and Anthony had landed in Le Havre the day before, spent the night at an inn, and started for Honfleur that morning. They were making the Chateau de Vienne their first stop because the comte had some paintings that Anthony thought Sarah should see.

The comte was a man of about sixty, thin and elegant, with a long, thin nose. His wife looked so much like him that Sarah thought they must be related. The comtesse graciously escorted her guests to their rooms herself, all the while chattering in French to Anthony about people whom Sarah did not know.

Sarah, watching the look on the comtesse's face as she
spoke to the duke, thought with amusement that even old
women took on a certain glow when they were around
Anthony.

"This will be your room, my dear," the comtesse said
to Sarah, as she opened a door and gestured for Sarah to
enter.

The bedroom was large, with French doors that opened
onto what looked like a private balcony. Sarah looked
around the room, which was light and airy and elegantly
furnished with some extremely beautiful painted furniture.

"How lovely," she said in the perfectly competent
French she had been taught at Miss Bates's School for
Young Ladies.

"I shall send a girl to you with water and a refreshing
tisane," the comtesse promised. "Your husband will be
right next door."

"*Merci, madame,*" Sarah replied, and stood in the middle of the lovely room while the comtesse escorted Anthony firmly away. He winked at her as he went out the
door.

Sarah walked around the room, examining the pictures
that hung upon the ivory-painted walls. Most of them
were views of local scenes. She recognized the Honfleur
harbor, surrounded by tall, narrow, slate-roofed houses,
and another view of the Seine estuary upon which Honfleur was built. The paintings were picturesque but unin-
spired.

While Sarah was inspecting the paintings, a maid came
into the room bearing upon a tray a pitcher of water and
the promised tisane. She was followed by Helena,
Sarah's personal maid, who began to instruct one of the

comte's footmen as to where he should place Sarah's portmanteau.

In order to get out of the way of Helena's unpacking, Sarah went to the doors that led out onto the balcony, opened them, and stepped out into the late afternoon sun. The narrow balcony looked out onto a formal garden, which was arranged in orderly fashion around what looked to be a statue of a young Greek god. There was an identical balcony set outside the windows of the room next to hers.

Sarah stretched her arms upward and inhaled deeply.

I am in France! she thought, and a thrill shivered up and down her spine. *I am really, really here.*

She leaned her arms on the smooth stone railing and thought back upon the past few months at Cheviot.

It had been a time of healing for Anthony. Max's betrayal had left a terrible wound, but he had been helped by the growing closeness between himself and Lawrence. Their mutual love of Cheviot had been a natural bond, but the brothers had many other interests in common as well.

Sarah sometimes threatened humorously that if she heard any more talk about horses during dinner, she was going to make them eat in the stable.

Then, in the middle of August, Anthony had asked Lawrence if he would like to manage Cheviot for him.

"I don't mean that you should be my steward," he had said. "Of course I shall employ someone to hold that position. But I shall probably be away from home rather frequently, and there ought to be someone here to take command. I can't think of anyone better than you, Lawrence, if you would like to do it."

At first Lawrence had been stunned by the offer, and then he had been touchingly eager to accept it.

"By Jove, nothing would suit me better," he had declared with a huge grin.

It was an arrangement that benefited both brothers. Lawrence would be able to remain at his beloved Cheviot, making use of his organizational talents, and Anthony would be able to leave home without worrying that his plans for the improvement of the estate would not be carried out.

Patrick was scheduled to go to Eton, Anthony's old school. At first he had not been happy with the idea, but then Sarah had suggested that Anthony invite several friends who had younger brothers to pay visits to Cheviot. Patrick had pronounced the visiting boys to be "great guns," and had been considerably more cheerful about the prospect of school ever since.

Unfortunately, the dowager duchess had announced in no uncertain terms that she did not wish to reside in the Newcastle house that had been part of her jointure. And Anthony, who had been counting the days until he would be rid of her, felt that he could not evict his stepmother from Cheviot while her sons were still in residence.

"I simply cannot tell my brothers that their mother is not welcome in their home," he had said to Sarah.

Gloomily, she had agreed with him.

As the weeks had gone by, however, and the household had turned more and more to Sarah for its leadership, the dowager had become more and more unhappy. She did not possess the temperament to accept being number two where once she had been number one. Shortly after it had been decided that Patrick would go to school, the dowager had informed Anthony that, instead of giving her the house in Newcastle, she would like him to pay for the lease of a house in Bath. She had friends in Bath, she said, and she would like to reside there permanently.

The duke had been delighted to accommodate her.

Sarah lifted her face to the warmth of the slanting sun and closed her eyes. After dinner, the comte would show her his pictures. And she would be able to look at them again tomorrow, in the full light of day.

Then, in two more days' time, they would be in Paris.

Sarah smiled and wondered how it was possible for one person to be so happy.

The duke listened to his cousin's wife talk on and on and he nodded and made the correct responses, and wished that she would go away.

Happiness pumped through him. Finally he had got Sarah to France.

He had never thought he would be glad to leave Cheviot, but in truth he had longed with all his heart to get his wife to himself for a while. The only time they had been alone together had been on their much-too-brief wedding trip. Ever since then, they had been surrounded by other people. It was for that very reason he had refused all invitations to stay with relatives and friends in Paris and had registered them at a hotel.

It would be nice to be alone.

Then, too, ever since their marriage, he had been spending Sarah's money to rescue his family and his home, and he wanted desperately to give something back to her. He wanted to show her the treasures of Paris. He wanted to spread them out before her, like pearls before a princess.

He wanted to give her the world.

"Oui, madame," he agreed with the comtesse. He glanced toward the bedroom door and saw with relief that his valet was coming in.

Finally the comtesse retired, leaving the duke alone

with Currier. After inquiring politely how his valet had found the carriage ride, Anthony went to the double doors that led to the balcony and threw them open onto the golden French air.

He stepped outdoors, feeling exhilaration surge through his blood.

They were here. He had promised her he would bring her to France, and he had done it.

A voice said, "I thought that balcony must belong to you."

He turned his head and saw his wife standing on the adjoining balcony. She was smiling at him.

Abruptly, his exuberance found a focus. "I'll come over there," he said.

Her dimple flashed. Then, as she saw him measuring the space between them and realized that he meant to cross from balcony to balcony, she cried out sharply, "Anthony, don't be foolish! It is too dangerous. Come through the passageway."

He didn't want to go through the passageway. He had been cooped up in a coach or on a boat for days, and he wanted action, he wanted danger. He assessed the wall and decided that there was enough of a foothold in the decorative ledge of stone that ran from balcony to balcony to let him cross.

"Anthony!" Sarah cried in panic. "Don't!"

Adrenaline was pumping through his blood. He glanced down to see if the space underneath him was clear. He didn't want to fall and kill someone.

The garden below was empty except for two gardeners, who were at a safe distance, trimming hedges.

The duke swung over the railing, put his foot on the ledge, and tested it. It held. He reached out, put down another foot, then let go of the balcony and committed himself to the wall.

The ledge was narrower than it had looked, and he had to keep his weight on the front of his toes. He concentrated on making one step at a time as he slowly inched his way toward Sarah.

At last he felt the balcony railing against his hip. Carefully, he reached down and caught the edge of the railing with his right hand. He moved his right foot, wedged it between the stone columns, and pulled himself from the wall to the balustrade.

He vaulted over.

"Are you insane?" Sarah demanded. Her eyes were enormous and he watched the fear in them change to anger. "What was the purpose of that exercise? You could have killed yourself!"

She had been afraid for him. He grinned and answered carelessly, "The balcony is not that high, Sarah. I might have broken a leg if I fell, but I would not have killed myself."

She was not appeased by this very sensible statement. "You could have broken your neck!"

"Well, I didn't." He walked to the balcony door and looked into the bedroom. Sarah's maid was busy unpacking her clothes, her back to the balcony. He said, "You may go."

The maid betrayed no surprise at the sound of his voice, but turned, curtseyed, and backed out of the room. The duke went back to Sarah.

"Helena will think you are insane, too," she said faintly.

He didn't deign to answer, but instead lifted a hand and traced his forefinger along her nose, which had turned pink with sunburn on the boat. What he was feeling right now was pure, unadulterated lust. He moved his finger downward, from her nose to her lips, her throat, between her breasts, and downward still, until he was touching between her legs. She stood perfectly still, but her lips parted and her eyes darkened.

He slid his hand up to her hip and gave her a gentle push. "Inside," he said.

She went before him into the bedroom. He stopped to open both doors to the balcony so that the room would be flooded with sunshine. When he turned again it was to find her standing by the bed, watching him. The room was cluttered with her unpacked belongings. The silence between them was charged with desire.

He stood in a pool of sunlight from the door and began to strip off his clothes. She sat on the bed, as if her legs had given out. She took off her shoes and began to unbutton her dress.

He finished undressing and crossed the floor. She sat upon the side of the bed and watched him come. Her eyes were huge and bottomless. He reached her, put his hands upon her shoulders, and pressed her backward, until she was lying on her back and he was leaning over her. Her breath was coming in soft little gusts and he could see the pulse beating in the hollow of her throat. Her hands reached up to touch him, one of them moving down his bare back, tracing the long scar that curved from his right shoulder to his armpit. Their faces were very close.

"Say my name," he demanded.

"Anthony." Her voice was husky with passion. He began to push her skirt up around her waist. She lifted herself to help him. In the end, he dragged the whole gown off over her head, leaving her clad in only her chemise. He pushed it out of his way and entered her.

Her legs lifted and wrapped around his waist. They

both shuddered, then went still, wanting to savor the moment, the feeling of that first connection.

"Sarah." It was almost a groan. He raised himself, withdrawing a little, then he drove again. She tilted her hips and bore him even deeper inside her than she had before. Passion beat through his blood like the insistent chiming of a great bell. He talked to her breathlessly in French as they rocked together, heart thundering next to heart, slick skin sliding upon slick skin, his body buried in hers as they ascended with mindlessly intense rapture to the shattering heights of sexual release.

A long time later Sarah said, "I hope you're not planning to go back to your room the same way you left it."

He was lying on his back and she was nestled within his right arm, her head tucked into the crook of his shoulder. Strands of her long hair spilled across his chest. She could hear the amusement in his voice as he answered, "I don't have the same incentive. I'll return by way of the passage."

She pictured the scene and felt hot color rush to her cheeks. "What will everyone think when they see you coming out of my room?"

He yawned. "What does it matter what they think?"

Sarah thought of the gardeners who had probably seen him climb to her balcony. She thought of Helena, so summarily dismissed. Her flush grew hotter.

"Servants are people, too," she said.

"Sarah." He sounded very patient. "You are my wife. There is nothing odd in my coming out of your room."

He would never understand her feelings in this. "I suppose so," she murmured doubtfully.

He moved his hand to let it rest lightly on her stomach.

"It's getting rounder," he said.

"Your son or daughter is growing."

"Life," he said in wonder.

The touch of his hand was so gentle that she felt tears sting her eyes. This baby had come at just the right time. It was one of the things that was helping him get over Max.

She turned her face a little and kissed his bare shoulder.

He said, "I had better send for Currier to come and dress me."

"What!"

Sarah bolted upright and glared down into his face.

He was laughing. "Do you expect the Duke of Cheviot to dress himself?"

He looked relaxed and happy and not more than eighteen years old.

"I am sure that a Duke of Cheviot who can climb across balconies is perfectly capable of dressing himself," she replied.

He sat up also, yawned again, then reached his arms up over his head and stretched. Sarah watched the strong muscles in his shoulders and back as they flexed under the smooth, ivory skin.

"All right," he said. His eyes glinted. "But you will have to help me."

"You are impossible," Sarah said. She folded her arms across her bare breasts, which were partially covered by her streaming hair.

"Of course, if you don't want to get dressed, I can think of something else we can do," he said wickedly.

Sarah leaped out of bed and handed him his shirt.

"Put it on," she commanded. "We have to get dressed for dinner. What will the comte and his wife think if we are late?"

"They're French," he replied. "They will know perfectly well what to think."

Sarah glared. "Anthony! Get dressed."

He grinned. He was having a wonderful time teasing her. She had to bite her lip to keep from smiling back and precipitating something that would make them late to dinner.

"All right," he said. "All right." He slid an arm into his shirt.

His eyes were brilliant, his skin was still lightly flushed, and Sarah made the mistake of going over to drop a soft kiss on the tousled brightness of his hair.

They were late to dinner, but the comte and comtesse were much too sophisticated to comment upon the fact.

"They'd kill me," he replied. "Then will know you teach well what is right."

Smith Jones said, "And let me reason..."

"..." said. "...back had a woman of good... for ... and to the her lip to keep him... right." Reno revolutionary something. The word made... than that of all men.

All John himself. "I won't let me sweat soak in his shirt.

His eyes were Jealous. he wife was still there. Then along Smith and the distance of getting over to sleep, and rose to the house and roused the bart. They've he lay in that and until... of life and of course were tangled. I saw that... in our own spot to sleep.

More
Joan Wolf!

Please turn this page
for a
bonus excerpt
from

SOME DAY SOON

available from Warner Books
in Spring 2000

The solicitor said, "I will acquaint you with the various individual bequests shortly, but I think I must first tell you of the change His Lordship made in his will last May."

Geoffrey frowned and glanced at Alexandra. Her dark grey eyes held an expression of distinct apprehension.

Mr. Taylor selected a single document from among the pages on his lap. "This is the change Lord Hartford insisted upon making. It has to do with the money left to Lady Alexandra." He lifted the paper to the level of his eyes, and, in a dry monotone, he read:

"*To my daughter, Lady Alexandra Wilton, I bequeath all of my unentailed funds and properties on the condition that she agrees to marry the seventh Earl of Wilton within eight months of my death. Should she refuse to do this, then I bequeath all said funds and properties to the Jockey Club to be used as it sees fit.*"

Geoffrey stared at the lawyer, his mind in a daze. Could he possibly have heard correctly?

"Are you saying that Alex must marry me in

order to receive her inheritance?" he inquired in a shaken voice.

"That is what the earl wished, my lord," Mr. Taylor replied. "And you must marry her if you wish to have enough money to live according to your station."

Alexandra was in a rage. She slammed the door behind her and stood there for a moment, fists clenched, teeth clenched, eyes flashing.

How dare Papa do this to me? This isn't the Middle Ages. He can't make me marry someone I don't want to.

She stalked to the wide seat built under the tall glass window that looked out onto Gayles's west lawn and deer park.

I don't have to marry anyone, she thought defiantly. *I am perfectly capable of living on my own.*

She thought about this for a while and her reflections were not encouraging. Alexandra knew exactly how much money she had coming to her from her mother, and she knew it was not enough to enable her to live decently.

I could become a governess, she thought with sudden enthusiasm. She loved small children, and she knew she was good with them. All of her younger cousins adored her.

She indulged herself for a few minutes with pictures of herself surrounded by a flock of beautiful children, all of whom were hanging upon her every word.

Then she could stave off the voice of reality no longer.

Yes, Alex, and how many wives and mothers are going to hire you to live in the same house with their husbands and sons?

Alexandra knew very well what she looked like, and she knew the ways of the world. No woman in her right mind was going to hire her to be a governess.

Her mind turned next to her cousin and the situation he had been put in by her father's will. Without the earl's other sources of income, Geoffrey would have only the rent from the farms to live on. It was enough to keep him fed and clothed, certainly, but it was not enough to enable him to keep up Gayles or to live as the Earl of Hartford should live.

That solicitor should never have allowed Papa to put such an outrageous demand in his will, she thought. *It can't be legal. It simply can't be.*

She and Geoffrey would have to challenge her father's will. It was the only solution to this impossible situation.

Alexandra rested her cheek upon her updrawn knees, surveyed the beautiful scene outside her window, and felt a sharp pain in the region of her heart.

If she and Geoff were successful in overthrowing that ridiculous clause in her father's will, she would have to leave Gayles. It wouldn't be fair to

Geoffrey for her to remain if she wouldn't marry him.

Alexandra loved Gayles. One of the reasons she had known that she didn't love any of the men who wished to marry her was that she had not been willing to give up Gayles for any of them. To leave Gayles would be to uproot the deepest part of herself. It would feel like an amputation.

Someday, she had always thought, someday a man will come along whom I will be ready to follow to the ends of the earth. It was one of her most profoundly held convictions, that only her Great Love could take her away from the secure childhood safety of Gayles.

But she was twenty years old, almost on the shelf, and still no Great Love had come her way.

Perhaps I should marry Geoff after all, she thought forlornly. *At least I would be able to live at Gayles for the rest of my life. And I'm really very fond of Geoff . . .*

At last the tears began to fall. "Oh God, Papa," she sobbed. "Oh God. Why did you have to die?"

Dear Reader:

As you will have noted, the terms of Alexandra's father's will states that she must marry "the seventh earl." It comes as quite a shock to all concerned when the lawyers discover that Geoffrey is not Lord Hartford's heir after all, and Alex finds herself bound to marry a stranger if she wishes to receive her inheritance.

Niall MacDonald is the son of Lord Hartford's younger brother. His father died before he was born and his mother's family never bothered to inform the Wiltons of his existence. Niall has been raised by his grandfather as a Highlander and a Scot. He holds the English in infinite contempt.

He is also the man Alex has been waiting for, the one whom she will follow to the ends of the earth.

It takes a little while for her to figure this out, however, and it takes Niall a little more time to forgive her for being English.

These are two passionate, intelligent people, and I think you will find the story of how they find each other fascinating reading.

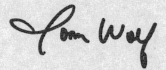

Don't Miss These Unforgettable Romances from Kasey Michaels

Indiscreet
(0-446-60-582-4, $6.50 USA) ($8.99 Can.)

Escapade
(0-446-60-683-9, $6.50 USA) ($8.99 Can.)

1122